THE LAST of the HEROES

To dear Joan,

a reminder of the happy days you spent here in Kerry

Billy Keane

THE LAST
of the
HEROES

BILLY KEANE

BALLPOINT PRESS

ISBN 0-9550298-0-5

Published by
Ballpoint Press Limited
4 Wyndham Park, Bray, Co. Wicklow, Ireland.

Layout, cover illustration and design: Mary Guinan, Temple of Design

Printed by GraphyCems, Villatuerta, Navarra, Spain

ACKNOWLEDGMENTS

I wouldn't have written a line but for PJ Cunningham.

A special thanks to readers of mad drafts.

Thanks to my agent Geraldine Cooke.

Take a lollipop out of the jar Mary Guinan for your patience
and craft in the design of my book.

Thanks to ace photographers Brendan Landy and Ray McManus.

Fair play to friends and editors Noel Twomey and John Greene.

The boys put structure and shape into my rantings with good grace
and a torrent of slagging.

Finally, thanks to my family for putting up with me.

DEDICATION

I would like to dedicate this book to my wife Elaine, our four children, my mother Mary, and the memory of my father John B.

THE BALLY BUGLE

TRUTH WILL OUT   October 23 · Edition 28

TUBBERMORE TORSO BEHEADED

By Harry Verdon, Chief Reporter

AN initial examination of the dismembered torso discovered yesterday in Tubbermore near the village of Glenlatin indicates the dead person may have been decapitated.

Sources close to the investigation suggest there are strong suspicions of foul play. It is not known precisely how long it is since the death of the victim but eyewitness accounts to the discovery of the torso seem to indicate that the cadaver was remarkably well preserved and "had a polished, leathery mummy-like appearance." Concerned locals have called the corpse The Tubbermore Torso due to the absence of the victim's head.

Gardai would make no comment other than to say the deceased may well have been in the bog for some considerable period of time. At this stage it is understood a specialist team will carry out forensic tests.

Sources say it is "too early" to begin speculating as to the identity of the remains. It is as yet unknown whether the torso is black or white due to discoloration. The gruesome discovery was made by Kerry County Council workers investigating alleged illegal dumping in the Glenlatin area.

Local people are said to be staying in tonight as fear has spread over this closely-knit rural village just five miles from Ballymore.

Parish Priest Fr Aonghus Fitzgerald called for "a speedy conclusion to the investigations to allay the fears of my terrified parishioners."

Mass will be offered in St Teresa of the Shingles Parish church on Tuesday morning next at 11am for the repose of the soul of the murder victim.

An urgent meeting of the Parish Council will be called in the coming weeks to discuss the implications for the village of the finding of the Tubbermore Torso. It is understood proposals will be put to the meeting to establish a branch of Community Alert in the locality.

A local man who is helping police with their inquiries is not a suspect but is being questioned in relation to a number of matters, including illegal dumping and the theft of an angle grinder.

CHAPTER ONE

October 23

THE FALLING VILLAGE, A LAZY MONUMENTAL SCULPTOR AND A WET DOG

THE SNIPE AND MYSELF hardly noticed the stiffness of the climb with the talk. We travelled up past the saddle and down over the summit of The Glen Hill. The Glen Hill is, I suppose, a bit of a contradiction. My grandfather, The Hero Sullivan, as usual sorted everything out. He nicknamed the rise Fat Arse Hill in honour of the zealous women who power-walk the loop from Glenlatin to Ballymore in the spring and early summer, the slimming season. Laid out before us is a perfect view of Glenlatin. The two-sided square at the top of Main Street is home to St Teresa's Church and my pub, The Mayo Bar. The square is named after my grandfather. The Hero Square.

You could spend your life figuring out why anyone decided to build a village on such a precipitous slope. It could well be that an ancient town planner advised the village founding fathers not to build a settlement on the side of the hill and they just ignored the advice for no other reason than they didn't want to be dictated to. They can be very thick in these parts when the mood hits them.

Smoke puffs up in fits and starts from a dozen chimneys. An unmanned ladder is lying up against a half-painted house. The whitewash on the house next door is flaking away as if it was suffering from a bad dose of dandruff.

Minnie May Murphy, the gossipmonger, is walking her bike down Main Street. She doesn't cycle because she might not be able to stop if the bike took off on her. A few hours earlier Minnie May would have walked the bike up the hill because she didn't have the strength to pedal up the slope. She uses the bike to carry her shopping on the handlebars and the carrier. No one has ever seen her mount the bike, or anything else for that matter.

Main Street and its offshoots are home to red hay sheds, thirty terraced small-windowed dwellings, one thatched cottage, twenty seven grey, unpainted two-storeys, thirty six newly-built council houses in The Hero Vale Estate and forty seven neo-the-one-next-door bungalows owned by commuters from Ballymore.

We look down on the wet fields. The early winter grass has the washed out anaemic complexion of an old man just holding on after a bad dose of pneumonia.

The Snipe is my first cousin and my best friend. We took his mother, Auntie Annie, over the hill to Tooreenbawn cemetery only yesterday. Funny, isn't it? Two removals in the one day. The Tubbermore Torso and Auntie Annie.

My aunt was the last of the old generation of The Heroes. The two of us went down this morning to take a look at the grave and say a few prayers.

The Snipe is tiny and wiry like one of those African marathon runners and he sets the pace. I stop for a breath and turn my back on the village. A row of bare tall poplars waves between the groves of Celtic crosses and piebald Italian gravestones in Tooreenbawn Cemetery down below.

"Well, that's it now Snipe, we're the last of the Heroes."

"Sandy, do you ever think . . . ?"

"Every day, and not just after the rubbish in The Bugle. Did you see the headline? Torso decapitated. How can you decapitate a frigging torso? As we're on the topic. Do you notice the grave two up from your mam's?"

"No Sandy?"

"That's just it, Snipe. No one knows who's buried in that plot, not even the old people. All I know is that I've never seen anyone stop to say a prayer or ask for help. It's as if they never existed. I tried to scrape away the blobs of yellow lichen and I even dosed them with a fungicide but it was no good. The monumental sculptor just didn't carve deep enough. I suppose he knew his clients wouldn't be around to ask for a refund when the weathering levelled the face of the stone down to the depth of the names."

The Snipe looks down towards the river. The Ballymore, in too much of a hurry to the Estuary, spilled over its banks wetting the land to such an extent you'd think you were looking at paddy fields in Asia if it wasn't for the cold wind coming down from the North East.

"Do you know something I was just thinking?" said The Snipe. "That memoir or whatever it is you've started writing. Will you do it right Sandy? And don't give up half way through. You might get a bit down in yourself when you get to thinking of the past. I couldn't do it. It takes me a full half an hour to think of what to put into a Christmas card."

The Snipe knows me better than anyone, even myself. I had intended to give up on the whole thing. Maybe not in a deliberate way. Postponement has always been my self-conscious trick for getting out of facing up to the unfaceable-up-to.

I can't bear thinking of the events that led to my losing my child.

"Get back at it tonight again, Sandy. Be honest. Don't be like the chancers who did that gravestone you were talking about. Carve deep. Tell all about how Mary O left and never came back. And how they put it out you did away with her. Tell about The Heroes and the village before it's all gone. Times are changing. The country isn't able to keep up to itself. So much happens in a single day that nothing happens. It might help you figure the whole thing out if you put it down on paper. It might even help you to put it out of your mind."

"I'm not sure if I'd be able."

"You will, and don't be too hard on yourself. The fact that Mary O was an unmarried mother was a bigger thing in those days. Maybe if your child did come back it might help him or her to understand the whole carry-on. See what you were really like. And it would always be there somewhere and wouldn't need any maintenance like the headstone."

I told my cousin of my terrible flashbacks. "I have these horrible wide-awake nightmares that my child was aborted. I see the baby floating around somewhere in the Thames in a wicker Moses basket bobbing up and down in the water like flotsam and jetsam."

It took The Snipe a while to take in the imagery. He wasn't shocked. My cousin was used to me waking up from nightmares when I was small. I used to talk in my sleep a lot with my teeth clattering and grinding into each other.

Then we gave each other a bit of time again. You know the way it is with someone who knows you well. There's no need to say anything if you don't want to and they take no notice of the silence. In a way, the silence is a form of communication.

We hit a short but steep rise in the hill before the rest of the descent. You'd have to catch your breath again in this part of the climb. We put our heads down like horses carrying a heavy load.

"Will you do that bit of a history, Sand? Keep at it for your child, Sand."

He was the only one who called me Sand - outside of my oul' fella that is. I could never refuse The Snipe. We're more like brothers than cousins.

"I'll start again tonight so, Snipe."

We shook hands. It was strange to be shaking hands with someone you meet every day.

I offered my friend a drive home but he declined. He wanted to clear the head.

He walks as if his thin bird's legs are picking out stepping stones at a ford in a river.

The knitting needle legs and the isolation and wetness of his nest in the marshy hill country gave rise to his nickname.

* * * * * *

I kept my word to The Snipe. He was right. The thinking back will be very difficult for me, but it might do me some good.

So here I am then, looking into my little laptop window at the past and out through the big window of The Mayo Bar into the present.

The pub is well closed at this hour and the few customers are all gone home. This is my thinking time and from now on my writing time.

An old banger bisects The Hero Square. The exhaust smoke lingers for a while before departing for a gap in the ozone layer. Two lovers are off to a lay-by for chips and a straddle of sexual gymnastics in the cramped back seat.

For a second the car lights up The Mayo Bar like a stage ready for the opening scene of a play. I'll do my best to give a true account of the characters, the village and the events that changed and shaped my life back in Act One all those years ago.

The street outside is deserted now save for Houdini on border patrol. He stops to urinate against a frontier lamppost. The village sentry is a bit down in himself. It's Monday. There's no fried chicken flying out of the windows of passing cars.

Houdini was thrown over the big bridge in Ballymore by a sheep farmer from the mountains of the West who was anxious not to pollute his own streams. Poor old Houdini just didn't have the legs for racing up the sheer slopes after finicky sheep in search of the sweeter grasses. The bandy-legged sheepdog escaped from a tied-up spud bag full of stones and swam ashore through a flood before he finally made it to the bank. He stinks of wet dog tonight but I open the front door and let him in.

So who am I writing for then? The Bugle piece will inevitably lead to rumours about Mary O's disappearance. So I'm writing to set the record straight. If my child comes back, it's for him or her. At least there will be an honest account of how it was I managed to lose my own kid.

Yes, it's mostly for my child and this account or record is addressed primarily to you. And it will be an honest account.

There have been so many lies. Our very name The Heroes is based on a lie, even if it is an hilarious lie.

Maybe this is my confession and as any theology student will tell you there is no absolution without sorrow and truth. So that's it then, this is an Act of Confession to my kid.

All I can promise you, my child, is that everything you read here is the truth. And I am so sorry, so very, very sorry.

CHAPTER TWO

CRUMBS LEAD TO A TORSO

THE BUGLE REPORTER PROBABLY didn't have time to get into the full story of the finding of the Tubbermore Torso what with deadlines and that. The Bugle's deadline is eight o'clock on a Thursday night and the torso was only uncovered a few hours earlier. Not that accuracy would bother The Bugle too much.

Everyone one of us here in Glenlatin knew there were outsiders dumping waste illegally in the Sucks' land. It was going on for years but on a small scale. Rusty prams, old baths, bags of rags, the odd dead dog, that sort of thing. I suppose it could be said the Sucks' holding was the ideal terrain for the concealment of rubbish since it was not really land in the true sense of the word. It was a kind of marshy bog, a type of amphibious land.

Not so long ago, the Sucks decided to take some environmental action but it proved to be their downfall.

When the animal crematorium in Ballymore was shut down for six months due to smells, a small army of rats converged on the dump to feast on the dead animals deposited by a steady cortege of knackers' lorries. The problem came to a head when Jereen Suck Junior found a rat in his bed.

Sammy, the clan leader, put a two-point plan into action. Firstly, Junior would have to stop taking packets of digestive biscuits to bed. Secondly, the rats would have to be culled.

Sammy had a brainwave. He trapped a rat by placing a lump of freshly fried bacon lard in a plastic land drainage pipe inserted into the ground and sealed at the bottom end with cement. It worked in much the same way as a lobster pot.

The rat was cut free from the pipe and left to starve for a week in a rain barrel. Then one day Sammy captured another rat. He was slow and soft from gorging on the bacon lard and at the same time stiff from his confinement. The Sucks climbed on to the roof of their cottage and shook the rat out of the pipe into the barrel.

The newcomer was disorientated from the tumble and was eaten up in minutes. The first rat was starved again. Then the Sucks piped him into the heart of the dump

The Sucks had trained a cannibal rat.

Sammy stole an angle grinder from the monumental sculptor, Tombstone Tim, for the cutting of the pipes. Sammy is the man referred to in The Bugle piece who is helping the police with their enquiries. Tim complained to the police in Ballymore. The Gardai had one look at the rat-infested dump, tucked their pants inside their socks and promptly sent word to The Council Anti-Dump Brigade.

Liam Lyons, the local police force, called in first thing this morning with the whole story. He seldom rose before eleven except on court days, and he hasn't been in court for years.

Liam is always welcome. He is small for a garda, very small for a garda. By all accounts, a sympathetic sergeant measured him up. Liam didn't shave even when he was on duty. Still the Village Police Force always seemed to have the same consistency of beard. He wore a red Manchester United fleece but no tie or tunic. A flap of his untucked blue Garda shirt hung out over his gut.

He's about my age, mid forties, but he's three or four stone heavier and about an inch taller. In fact we look alike around the face and people say we could pass for brothers. Liam is nearly bald but I have a good head of blond hair with grey highlights. I caught Liam rummaging through the bathroom cabinet for Regaine, hair dye and Viagra. Police have to be investigating something. They can't help it.

Liam is smart in the head if not sartorially. He could have risen higher in the force had he wanted to but he is more than happy in The Glen. As he said himself: "It is the last of the cushy numbers."

Liam gave me a blow-by-blow account of the raid on the Sucks' place.

"They went stone mad. Sammy Suck was carted off to Ballymore in the squad car. It took six of us to quieten him," he said. "I tried to get him to come for a drive with me in my Panda van but the lunatic refused. He said he wanted to be arrested in a proper polis car. I did my best to explain I wasn't arresting him. I was just taking him for a drive until the situation calmed a bit but I should have done my homework. It was the day of the Full Moon. I wonder do any of those gobshites in the council have a calendar showing the lunar cycle. Sammy kept on roaring out the Suck war cry, 'We rode half the country and bate the other half.' Still, the rest of them quietened a bit when he was handled."

"Was it bad, the dump like?"

Liam looked away from me for a second. He was revisiting the scene in the editing suite in his head, focusing on the wall as if what he was about to tell me was projected by his eyes.

"The Environmental people from the council moved in a fleet of diggers. It was the end of the world. The councilmen were dressed in moon-walking gear and were walking around with big long steps. The Sucks were cordoned off behind a rope. They kept trying to get into the dump, sneaking around diggers and dodging in and out through the squad cars and the dead lorries. The rats were everywhere. It was if the very ground itself was moving when the diggers started to shift the carcasses. The newly-dumped cows were lying on their backs in the digger buckets with their stiffened legs and paps pointing straight upwards, parallel to each other. A fresh enough looking sheep's head fell off the overloaded digger shovel and rolled right to my feet like a football. He had only the one eye and it was looking at me.

"The stench was vomity, stomach upsetting. I had to put on a gas mask thing. Rats were jumping off as the diggers were rising up to shift the cows into the dead lorries. The council boys told me the rats had set up home inside the dead carcasses. They kicked their legs around flapping madly as if they were trying to fly when the digger driver changed the height of the shovel sudden and jerky to get them to fall off. The rodents were tossed up into the air like acrobats and then when they hit the bog pools they tried to swim. And rats aren't an awful lot better at the swimming than the flying. I'll take it with me to the grave," said Liam, who loves to embellish a story.

"The squeals when a councilman cut off one of their heads with a shovel and the rest of the rat didn't know the head was gone and just kept on kicking away. The rest off them ran off madly in every direction. The village will be alive with them. I hate rats. Fuck me, but I'd face an army of mad druggies and drunks outside a chipper in Ballymore before I'd face a rat. I had this thing always that a rat would run up the leg of my trouser and bite the balls off me or a gang of them would jump at my throat and tear me to pieces. Like a phobia sort of a thing. Do you know what I'm saying?"

I informed Liam I knew exactly where he was coming from and that I was no great fan of ratkind myself and would he ever shut the fuck up, talking about rats. I resolved to wear steel underpants from then on.

Liam took a good sup out of a tumbler of whiskey, his usual tipple early in the day.

"Sandy, of course, you read The Bugle. You know the Council found a human torso in a boghole."

Liam is a friend but a Garda is still a Garda especially in a possible murder inquiry.

"What's the story, Liam?" I decided to take a cautious approach.

"Ah, it's probably there for years. Mummified by the bog probably."

"Christ Liam, that's serious?"

"Ah, I don't think it is Sandy. Except for maybe the owner of the torso. That kind of thing is a regular enough occurrence up in the state bogs in the midlands but it was some shock all the same. And The Sucks went crazy. If only the shagging thing was killed on a sane man's bog."

Liam reckoned the forensic people would come tomorrow to take the torso away for examination. The scene had been preserved.

"I'm going up there tonight to guard it until the experts come to take it away. Jesus, but I'm going to get rightly drunk before I face into it. Bollix to The Bugle and all who sail in it. The phone hasn't stopped ringing with newspapers asking for details and asking where the head is gone. You'd think the body was only murdered the other day from reading the piece."

Liam had no doubt that one of the ancient Sucks chopped a soft Viking or a dopey Norman and dumped the poor bastard in the bog. It was Liam's professional opinion, based on years of policing with the Sucks, that they probably ate their ancestors and boiled the heads with cabbage when they ran out of pigs.

There was a problem with the forensic people up in Dublin, he explained. Loads of old corpses were being discovered with the new motorways and the building boom in the east. It could lead to long delays in the forensic examination. The archaeologists will probably take the body away with them and put it in storage.

"And you know what they'll say, Sandy? Don't you?"

"What who will say, Liam? The forensic science gang? They will probably say there's no point losing the head over finding a thousand-year-old torso."

"It's the shagging Rumour Factory, Sandy. Don't be messing with me. You're going to have to face up to this. You know what that crowd are like once they get the whiff of a scoop."

The Rumour Factory are a bunch of elderly female desperadoes who congregate outside Mass every morning to slate and gossip after snapping digits off the priest's fingers in their haste to receive Holy Communion. The Hero always maintained that the gossip was a substitute for sex, or a life, or both.

"No, I don't know what the Rumour Factory will say Liam. And anyway bollix and double bollix to the Rumour Factory and all that sail in her as well."

I knew only too well what the Rumour Factory would say. They were the Reuters of The Glen, except more often than not they managed to get their facts arseways.

"Well, think about it Sandy. You know what they're like. And The Bugle . . . The Bugle even had a story on the front page last week, 'Ballymore Boy Loses Dog'. You can guess how excited they are going to be about someone losing a head."

"I know Liam. I'm sorry. Thanks. Hopefully they won't put two and two together to get five. Anyway, in a few weeks the results will be out and that will be that."

"I hope so Sandy because the initial report from the County Archaeologist is that the body was that of a woman. And it's only a matter of time before the Rumour Factory change Jane Doe to Mary O."

There wasn't much I could do except wait and hope that nobody would make a connection with your mother's disappearance.

* * * * * *

I think it's the unfairness of rumours that bothers me most of all. When your mother disappeared they carried out a campaign against me. I murdered her, they gossiped. Natural justice doesn't seem to come into it at all. No one knows who started it but The Hero was pretty certain it was Tom Tie, your maternal grandfather, aided and abetted by Minnie May. Tom Tie did it out of badness. Minnie May hadn't much else to do I suppose. The quest for news after ten Mass probably gives her a reason to get out of bed every morning. It's funny enough, I suppose, unless you're the subject of the rumours.

People believe gossip without ever asking the victim for his or her side. What starts off as supposition turns into fact with the telling and retelling. It's impossible to trace the originator and even more impossible to stop a rumour in transit.

I know some rumours turn out to be true or some might have some bit of the truth in them. And these are the most dangerous rumours of all because the bit that's true validates the lie. But many are just full lies. Then the rumour gets repeated and the repetition somehow gives credence to the story. If two people meet and tell each other the same rumour they walk away happy in the knowledge they have their facts right just because the other person has the same version. Repetition is validation.

There was a boycott of sorts when Mary O went missing. There were no placards or daubed walls. People just stayed away. Tom Tie was behind that alright. He let it be known that he believed the stories that I did away with your mother or maybe had her kidnapped and brought to England. We had only a handful of customers and The Hero was going nuts from the poverty and injustice of it all.

Monopolies are not necessarily a bad thing, particularly when you own the monopoly. The Mayo Bar is the only licensed premises in Glenlatin and when two or three of the boycotters were caught for drunken driving on their way back from the nearby town of Ballymore, the tide turned and gradually the business came back. The Superintendent in Ballymore issued a statement to the effect that I was not a suspect and that he was satisfied Mary O was most probably in England.

The Hero was a close friend of the Super's. In fact, The Hero was a close friend of every Chief of Police who ever held office in Ballymore since the foundation of the state.

The worst thing that could happen now was that Paula, my niece, would get to hear the whole story of your adoption.

Paula was adopted too. Her adoptive parents were my sister and her husband. They are dead for a good few years now. Paula is, I suppose, your cousin but she is also your sister because I regard Paula as my daughter. Complicated isn't it? We are very close. She is a pretty girl in her final year in engineering in Dublin. Paula has the blonde hair without recourse to a bottle and can hold her own in any company. She has the bit of height too unlike myself and has The Hero's brains and his way of getting around people. But unlike him she's an honest girl. Well, honest enough anyway. She's mad for the craic and drinks a lot more than she should at times but at least she doesn't do drugs.

The second last time she came home she emptied out her bag looking for keys or her mobile and a half dozen condoms fell out on the kitchen table. I was mortified but relieved in a way she was taking precautions and wouldn't end up like your mother.

"Did you ever see these yokes before, Uncle Sandy?" she asked and then after a fit of laughing she piled them back into her bag.

"Aren't you always asking to me to be careful and not to get myself pregnant. Well, aren't you?"

I was amazed that she wasn't in the slightest bit embarrassed. I told her to watch herself as the country was full of burst condom babies. She just laughed and laughed.

"Is that what I am so Uncle Sandy, a burst condom baby or maybe I'm a broken test tube baby?"

A few minutes later she was texting someone. I was sure she was relaying my comments as to the fallibility of condoms.

I was going to give her a lecture on her morals but I was too embarrassed to talk to her about such things. And anyway I didn't feel very much like providing any more copy for her texting.

I think she knows nothing of your existence. I'm afraid that if she found out I was responsible for losing my own child she might turn against me. And that would be the worst thing that could happen. I'd say she would give me the benefit of the doubt being Paula, but it's a chance I would rather not take.

Paula was in a bad way when she came to me. She was only seven.

Her mother, my sister Mary, died first from cancer. Her husband Jim went the same way a year later. It was all so sudden. I was the double orphan's nearest relative, a hard-drinking hedonistic uncle with a disastrous past.

There was the first day she came to stay with me for good in The Glen. Her little carry bag. A tatty old teddy by the name of Martin who she pretended was her baby brother. Thin legs with sliotar knees. A mop of uncultivated, golden curls. Red-rimmed eyes peeping out of a pale face. Old fashioned clothes bought by her Dad. Head low. One sock up and one sock down. Broken, lost looking and very small. It seemed as if I was looking at her through a pair of binoculars the wrong way round. Whatever was in there behind those limpid brown pools of eyes of hers was very far away and hard to get. It took her a month to say anything much but once she started she was full of talk and we grew very close.

Paula has her own mind and you could never get the better of her. Even when she was an apprentice woman at sixteen or seventeen she called the shots. There wasn't much I could do. I tried to control her a bit but it was no good. I had to hold on and hope she would come good. She has settled down a lot but Paula is different to the girls of my day. Open is the word. No secrets about boys or anything else. She just tells me she is staying over somewhere and all I say is 'well call me in the morning to let me know you're okay'. We're close though, but we have our rows. We're the same as a father and a daughter, only better. I hope that some day maybe she will be like a sister to you.

Mary O, your mother, became pregnant when she was seventeen. I was nineteen and in first year in College. She was doing the Leaving and leave she did. She left when she was three months' pregnant with you.

Your mother never came back and never even contacted her own mother since the day she left. When Mary O was gone a few days the Gardai were called in by her father to investigate "the matter".

The Rumour Factory swapped "matter" for "murder" and the rumour train left the station for destination everywhere.

CHAPTER THREE

TRACING OUR SIDE

I ALWAYS SAID THE day I started tracing I'd send word to my closest friends to sneak into my room in the old folk's home and smother me with a pillow like the big Chief did with Jack Nicholson in 'One Flew Over The Cuckoo's Nest'. And now here I am at it myself.

I know from Paula how much she craves knowledge of where she came from. There were times when she drove me crazy. "What if I'm a schizophrenic or a frigging nymphomaniac or a kleptomaniac or just a plain ordinary regular maniac with cheese and fries? What if some hereditary disease kills me before I get to college? I haven't a clue what frigging genes I'm carrying around."

I'd eventually lose it and scream at her.

"For Jaysus sake will you shut the feck up. Stop making things worse than they already are. I'd say your poor parents must have been the lead players in a court of neurotic drama kings and queens."

Then she'd do her usual exit pushing the door back out as far as it would open and then slamming it shut with a big bang at the end of the back swing. It might take us until the following day to make up. I always insisted on waiting for her to apologise first. Then I'd say I was sorry for shouting at her and say she wasn't a drama queen, well not all the time anyway. We'd laugh and get back to normal until the next blow up when she arrived back three hours late and falling off her high heels after a feed of alcopops at a disco.

We once tried to get my lawyer Tommy Junior to find her folks but to no avail. Her mother just didn't want to know.

I'm pretty certain you are in the same boat. You must be. You will be glad to hear that there were no lunatics in the family. Complex yes and eccentric maybe but not boring, except for maybe my oul' fella, your Grandad, who was a very safe but very loveable man.

It used to drive me nuts listening to my own grandfather and your great grandfather The Hero when he started at the tracing.

The Hero could trace a connection to anyone anywhere in the world through marriage or directly through blood or by virtue of the fact they both had a fondness for semolina with a dollop of red jam. There was no such thing as degrees of separation. The Hero was reared by at least twenty different families. That was a great one by him. Some young lad would come in for a quick drink on his way to the lively spots in Ballymore. The Hero would limp theatrically over to his table and tell him how he, The Hero, was reared by the boy's great grandmother. The young lad would be told all the stories about mugs of milk and duck eggs being given to The Hero by the young lad's family in bad times. He might also mention casually that the young fella's great nanny hid The Hero during The Troubles. Knowing The Hero, he probably threw a leg over her as well. If The Hero stayed in as many houses as he said he did, The Troubles would have had to have lasted about fifty years.

The young lad would soon be on his mobile telling his girlfriend to get a taxi out to The Glen so she could hear at first hand about the old girl's part in the struggle for independence.

"I'm setting up the business plan for the next generation," The Hero would say. "I'm one of the oldest still with his marbles. There is no one to contradict me. Tracing is dead and gone and you can say you're related to anyone you want. I have a few we need to forget we're related to as well. We'll delist them like the Vatican did with the redundant saints and in a few years when the old people die off no one will be any the wiser."

Our immediate family, the Sullivans, are known collectively as The Heroes. We've been here in The Glen for a good few hundred years at least. Your great grandfather was the original Hero and my Dad Liam was, of course, his son.

Dad did most of the work in the pub and all the cooking and the washing. The Hero played the role of the country squire and invented the concept of early retirement long before anyone else had thought about it.

The Hero loved clothes and took great care with his appearance. Up until very near his death he used to flirt with the young mothers as they walked around the square with their prams and full blouses. You could see they were delighted to see him as they'd immediately put the brake on the pram and moved from the front handle to the side to be all the nearer The Hero. Sometimes his elbow would surreptitiously, almost subliminally, brush against a proffered breast.

The Hero had a fine head of silky-silvery wavy hair combed back and up in the fashion of a thirties film star and sprayed with a mist of some kind of woman's holding foam. The Hero was well aware of all the advances in skin care from his in-depth study of women's magazines. He discovered the beneficial effects of anti-wrinkle cream long before any of the women in the village. Even when he was very old his eyes were blue and bright like a young fella's on Christmas morning - and full of roguery. My Dad had grey eyes but I have the bit of blue. The Hero engaged any woman he was talking with full eye contact and made them feel beautiful and special.

No more than myself, The Hero had a long enough nose, I suppose. The Hero nose, my father called it. Of course my father didn't have it himself.

The Hero's mother was a Fitzmaurice – a family that hailed originally from Normandy. Even though the Fitzmaurices left for Wexford about eight hundred years ago, The Hero acted as if the boat had only just docked in Bannow Bay. His grandmother was Molyneaux, a Huguenot name. The Hero maintained he was more French that Irish. He had the sallow French skin and a half an hour in the sun turned him as brown as any continental.

His smile was his greatest asset. It opened his face up as wide as the Ballymore Estuary. The smile took a while to come up. Like the moon it appeared in stages until after a few seconds it radiated in its full glory.

Dad and Grandad used to fight like cats and dogs in the family kitchen in the back of the bar. But once they went in behind the counter, on would go the shop face and you'd think they were the two most compatible and happy men that were ever born.

My father rescued us from ruin when The Hero attempted to pour the deeds of The Glen Bar down the throats of his friends and relations. The Hero saw a chequebook as his own mint. My Dad on the other hand was careful with money. He had to be. A small pub could go bust in six months if you didn't watch it.

Dad was a big, strong man with a thick head of fair hair from his mother's side. He always squinted a bit when he was looking at people for the first time and it was a bit off-putting but all the locals liked him. He was reliable and straight.

The Hero and myself were always at him to get a pair of bifocals but Dad felt if he bought a pair then his eyesight would get worse and worse.

The Hero was constantly on the road, away at some funeral or going to Ballymore to see the accountant or heading off to the chiropodist. "I must go to the forge to have my hooves paired," he'd say in a booming voice, and that was the last we'd see of him until teatime.

Dad reminded me of one of those travellers' horses you see tied to a paling post on the side of the road. The horse's world was the radius of the rope. I think you could say Dad was spancelled to the bar and to me. He had a tough old time of it. There just wasn't enough of the rogue in him for the bar game. He was too honest.

Dad died when I was twenty-one. Just two years after you were born. They say great trauma can sometimes bring on cancer. He was gone within a few months of being diagnosed.

Every now and then I think of him. The other day I was sitting in the car at Ballymore railway station listening to the radio, waiting for Paula's train home.

'The Black Hills of Dakota' came on. It was one of your Grandad's favourites. And I was very sad when I thought of the singsongs we had in the bar. The Hero was MC. But Dad was the star. For a shy man he was a lovely singer and never had to be begged to sing.

"One dog, one bone," The Hero would shout when some unfortunate got a bit carried away and joined in a verse before Dad got to the chorus. The Hero was very proud of my Dad's singing even though he never told him as much. Still I'd say my Dad knew.

Even though I took the scenic route through the exams, Dad never gave out and of course he stood by me during the terrible time of your adoption and the murder accusations, which hopefully will not now be resurrected by the rising up from the bog.

Mary, my sister and Paula's adoptive mother, was constantly badmouthing me. But he really did believe in the whole prodigal son thing. It was only after he died it dawned on me how much he lived the parable.

When the son came home from his wanderings the father didn't just slaughter a fatted calf. The big thing was he didn't ask the son any questions about his life when he was away.

Dad lifted himself up from the bed in the hospital to kiss me before he died and I kissed him back. The last kiss was our first in years and years. He died later that night.

I miss my mother too, even though I never knew her. I think it's a cumulative thing. I mourned for her for as long as I can remember. It was the unfairness of her death that bothered me as much as anything. I'm older now than my mother was when she died. Imagine that, I'm older than my own mother.

My mother, I'm told, papered the walls when she moved in to The Mayo Bar.

She must have been like most young women who want to put their stamp on the family home. The wallpaper is a faded brown now from cigarette smoke and stained with spilled porter and torn in places from scrapes of hobnailed boots and the friction of high stools. I am often asked if it's left there just to maintain ye olde trendy look like the mock bars in the city with currachs and bicycles hanging off the ceiling, but it's the only evidence I have that my mother was once mistress of The Mayo Bar.

I place my fingers across the veiny texture of the wallpaper like a blind man reading Braille, feeling the ridged fleur de lis and the raised embossed contours of oak leaf and laurel garland. I smell the fusion of the cool musty wood smell of the wall and the paper. It has the scent of an old book rescued from an attic.

I feel a sense of duty to keep the pub right and to run a good shop. I owe that to those who came before me.

The old two-rung stools line up at the counter, soldiers on parade, so smooth and polished from the bottoms of generations of Glen men and women that a girl in a silk kimono with a drink too many could easily slide off.

I thought of Paula in her flat in Dublin and how I'd love to have her here for company and a chat and how I missed the drink at the end of the night with Dad and The Hero.

CHAPTER FOUR

Tom Tie, The Facts Of Life, Calling Women Man

MARY O'S DAD, TOM Tie, your Grandad, had a wide back, thickening and stiffening into his short, stumpy bullock's neck. His floppy cow's low belly spilled out over the top of his pants and then stopped, defying the laws of gravity as if it was trussed up by a wire-enforced corsetty bra. All this was supported by tree trunk bandy legs which turned the area from his crotch to his toes into an almost perfect diamond shape.

The bandy legs led to a bad back which led to an erect posture like a monkey learning to walk during one of the transmissions from crawling ape to Homo Erectus. It was all down to lifting multiples of his own body weight since he was a small boy.

I'd say Tom Tie formed a limited company, with the belly as its main asset so as to separate it from the rest of his body. Every now and then he'd pat it and say, "it cost a pile a money to put that there". His mouth seemed to be always open as if he was on the look-out for flies to swallow or he was permanently in awe. He also had a habit of rotating his false teeth, making a swishy sound like spitting out at the dentist's.

Tom Tie was a conservative Catholic who was very strict on his wife and children. But like most conservatives he wasn't that hard on himself. He held on to the sixties' sideburns and his fifties' attitudes. The collar and tie was as much a status symbol as the stomach. He was no ordinary navvy but a gangerman. A mini boss in the feudal chain of the English building sites.

When he came home first a few smart boys caught him for a few bob. Loans of a fiver, or overcharging him for the occasional odd job he couldn't do himself. He was tipped off by supposed friends in The Mayo Bar and it turned him into the meanest and most suspicious man you could ever meet. He thought the locals were trying to do him and were laughing behind his back when they did.

All the Mary O's ancestors on both sides slaved in England. They were long-distance men, travelling the length and breadth of Britain from job to job. Some came home. Most didn't. They were the men "who built Britain". Their inheritance was the start in England.

For the first couple of years Tom Tie tossed his wages up on the counter on a Friday night and stayed drinking until it was all gone. You cash your pay cheque in the pub for a one per cent commission. Then over the next three days you leave them the other ninety nine per cent. The big spending stopped when the navvies were all worked out and past their sell-by date. They became a drain on the state they helped to build. But I'd say if their contribution was placed on a balance sheet they'd be well in the credit.

Your grandfather became aware of all this. He also wanted to get to know his family through the different stages of their upbringing and keep them all at home. Your grandmother, Molly O, was sensible and looked after the money. She took a job cleaning houses when the children were at school. Her employers liked her and being English treated her fairly. She managed to save up on their generosity. Tom Tie only started to get ahead when he became a gangerman. Tom Tie and your Nana eventually bought a small bit of land and exchanged one form of slavery for another.

But at least your grandfather was home in his beloved Glen. And he was home the twelve months of the year. He used to imagine Mary O up on his shoulders and her hair being tossed by a leafy sycamore on the banks of the Ballymore River when he was working in the back of beyond in Scotland building the hydro-electric stations.

Mary O had a small hint of an English accent when we started to go out first but I'd say she had been living in The Glen since she was about ten. Mutual friends told your mother and I we fancied each other. That was the way it was done.

"Hey Sandy, Mary O says you're not the worst of them."

"Hey Mary O, Sandy says to tell you you're not the worst of them either."

The negotiations took place over a period of about two years.

She was fifteen when we started to walk out with each other.

It started off well before that with games of spin the bottle. I became adroit at spinning the bottle exactly at where Mary O was sitting when it was my turn. It was another advantage of being reared in a pub.

I remember the first time I kissed her I swallowed the silky strands of her long brown hair. Mary O's hair was light and beautiful with natural strands of intertwined auburn. It could be blown around by a puff of your breath and went down well beyond her shoulder blades. Her eyes were deep brown, a dark brown, the colour of conkers when they come fresh out of their pods in the autumn, and when we were together her sensuality was there for me in the eyes. A look would drive you wild.

By the time she was seventeen Mary O and I used to make love in our own secret place in the long moulting meadow grass near a little stream hardly anyone knew even existed. Our toes touching in the clear, cool water, turning over a stone with them and the kissanes disappearing into the deeper shallows with wriggling tails waggling and propelling. Home after to Mary O's from the well. The clear well waters caressing the blue rim of the white bucket. Brown speckled legs. Clip clap of the flip-flops in perfect time to the rhythmic swinging of the bucket. Her hair blowing into her face in little wisps. Down the old dusty bohereen in our own time. The 'I am yours' look over at me as we walked. The stencilled shadows of the trees projecting perfect shapes of oak and beech, ash and sycamore, weeping willow and the supple sally. Preening the tell-tale grass seeds from our clothes and hair. Interlinking our fingers and squeezing them just before we reached Mary O's cottage. A look. Then we'd release and walk in as if nothing happened.

I was the star turn at dinner in her house. And how I loved entertaining. I had a hundred riddles and a thousand jokes. The Hero's grandson had to be able to talk. I was trained from the time I was a little boy into making people comfortable. They liked me and I could do anything I wanted with them. And I did. Tom Tie was suspicious of me at first and spoke to me in a series of grunts but after about a year he loosened out and treated me well enough. He eventually got my name right. It was Rusty or Corky or Blondy or Blackey or Skin at first. I tried to crack a joke when he called me Skin. "Can you imagine what would happen Tom if a golfer hit a stray shot and called out Fore . . . Skin?"

He didn't laugh.

"Did you get it, Tom?"

Mary O used to love it when I took the piss out of her father.

"Of course, I fucking got it. Do you think I'm thick or something? Golfers is it? Golfers are a shower of snobby bollixes and West Brits."

You couldn't talk to the man. He had a chip shop on both shoulders.

There was an unspoken agreement between your mother and myself that I would look after her if anything happened. This was the only condition she attached to our lovemaking, even if it was only implied. I was never in any doubt as to that.

There was little or no education in sex in those days. I'm making excuses for myself but I was well educated in every other area of life. In fact people didn't even call it sex. It was usually referred to as 'the other thing', or by its Irish title 'Conas tá d'athair?' How's your father?

But when you did ask your father about how's your father it was a case of ask your mother. But I had no mother so my father told me to ask The Hero. It was the funny thing about my Dad but he could spend ten minutes threading a reluctant worm onto a hook but he wouldn't give a second telling you about your dead mother or the facts of life. Men didn't open up much in those days. It was as if it wasn't a manly thing to do and most of us picked up the brave face from our fathers, who in turn took it down from their fathers. It killed half of them when they put up with all kinds of pain before they would get to a doctor by which time it would be too late.

I asked The Hero to explain the other thing to me when I was fourteen. He pulled me into the corner of our sitting room even though there was no one else around. He put his arm around my shoulder and said: "Sandy, my great friend, there's only one bit of advice I'll ever give you going through life and it is this. Now listen carefully and never forget what I am telling you. My venereal friend you must never put your pen or your penis anywhere without careful consideration." A conspiratorial wink and off he went, delighted he had brought the whole carry-on about the other thing out in the open.

Biology teachers taught a module on the reproductive organs of the rabbit. This usually consisted of a chalk-drawn diagram of a round ball with a few squiggles and smaller balls joined up with more squiggles and with what looked a bicycle pump lording it over the whole lot. There was a cloudy smudge in the middle. I could never figure out whether this was some form of ovarian plasma or the remnants of the inept brushings of the geography teacher who was a dab hand with the chalk and could easily have made a living as a pavement artist.

My first textbook on female anatomy was a copy of 'Playboy' smuggled in from England from a friend who bought it in Heathrow Airport when his mother was gone to the ladies.

The second lesson was from a late night documentary shown about a tribe in Africa where everyone went around naked. We couldn't figure out why the men didn't walk about with permanent erections. The merest thought of a naked woman was enough to trigger us off. For some reason the TV only showed naked black women or jungle girls in documentaries made by anthropologists who knew the only chance they had of selling their work was if they were to show a bit of nakedness. If white women were shown naked the keepers of all that's good and decent would have bombarded the papers with letters.

And as for Mary O, well she trusted me implicitly. It was the first time for the two of us. She loved me and gave herself to me body and soul with a passion that was so intense it blocked out the world.

All in all, I suppose, we only had intercourse about a dozen times but once can be enough. I'm not saying I didn't know there was a risk of your mother getting pregnant but it's like car accidents or cancer, you always think, 'not me'.

When I went to college I suffered from terrible loneliness for The Glen, Dad and Grandad. And for Mary O most of all. But it was a relief to be free from the benevolent plutocracy of The Mayo Bar. I worried that I wasn't good enough for the Arts course in college and was afraid of my life everyone else was my intellectual superior. I missed the camaraderie of Ballymore Secondary School where I first made friends with the fast-talking, laugh-a-minute Ballymore boys. The teachers there, for the most part, treated us well. By the Leaving Cert year we were kings of the school, mature and sure of ourselves. Then in college we were shy, pimple-counting country boys.

After a few months I settled into college and discovered that everyone else in the fresher year felt the same. The older lads from Ballymore introduced us around and I became a proper student with a scarf and roll-your-own fags.

At the beginning of my second year in college I fell in with the trendy dope-smoking gang after watching 'Easy Rider'.

* * * * * *

I first met Rachel at a party. There was no furniture of any kind in this big room with high ceilings in a huge house up on Patrick's Hill. The house was divided up into twelve flats and rented out to students at rack rents. We sat cross-legged on the floor in a square, backs up against the wall. This guy beside Rachel was wearing German army surplus gear and hobnail boots. I forget where he was from but it was some place far away and so remote that it wasn't on the maps and didn't even have a pub. He asked Rachel if she "was going to Varna, man" even though she was a woman.

The cool heads always called women 'man' at the end of every sentence. Varna was a reference to Lisdoonvarna where there was a big rock concert that summer.

When a Gallagher, man, guitar solo came on his head shook as vigorously as Houdini after a wash in the Ballymore. It was like a snowstorm from all the dandruff. There was a huge epidemic in Ireland around this time. Long hair was in fashion and the dribbling showers were so bad that it was impossible to wash out the gallons of shampoo needed to keep the hair shiny clean. There was a gooey blue antidote called Head and Shoulders, but no one bothered with it, preferring an apple-flavoured shampoo that smelled like cider and would strip paint off a wall.

"Like 'Frisco, man," explained the cool dude when I - taking the piss - asked him where Varna was . . . man?

"Have you read 'Ulysses'?" The blonde girl with white skin passed the joint without taking a drag.

"Seventy seven times," I replied, taking a deep pull and nearly coughing up. And then I added: "Man or is it babe? Man."

That did it. She laughed. It was as simple as that. I fell for her immediately and I passed her test.

Rachel's father was a barrister. Plenty of old Cork money. They lived in the most affluent part of the city "and drove a yacht". She was a medical student. She was pretty and smart. She had never met anyone like me before and I definitely had never met anyone like her. We started to see each other.

Rachel explained the intellectuals at the party were not real intellectuals and almost all of them failed the exams. She was liberal and a socialist. She told me they were all phoneys in that room and were best left to themselves. My friends in the Gaelic football club were greatly relieved when I began to show up for training.

There was no sex, well not full sexual intercourse anyway. The Pope had been to Ireland the year before and his charisma won everyone over, especially the young girls. The minute he said "young people of Ireland, I love you" it spelled the end of the lovemaking for us young blades.

I wouldn't mind but the sexual revolution was just about hitting Ireland when his Holiness's Holy War on sex put an end to the whole movement. There was lots of groping and panting and furtive sighs and pushing away of hands, or, more technically, moving of hands from the crotch area to the breasts.

Maybe one of the Pope's acolytes put out the word on the QT that outside breast touching was alright. Or, as it was known technically at the time, "outside tit". The technical term in the confession box for groping down below, a rare enough event, would have been "heavy petting". And there was always - oh yes, how could I have forgotten - a chorus of "I'd love to but it's wrong".

And that was about as far as it got. On our first date Rachel and I kissed against every tree on the College Road. I still remember the shape of her breasts in my hands. It was as if they left a permanent imprint. And the sweet taste of her mouth still lingers. Even her perfume stays with me. It was strawberry sweet and young and summery. It went nicely with the apples.

I have this permanent image of her under a flowering cherry tree in early April. It's still cool. She's wearing a big, bright rainbow sweater, faded painted-on blue Levis, multicoloured socks with the ends of the jeans tucked in. Her hair is light brown and long and wispy, almost like Mary O's. She's sitting on a bench under that tree in the Quad in UCC waiting for me on my way back from football training. The big blooms are hanging down near her from the drooping branches. There are books on the bench and red and yellow mittens. She looks up every now and then from the one she is reading. Scanning with the pale, blue dawn-all-day-long eyes. Looks up for me.

I think Rachel liked people who were different. We used to go out at night with the Simon Community giving out mugs of soup and cheese sandwiches to cracked oul' lads living in shacks by the city dump. The rats nibbled at the down and outs' bars of soap and you could see thousands of them scampering around in the car light as we entered the dump. Rachel held on to me. Trusted me. That was the first night she said the words. On the way home. "I love you, Sandy."

It was funny but Mary O never said the words. She was quiet, your mother. You'd never know what would be going on in her head. You always felt there was a place in there only for her but Rachel wanted everything out in the open. Whatever it was that was going on in her head would come out sooner or later.

Every now and then my flatmates would head off home to the country for the weekend. We'd usually meet up in the Old English Market just off Patrick Street. Rachel never seemed to have any trouble being on time. Everything she did came easy to her. I couldn't organise a booze-up in a brewery. I was always losing notes and forgetting books on buses but Rachel kept beautifully written up folders with little annotated plastic quickfind inserts on the edge of the pages. Even then, something told me Rachel would sort me out. Put structure and direction into my life forever. Be the makings of me. I was very proud to be with her as she was a beautiful looking girl, not that your mother wasn't pretty. She was very pretty but Rachel was striking.

There was a benefit in the lateness. Before I would go up to her I would take a few minutes just to look at her from behind a stall or pass myself off in the crowd of shoppers so I could examine her from every angle. She looked good in everything she wore. Rachel was tall and elegant. Taller than me but we looked right together. When we danced she was light in my arms even though I was very awkward when I waltzed with anyone else. We just seemed to fit.

I loved walking with her through the beautiful old indoor English Market, picking up bits and pieces from the stalls or just looking.

The Cork people are like the Chinese. Nothing goes to waste. Skirts and bodice are not articles of women's clothing but ribs and pork bones. Sheep hearts and pig livers lay in silver-papered platters waiting to be transplanted to ovens and pans. A chorus line of lambs' tongues were staked with wooden skewers and set out in stainless steel trays; the stiffened tongues stuck out like Holy Communicants ready to receive. Tripe made from bellies slithered in its own juices. Heifers hung cross-sectioned for the shopper's autopsy. There was the banter and the patois. We were very much a couple. The stallholders seemed to like us, got to know us in time and threw in an extra fist of mince or a few free onions or a couple of extra chops from Lilliputian sheep with a tiny eye of meat and a long inedible tail with meat and fat layered like lasagne.

I loved every day I spent in Cork. They were interested in your story and if I didn't mention I was from The Glen there was no talk of The Hero. Students weren't just tolerated they were seen as a resource and a diversion.

Up steps, down steps. Pulling each other up hills. All the hills in the

THE LAST OF THE HEROES

THE LAST OF THE HEROES

city seemed to go up. It didn't matter where you were going it was always uphill. Every now and then we'd let the shopping bags down and stop for a bit of a kiss.

There was a punctured bike docked in the hallway of the flat. The linoed floor was littered with unopened bills for long-gone tenants.

The sign for flat number 9 fell down in such a way that it read flat 6 and nobody really bothered to fix it but everyone knew instinctively it was flat 9 and not 6.

The menopausal woman in flat three complained about the noise and constantly advertised for an apartment "for a mature semi-professional lady" but always balked at the higher rent which might inhibit her consumption of supermarket wine. You could hear her ranting to herself when she was jarred through the paper-thin party walls.

"Fuck 'em," she would scream, "fuck 'em all." Then the next morning she would head off to work with her superior manners, grand accent, cocked up nose and tweed suit.

Up the windy stairs as fast as we could before a push-in light sprung back out to switch off the bare yellow bulb hanging over the stairway. In then with the two of us to a tiny kitchen overlooking a neighbour's back garden.

Clotheslines with long johns and double gusset passion-killers danced a can-can in the wind in the stairs window looking out onto a small yard. Jockeys hung on to the one peg like a trapeze artist holding on to the swingy thing.

Linoed floors, narrow beds for men with short legs. Displaced cats tiptoeing the glass-topped party walls on the way to the sunniest window sill. A mouse family that seemed to survive any amount of culling. The black and white TV with rabbit's ears which sometimes picked up Spanish TV if atmospheric conditions were right. Stuck windows that left in draughts in winter and no air at all in summer. Beauty board bulging in the middle making the bedroom walls look pregnant. Emergency condom glued to the back of the headboard with chewing gum. A plastic toilet seat with a crack that could pincer your arse if you didn't take care. A collapsed jute bag with the green shoots from withered potatoes fighting for territory in their search for extra light.

I did nearly all the talking and Rachel listened and laughed a lot as if she was enjoying everything I said. It was nearly always Spaghetti Bolognaise for lunch and a session of medium to heavy petting on the springy couch for dessert.

The cooking had to be minimal. Rachel was used to mammy having everything perfect. Our cooker had only one working ring and an oven with first cousins of mushrooms living in it.

I managed to set fire to the landscape of a West Cork scene by the owner's mother who had taken up painting as a hobby after the husband died of a heart attack on the twelfth tee at Little Island golf course. She proudly presented it to her son. The son's wife told us she hated it and the mother-in-law as well so she dumped it in the investment.

There was a faded print of St Joseph, the Virgin Mary and the Baby Jesus and a very small donkey with legs as thin as Jerry Daly, the Manchester United soccer player.

Our landlord must have been very religious as we also had a print of the Italian bleeder. The eyes followed you everywhere. No matter where you were in the room or at what angle, the stigmatist was looking directly at you. I always took him down when I brought Rachel back.

More 'No Sandy, I want to but it's not right'. And a lorry load of 'Sandy, I want to too, but what will you think of me after?'

"I would think even more of you, you know that."

"You mean you would think more of me if we had sex? Is that all you think of me? I have to have sex with you for you to think more of me."

There was none of this stuff with Mary O. It just happened without any discussion. As if it had been decided on but never mentioned.

I'd brandish my solitary smuggled condom bought well above the retail price. I'd tell Rachel everything would be fine. Frenchies, as we called them, were illegal believe it or not. You might ask why I didn't use condoms when I was with your mother. We just didn't see condoms as a form of contraception but as a method of getting women to sleep with us. The convent girl in Rachel always won. The girls around that time had another big fear and that was that boys would talk. Boast to their friends. The girl would be branded a 'fla' - a woman of easy virtue. The physical attraction was intense but Rachel managed to hold out, just.

Your mother didn't suspect anything when I failed to come back home most weekends. I told her I was studying.

'Blind from it' was the expression in vogue at the time. She wrote twice a week and I'd reply once a week. My letters became shorter and shorter as my relationship with Rachel intensified. After a while I wrote in a kind of abbreviated English, similar to text messaging.

Dear M O. OK. Hard at it. Love Sandy.

The phone system was a disaster in those days so we hadn't much contact in that way. And you'd never know who'd be listening in. Mary O was dying to come to Cork for a weekend but Tom Tie wouldn't let her and I was just as happy. Her plan was to join me in college the following autumn. I felt guilty but I would break it off before I went to the States for the summer. I'd be gone for three months and maybe she'd find someone else and I'd be well out of the way of the fall-out. Your poor mother must have trusted me completely because she never suspected a thing.

I thought I had outgrown your mother and The Glen. I persuaded myself the only reason we were going out together was because there was no one else to go out with. I think I might also have felt that because she had sex with me she was in some way flawed. Even though I was very liberal, or so I thought, there were still big chunks of Catholic irrationalism subconsciously controlling my thought process.

I didn't understand sex or women. Many of my generation went straight from puberty to the menopause. Even though we were dying to get women into bed, when we did in some way we lost respect for them.

Still that was the time and that was the place when God moved his heaven to a small flat over a little shop on the top end of Blarney Street in the beautiful city of Cork. I was full of hope and confidence. I felt I could do anything I wanted. Be anyone I wanted. I didn't know then I wasn't equipped for many of the things I wanted nor would I ever be.

At that time I felt I had everything. Two girlfriends. A good home.

Loads of friends who would party with me until dawn and were always on the look-out for something funny to say or to happen. There was no such thing as failure or sickness or unhappiness. I hadn't a care in the world and I was in love with Rachel. And I didn't know your poor mother was pregnant.

It was the happiest time I can ever remember.

CHAPTER FIVE
MASTER BATER

MASTER MORAN, THE RETIRED teacher and child hater who seldom misses a burial in the forlorn hope of attracting a big crowd to his own, is red-faced from his manic rush to the church for a special Mass for the Tubbermore Torso. It is only five days since the finding of the remains, and it seems new theories are emerging every hour.

Already Fr Fitz and Moran have turned The Torso into some kind of martyr. The Torso is now almost a relic. One of the theories doing the rounds, no doubt propagated by the priest and disseminated by The Rumour Factory, is that the Torso was a nun beheaded by Cromwellian troops. The Torso refused to change her religion to one that was almost the same as the one she had herself with the same God and the same Bible. At this rate the bones will be upgraded to the status of blessed and will be carried around the country for veneration. If the hysteria that followed the epidemic of moving statues a few years back is anything to go by, there will be calls for canonisation before Christmas.

Moran calls the shots in the parish. Fr Fitz is a weak, old-fashioned priest. He does the sick calls, says his masses, hears confessions and buries the dead and all with a certain kindness and simplicity but Moran is the real power. There's no doubt about that.

Since the discovery of the torso and The Bugle's splash, Moran has the people terrified. The Rumour Factory are going nowhere without a panic button. Most of them have been over to buy second hand golf clubs at the Ballymore pro shop to keep next to the bed.

Moran's wife is a nice, harmless, inoffensive little woman. Moran strides out at a fast pace, hands swinging, legs kicking in the rhythm of a soldier marching. Mrs Moran follows on behind her husband shuffling along like the spancelled Japanese women who had their feet bound in tight bandages in the old days so they couldn't run away.

Moran looks out over the top of his gold-rimmed specs. The narrow slanty eyes do not fit into the symmetry of his wide shoulders and his crew-cut, square head. Staring people down was a favourite intimidation trick of his. I'd say he often practised it in the mirror.

He greeted me for the first time in several years.

"Bad business in the bog, bad business, bad business. My village does not deserve this terror," he said. "You may say it does not. Oh you may say it does not. The perpetrator will be brought to justice as sure as day turns into night. Oh you may say he will. You may say he will."

"Oh, you mean the stealing of the turf, Master Moran. Oh, it's a bad business and all the work that went into the cutting. Not to mention the drying out and the bringing home from over in Mullaghdearg. I'm a great man with the sleán myself. My blade is as sharp as a guillotine. Oh you may say it is. You may say it is."

"The cutting?" Moran took a step back at the end of his delivery as if

I was going to behead him there and then and his substantial sconce was falling off his shoulders into a creel of turf.

"I mean the cutting of the turf and all the trouble that went into it."

The teacher gave me another one of his intimidating looks, the kind that used to terrify me when I was incarcerated in his class.

"They say the tests will reveal a lot – an awful lot, Sullivan. A fibre or a hair can turn a suspect into a convict."

Moran looked at me again through the bottom end of the glasses and hit off at a mad pace. His wife kept her head down. I couldn't say anything. He obviously had some notion that I buried your mother up in the bog.

The teacher kicked the flaps of his trench coat out in front of him in his anger, probably imagining booting spelling miscreants or sum delinquents up the arse. He was very rough on us kids, even by the standards of the time. It was funny but the few slaps never bothered me. Slapping wasn't too bad if administered without too much backswing. It was the sarcasm and the threat of the slaps that was the terrorising thing.

I finally broke down after three years of daily terror and told Dad and The Hero how badly Moran was treating The Snipe and myself. Dad wanted to give him a good hiding. My father always took on bullies in the pub and was well able to handle himself. The Hero urged caution. He visited Moran's hometown in the midlands, checked schools where he previously taught and had his police contacts make discreet inquiries.

The Hero then called to see the teacher one day at the three o'clock going home bell. Moran never laid a hand on us again.

The Hero told me he promised his informant he would never reveal the information passed on to him about Moran but he had the goods on the teacher. Make no mistake about it. But I wasn't privy to that information. The fact that Moran suspected me was worrying. He's a bad bastard. Word could soon be out that I was in some way linked to the torso. Then again, maybe I'm reading too much into a series of throwaway remarks.

CHAPTER SIX

The True Lies Of The Hero's Fight For Irish Freedom

GOING BACK IS SENDING me into the pit of despair. The Hero, paraphrasing Churchill as he often did, called it 'The Black Bow Wow'. Wish he was here. The Hero that is. He would talk me out of it. I've spent the last few days feeling sorry for myself.

While I've always had the consequences of my actions rolling around in my head like marbles in a wooden drawer, the actual circumstances of the events leading to your adoption have been suppressed for many years. I know some day I will have to set it all out for you. I promise I will. In the meantime you will have to make do with the story of how we came to be known as The Heroes. It will give you a good insight into Ireland's greatest rogue. The Hero was as central as anyone else in your mother's leaving. Maybe he was as much to blame as I was.

It was about six months after we took my father over the hill. The Hero wasn't well himself.

"Ah Sandy," he wheezed and coughed, "either a good ride or a bad dinner would finish me off."

You'd never know with The Hero whether he was putting it on or not. I laughed but I sensed he hadn't much time left and I was right.

"Grandad," I asked him that night, "do you still have nightmares about the old days? It must have been a terrible thing to have to look a man in the eye and kill him."

He turned his back on me for a second and I saw his shoulders shake and when he turned round to face me he was in stitches laughing.

"Nightmares my arse, only deadly fits of guffawing. I told your dad I suppose because I thought he'd tell you in case you felt under pressure following in the footsteps of an icon. I always hoped your Dad would bury me. It's not in the nature of things to live longer than your son. I had a terrible job to persuade him from making me tell the truth. You know what he was like?"

I nodded. My oul' fella was as straight as the road to Ballymore.

The Hero was never one to stay sad for too long. His brain was too quick to dwell on any one topic for more than a few minutes, particularly a sad one. He was always on the look-out for himself and managed to shut out the world if it became too unpleasant.

"I'll have to swear you to secrecy on this one, Sandy, but it's important the real story of my heroism is passed on."

"Consider me sworn, Grandad."

"You will tell Paula when the time is right, but no one else." I think if he had thought of it, he would have included you too. "Watch out especially for telling women after having a bit of the other thing, or if you're half cut. If the papers got a hold of it or, worse again, a revisionist historian, we're all finished.

"It was 1921 and those murdering bastards the Black and Tans were everywhere, even in The Glen.

"The Tans shot a man outside this very door for no other reason than they were drunk and he was standing where he was. The people were terrified and so was I but I was even more terrified of something else and that was a horrible nickname.

"I was fair game for the nicknamers. I had the same lame leg as I have now and a terrible stutter. What's more, I left myself down badly with a young semi-professional lady from Ballymore who would pull your wire for two shillings. A great treat in those days.

"It was the first time I ever had my hand on a vagina and I'm afraid I suffered from a slight touch of, eh, premature ejaculation. She was a half-eejity, yap yap apey type of a girl so I knew it was only a matter of time before she told one of my friends of my little bit of misfortune. The nicknames stuck forever in those days not just to the nicknamee but also to the family in perpetuity. The Up and Down Browns of today are so called because their great grandfather, the original Up and Down, was a manic depressive in the days before medication and was always being carted off to the mental.

"Where was I?"

The old man was beginning to slip a bit. In another few years he would be taken over the hill but he was anxious to finish off my education.

"The War of Independence, Grandad. How we were christened The Heroes."

He straightened himself up and pushed the silver lick in front of his forehead to the unparted side. He took a second to catch a breath and then he smiled that fine open smile. He gave a little laugh to himself, pulled his shoulders up to his neck and closed his eyes to enjoy the laugh all the more.

"Oh right, Sandy. I made out that if I joined the struggle for Irish freedom it would have three consequences. One would be the boys would be terrified of being tarred and feathered or maybe even executed if they called me Touch and Go Joe Joe. Two, I might even be given a very nice nom de plume. And three, I might get murdered by the Tans.

"I formulated a plan to ensure consequence one and two would come to pass and consequence three would be avoided at all costs. Being a hero, I decided, would suit me a lot better than being a martyr.

"I decided to carry out a raid on an uninhabited RIC barracks in Mayo, which was so far out on the edge of a cliff that it eventually fell into the sea.

"If I went off and attacked the old ruin on my own no one would believe me. I needed witnesses. I rounded up a couple of sons of the revolution and we hit off for the West. I managed to persuade Tom Twomey and Tony Shine to come with me on the promise of a jump from a woman by the name of Thunder Thighs in Limerick docks who'd ride anyone for small money. It was the way of Irish women in the old days either to ride no one at all or ride the whole country. There was no in betweens like you have now. The three of us were virgins and were anxious to get in a bit of practice so as not to let ourselves down when we got married.

"The encounter with Thunder Thighs passed off successfully enough. Times were bad and she did three of us for the price of two like the supermarkets do today. We transacted our bit of business in an old coal store on the docks. When we came out we were as black as the ace of spades. Camouflage for night-fighting, we later called it. 'Martin,' she said to me – I gave a wrong name – 'you weren't the best ride I ever had but you were definitely the fastest'.

"The two boys were worn out after the ride and the cycle. I had a fierce job getting them to carry on. It was a long, hungry cycle to Mayo as we spent nearly all our money on the whore.

"We had another crisis about two days after the coal-shed romance. Twomey called me aside for a private chat while Shine was gone off to see if he could bum a few eggs off a small farmer. 'Joe Joe, I think I have a dose of the clap.' He was in an awful state from piles brought on from the cycling on bad roads as it was. We were aware of such diseases from the returned soldiers from The Great War. One man was blinded from it and another was mental. Word had it that it was an English plot to weaken the Irish so they couldn't put the skills of warfare they picked up at Verdun and Ypres to use against their old teachers. 'What's up with you?' I asked him. 'Shine said the other night his john tom was covered with anthracite. I'm fierce itchy down below Joe Joe? Will I go blind and disgrace myself, going around using bad language at everyone? Is there any cure for anthracite?'

"I explained to my comrade in arms that anthracite was another name for coal and not some terrible disease. The itchiness wasn't imagined though and we nearly tore the willies off ourselves with the scratching. I'd say we drove all the way to Mayo with only the one hand on the handlebars. 'I found something crawling around underneath, down below you know where, Joe Joe. What is it at all?' 'So did I,' said Twomey. 'Coal mites, lads,' I said, 'a thing of nottin'.' And we carried on. If I told them the truth they would have cracked up on me.

"The boys lost their nerve as we neared the barracks and refused to go any further but I marched on. Twomey was nearly crying, 'If there's no one there,' he said, 'come back for us.' 'And if there's Tans or real soldiers there pretend you're lost,' added in Shine, who seemed to have suffered more bites than we did, 'and ask them if they has anything for the itch.' 'That's right,' said Twomey, 'and if you get shot and you're not dead fire two shots one immediately after the other so we can get a good head-start on the Tans.'

"I left the boys shivering and scratching where they were and prayed the information I was given about the Barracks being deserted was accurate. I checked to make sure there was no one inside the half tumbled down ruin. When I was sure of my ground, I let go a shot from the old gun my Dad kept for scaring off crows and barrel thieves but I missed the barracks, even though I was only the width of the pub away from it.

"I reloaded, fired another round which broke a window and set fire to an old oil lamp. In no time at all the flames were rearing up, throwing out clouds of thick blue smoke and lighting up the cliffs and sea below, sending sea birds squawking and me running. Bad leg or not I ran as fast as an Olympic sprinter but I needn't have worried. It was weeks later before the fire was discovered. I had to tip them off.

"The local newspaper reporter from The Western Sentinel, probably hard up for a story, described the attack as 'a daring raid on the heavily fortified clifftop fastness executed by ruthless marauders and arsonists from The Rebel Kingdom of Kerry'.

"The boys bolted when they heard the gunfire. I finally caught up with them in Limerick when they stopped and tried to persuade Thunder Thighs to give them a credit arrangement. They failed of course. When we arrived back home my companions, who subsequently became known as Sure Shot Shine and Turpentine Twomey, praised me to the moon and of course I reciprocated. It was a bit like where you say to a fella after a football match 'you played great, how did I play?'

"The boys couldn't contain the excitement even though they were sore back and front, but happy to be back safely in The Glen. I warned them to keep their mouth shut for a while but of course they couldn't contain themselves. Sure Shot was a terrible blowhole. 'The air was that thick with the bullets lads that the seagulls had to walk.'

"With that kind of shite being pumped out it was only a matter of time before the local IRA got to hear of The Mayo Job. I was asked to go out at night with them. I told them I couldn't go as my mother wouldn't let me. The leader of the Flying Column informed me if I didn't go out they would tell my mammy about Thunder Thighs. I think they might have suspected we weren't real heroes. We were being checked out. I was a natural liar and had to be begged and then ordered into debriefing The Mayo Job details. They were taken in by my modesty and my calm demeanour on the nightly patrols even though I was scared I would be killed by The Tans who were as low as you could get.

"The rest of them were real heroes and were afraid of nothing. We were hiding in a ditch one night waiting for a party of Tans. After four hours Tom Kilter, our leader, ordered us home. 'They'll hardly come now lads. I hope nottin' happened to them.'

"As luck would have it, The Truce was called a few weeks later while I was on the run with Turpentine and Sure Shot in the snug of the now defunct Half Way Bar two miles from Glenlatin on the road to Ballymore, a full five miles away. We were afraid of our lives a Tan would arrest us. The country was full of informers. We would have been mortally embarrassed if the Tans made us strip off as the three of us were shaved as bald as coots down below you know where to get rid of the anthramites as the boys called the little bloodsuckers.

"When we came back home to The Glen I pleaded my case but I was cunning. 'Lads, I hope ye won't be doin' the same as them horrible low types over in Ballymore and go calling me The Hero or anything now just because of The M-M-M-Mayo job.'

"This was enough. The fact I seemed embarrassed by the title persuaded the village to confirm the name. They'd never give you a nickname they thought you might like. And so I became known as The Hero Sullivan.

"The reference to The M-M-M-Mayo job gave the impression that there were other jobs and the legend grew. I tried to stop it but such was the desire around here for a local hero it was an impossible task.

"The stutter all but disappeared within a year or two of The Mayo Job. As for the, eh, premature ejaculation, that went as quickly as it arrived. I was besieged by women wanting to do their bit for the cause and that in times when you'd have to go through a draper's shop to get a feel of a girl's purty."

"And Grandad, did the real heroes ever find out?"

"No Sandy. I was a bit embarrassed because some of them were really brave men. Real patriots but it was survival for me. Nothing else."

Now I'm known as Sandy The Hero, grandson of The Hero Sullivan. I'm vice chairman of the Glenlatin Development Association, honorary president of The Glen Heroes football club, which has no team due to falling population.

I love Glenlatin and will do all I can to keep my home village alive. It won't be easy. There's a small farmer selling out every week now at the cattle mart in Ballymore.

When the smallholders move in out the diggers move and row after row of conifer trees stick up as innocently as a handkerchief in the top pocket of a First Holy Communion suit.

I remember my black days after your mother left. I couldn't face outside the door. My father coaxed me out and made me walk down the Main Street and round the Square with The Hero. Most had a salute, a kind word. It was as if they knew I was weak and wanted desperately to see me come up. The village embraced me. Even the Rumour Factory. I was beaten and broken but I felt safe. I went back into the womb for a while. Their forgiveness was my salvation. They never cut the cord on me.

THE LAST OF THE HEROES

CHAPTER SEVEN

THE BLACK BOW WOW HAS PUPS

ANOTHER BAD DAY. I know I did wrong but Jesus am I suffering? Outside the bedroom window a grey-winged carrion crow sits on the apex of one of the naked silver birch trees. Except the birch bark is not silver. It takes the grey death pallor from the gloom. The silver birch is a chameleon tree. The crow is looking for dead meat or a soft live target. I wish I could get up, shout at him, clap my hands together to simulate gunfire, get him to fly off and visit death on someone else but I can't. I'm transfixed by him. The crow is soon replaced by a magpie, another murderer. One for sorrow, two for joy. I watch for a few minutes but no one joins him on his improbable perch. I turn away from the window but I can see grey clouds pass by in the wardrobe mirror.

The radio DJ plays a request for me. Says I'm recovering at home from flu. Probably some smart bollix I barred from the pub sent it in. I can't even get angry. I feel nothing now, not even pain. I will be here forever. I turn off the radio.

Death doesn't bother me. It's the unfinished business that bothers me. The sense of dying without sorting out the whereabouts of my child and Mary O. I have this vision of myself lying in a cream-coloured, satin-lined coffin. Paula and The Snipe stand to the rear accepting all the commiserations. I'm just lying there watching, fully aware of everything that is going on but I'm calm, resigned as if I was on anti-depressants. Troubles over, race run, no more to be done.

CHAPTER EIGHT
THE BLACK BOW WOW GETS THE ROAD

THE SNIPE CLIMBED IN the back window and managed to get me out of bed this morning. The whole place had been locked all day yesterday. He cooked dinner and was handy enough with the pan but I couldn't eat a bite. Paula phoned. Apparently her landlord threw a fit after the neighbours complained about excessive noise at a party.

Paula must have copped something or maybe The Snipe told her I wasn't feeling the best because she was down home that evening. The sight of her brought me back to myself. I owed it to Paula to keep going.

She called me "self-indulgent and lazy". And then she told me she didn't really mean that. It was just that she had no one else and I wasn't to go cracking up on her.

Her enthusiasm buzzed up the place. It was great to hear noise around the house. In another day or two I'd be screaming at her "to turn the shagging thing down".

Paula would pretend she didn't hear a word I was saying and just carry on with The Fine Young Cannibals or Dogs Die In Hot Cars.

When she was a little girl I thought she was deaf and carted her off to a specialist. A friend of The Hero's. Luckily, he was good at his game. The best in the country. He asked her in a low voice that only a dog could hear if she'd like chocolates and Barbies. "Oh yes," she replied. We knew then it was just her way of getting the better of me.

The love of Paula and The Snipe brought me back a bit. The self-loathing has diminished, if not disappeared. If two people like The Snipe and Paula could think so much of me I can't be too bad.

Paula played Madonna's version of 'American Pie' and was astounded when I joined in. We sang it at the tops of our voices accompanied by air guitar. Paula couldn't believe that I knew every word. I told her Madonna's version wasn't a patch on Don McClean's.

"I'm surprised at you Uncle Sandy. I thought menopausal men loved women with big boobs."

It reminded me of the time Don recorded the 'Mountains of Mourne' and my own Dad said Percy French would be turning in his grave.

"Cover versions really piss off the dead Uncle S," said Paula.

Cure completed, Paula hit off for Dublin the next day on the early train. I was close to telling her about you, but I just couldn't do it. I am only barely able to keep going as it is. I think if I can get it down on paper I might be alright.

CHAPTER NINE

THE STORY OF AN AWFUL NIGHT IN CORK

HERE GOES. I'VE HAD a couple of good-sized brandies to get me over this bit. In a way it's a relief to actually get down to the telling. A bit like Confession.

The UCC rag week was usually held during the term before Easter. It was the social highlight of the college year. And the biggest day of that week was the boat race. A flotilla of patched-up rafts sailed up the river through the centre of the city. Everyone was either drunk or getting drunk. I was petrified. I couldn't swim and clung to Rachel who was well used to boats and totally relaxed. Flower bombs were thrown at us from Patrick's Bridge and the onlookers were hosed by some hydraulics genius who'd set up a pump that sucked up water from The Lee and then spewed it upwards. Rachel's friends were beginning to accept me. The rest of the day was spent drinking and bouncing repartee off new friends with diverse backgrounds and personalities.

This is the life, I thought to myself. I had it all figured out.

Rachel's parents were away for a break in London. She was to stay with me that night. It could well be the night, I thought, as I secreted my solitary smuggled condom in my sock and wondered if it could be reused when I spotted a sign for 'Fit Kilkenny Remould Tyres'. The ad jingle came into my head.

'Fit Kilkenny remoulds rule the road.'

The parody just wouldn't leave me. It kept on replaying.

'Fit Kilkenny remoulds ruin the ride.'

I carried that condom everywhere with me like one of those organ donor cards in case one of my flatmates stole it or Rachel might relent. We drank too much and stumbled up the hill to Blarney Street. There were people talking in the kitchen so Rachel and myself headed straight for the bedroom. I spent the morning tidying it up. Dirty socks were kicked under the bed. Past issues of the Sunday World were stored on top of the wardrobe under 'Middle English For The Advanced Student'. A friend had nicked a clean set of sheets from a city hotel and lent them to me for the night.

We were lying on the bed kissing when I heard a feeble knock on the door.

"Sandy, are you there?"

It was your mother.

"Just a minute," I said as I tried to get dressed.

"Who's that?" Rachel asked.

"My sister," I lied.

Mary O opened the door of the bedroom. She saw Rachel lying on the bed with her top off.

Mary O let out a sharp wail.

Rachel kept repeating, "Oh Jesus, Oh Jesus."

The Snipe, of all people, emerged from the kitchen when he heard the commotion and stopped Mary O from running down the stairs.

Rachel dressed and went into the kitchen after Mary O.

"I didn't know," I heard her say. "I'm so sorry I didn't know."

Still feeling the effects of the day's drinking, I sat silently on the bed with The Snipe. Neither of us said a word. It was the same when we got into trouble as kids. We used to just look at each other and wait for Master Moran to calm down knowing that no one could keep on going mad forever. We just sat there waiting, saying very little.

Rachel arrived back in the room about ten minutes later. The Snipe went back into the kitchen to your mother.

"She's pregnant, Sandy . . . Jesus, here I am thinking I'm your girlfriend and that poor girl back home in Ballygobackwards or wherever is pregnant. Pregnant. I just can't believe this is happening. You'd better go in to her. The very sight of you makes me sick."

"I never knew she was pregnant Rachel, I swear."

"So you're flaing your sister, is that it Sandy? You lied and that's a lie too. And the other lies you told me. How much you loved me. You just wanted to get me into bed. I was lucky you didn't put me up the pole as well and dump me."

"But Rachel, I have a condom."

"Why didn't you use a condom with that poor girl, Mary whatshername."

"It's Mary O . . . and I only had the one."

"Sandy, you are sad, so fucking sad. And what's worse than the lie is that she's nice. She's really nice. I never felt so ashamed in my life."

She kept going on and on, working herself up from tears into semi-hysteria.

There was the barest of knocks on the door. The Snipe baled me out. He offered to drive Rachel home.

He was shaking and it seemed to bring Rachel back to herself to see him so distraught. She accepted the offer of the lift and left without another word. I went back into the kitchen to your mother.

She looked like death warmed up. Her right cheekbone was half closed up like it was winking at someone and her nose was swollen.

"I'm pregnant Sandy."

"Rachel told me . . . You sure?"

"The doctor did two tests. I've been sick a lot."

The room seemed suddenly cold. The window was jammed about an inch from closing. I got up to try to push it up the full way.

"It's okay. Just leave it," said Mary O as she turned her back on me and stared out the window into the yellow glare of the street lights. She stood absolutely still and thin like a heron waiting for sight of fish at a ford.

"What are you going to do?" I said, trying to break the tension.

"She's pretty Sandy, and nice too. Why didn't you break it off with me?"

Mary O's eyes darted around the room in every direction. She removed the top of one of her nails down to the red with her thumb.

"What happened to your face?"

"Sandy, she must think I'm an awful slut."

"Rachel, what happened to your face?"

"My name is Mary. Remember Sandy."

"Mary O, sorry, what happened to your face?"

"My father hit me when I told him."

"Jesus."

"He called me a whore and told me to get out of the house. I cycled up to The Snipe. He borrowed his mother's car and brought me here. I had nowhere else to go."

"I'm sorry Mary O."

"What will that girl think of me, Sandy? What will everyone think of me?"

"What will you do?"

"What will I do?"

"What will we do?"

"My mother wants me to get married but you have Rachel. I don't think I could marry you now Sandy anyway. I can't believe you could do this to me. I just can't believe it. The deviousness. Never. I just cannot believe you would do this to me. It's . . . it's . . ."

"It's not the end of the world. I'll help you."

I moved over to put my arm around her. She pushed me away but not that gently.

"Were you doing it with her as well, Sandy? Was she better than me at it Sandy. I suppose there was more. Was there? Well?"

"No, there was only the two of ye."

The moment I said it I knew that was the end of calming down Mary O.

"Only the two of us. Is that all? Aren't you a great man just to keep it to the two? It's no wonder they call ye The Heroes."

She stopped and looked out the window. And then she started to cry.

"What a mess . . . Oh what a mess."

There was another period of silence before The Snipe returned. Mary O went to him at the front door and I followed.

"Take me home please Snipe. I know where I'm not wanted."

"You can stay here tonight Mary O. It's too late to go home."

The Snipe had left her bag back down in the hallway.

"I'll go home Sandy. Anyway you'll probably try your case again. No danger of getting me pregnant a second time. What's this they call it down here. Sandy's Fla. Wouldn't it be a lovely name for one of my Dad's greyhounds?"

The Snipe looked down at his shoes. I said I was sorry and asked her again to stay the night in my room on her own.

The Snipe brought her battered old capillary-veined leather suitcase down the stairs. It was held together by a belt. Then it dawned on me why Mary O didn't have her own overnight bag. She was never away from home in her life. Tom Tie bought that old case for two and a tanner from a huckster's shop in Covent Garden. That suitcase had seen its fair share of anguished comings and goings. I felt so sorry for her.

Mary O, your mother, just said "goodbye Sandy" in a quiet, almost inaudible, voice caught in a sigh.

But I let her go and I haven't spoken a word to her since.

All the anger was gone in that goodbye. It went through me, the way

I treated her. Maybe I should have asked her again. I didn't know what to do. She gave me such a savaging when The Snipe drove Rachel home I was afraid she'd start off again.

I'm experienced enough in the ways of the world now to know that if I asked her again she would have broken down and stayed. After all, she was only just a bit older than a little girl. The anger was justified and so were the harsh words. It was her way of keeping her bit of dignity. She was too proud to beg for my help. It was up to me to do the begging and I didn't do enough of it.

The Snipe was back up the stairs a minute later.

"She's in the car Sandy. What will you do?"

"I haven't a clue Snipe. It's a bit of a shock."

The Snipe was even thinner then than he is now. He looked very sad, like a jockey on a diet.

"Sorry about barging in Sandy but I never knew you were tipping around with the Cork girl. I can bring you home. The two of ye can work something out. Your father will have to be told. He won't be too hard to talk to, I'd say. We'll go home tonight and see it through."

"No Snipe, I'll get the train to Ballymore at the weekend."

The Snipe was more worried than I was. He knew what was coming whereas I just put everything out of my head. I might have had more brains but he definitely had more cop on.

"Jesus Sandy, you're in a spot. Make sure you come back soon. Your Dad only loses it over small things like stealing socks and blunting razors. He's all right with the big things. And Sandy . . . sure he's your Dad."

THE BALLY BUGLE

TRUTH WILL OUT   October 30 • Edition 29

GLENLATIN'S STREETS OF FEAR

By Harry Verdon, Chief Reporter

FR FITZGERALD, the chairman of the newly formed Ballymore Community Alert committee, has admitted to The Bugle that the village of Glenlatin and the surrounding areas were vulnerable to attacks.

There were many people living alone in remote areas who lived in fear since the discovery of The Tubbermore Torso, he said.

It is understood the committee is to make representations for an increased Garda presence in the area.

Minnie May Murphy, a seventy-eight-year-old pensioner asked that "stun guns be provided for all those living alone."

Fr Fitzgerald considered that this may be excessive when told of Ms Murphy's request but he did offer a recommendation that all people living alone should be provided with panic buttons for their safety and security.

Retired schoolteacher Mortimer Moran blamed drink on most of the probelms in the parish.

"The drink culture in the area is pervasive and dangerous to society as a whole," he said.

Fr Fitzgerlad added that the police must broaden the investigation but declined to elaborate what he meant by this request when asked by The Bugle, other than to say "there must not be a witch hunt or unfair targeting of innocent individuals."

In the meantime, there is still no result from the forensic examination into The Tubbermore Torso. However, The Bugle has learned from sources close to the investigation that the body is that of a woman.

Fr Fitzgerald commented that "women are particularly vulnerable to cowardly and brutal attacks of this nature."

He urged people to stay alert and asked that "a special look out be kept for the missing head."

CHAPTER TEN

Shop Faces And Incestuous Mummies

I WAS WORRIED PAULA might have seen The Bugle on her way back to Dublin or heard of the story from one of her student pals from The Glen or Ballymore. I phoned first thing Saturday morning just to see if someone went a bit further than The Bugle and maybe gave her the whole story, the unedited Rumour Factory version.

As it happened she had already read the article in Easons for free.

"I'm looking for the news behind the news," she said. "Come on, I'm dying to hear."

I repeated Liam's theory about the torso probably being a Viking or a Norman. She was in hysterics with the laughing.

"That's The Glen for you. Brilliant. You know when I went away first I used to say that I was from Ballymore. But there's no place like The Glen. That Bugle is evil. Brilliant."

I joined in the laughter, but it was shop laughter. It was a good job Paula couldn't see my face. She would have copped straight away.

"Hey Uncle Sandy, we might even make a documentary on the Discovery Channel. Like a one where they discover hundreds of mummified corpses with tufts of hair and jewellery. 'Here we are in

Glenlatin, home to the largest collection of incestuous mummies in the world. Notice the three thumbs on each hand'."

And then she put on a deep, hoarse, whispery English documentary accent as if she didn't want to wake the dead mummies.

"The startling discovery of the remains of sheep in wonderfully preserved leather gear and chains leads to a belief that the ancients were immersed in animal worship. The ancient Egyptians worshipped the cat and the Glenlatinos shagged sheep."

She had me in stitches for real this time. Of course, Paula sensed I was putting on the shop face. Like The Hero, she always knew when I needed a bit of stand-up.

"Love you, Uncle Sandy. See ya soon."

CHAPTER ELEVEN
CUSHION SOFT, LISTENING

"DO YOU KNOW," THE Hero said to my father, "it wouldn't surprise me at all to come back here some evening to see the toilet paper hanging out to dry on the clothes line."

"Well, you never hung anything out to dry on the line in your life. Only throwing your swanky gear in a heap and expecting the clothes to appear in the hot press cleaned and pressed as if fairy elves got up out of bed to do the laundry in the middle of the night."

Dad's conversation, even years later, was full of metaphors from the fairytales he used to read for me. The two were having a go at each other every minute of every day since the news broke of your mother's pregnancy.

The toilet paper rationing triggered off a previous incident in The Hero's mind.

"And what about the time you embarrassed me in front of Jones the commercial traveller?" he asked.

"That Jones was some robber," Dad replied. "He should be wearing a balaclava. If he ever darkens the door here again, I'll shoot him."

Jones sold The Hero twelve gross of Cushion Soft toilet paper at a 'bargain price' because he said he liked The Hero. Your Grandad was out for once. Jones knew when to hit The Glen, the first day of the fishing season. The following year Jones called on the very same day but your Grandad was waiting for him. It was a huge sacrifice for my father to give up the first day's fishing in six months but Jones had to be hooked and bagged.

"What are you selling today, Mr Jones?" asked The Hero.

"Toothbrushes, Toothkind Toothbrushes with fortified bristle and a bend mould handle."

"How much are they, Mr Jones?" asked The Hero, clearly impressed.

"If you buy three gross I can let you have them for six pence each."

"That's a great deal Mr Jones, six pence each only. We can sell them for a shilling at least."

"A hundred per cent profit," volunteered Mr Jones, ever helpful.

"How many different colours do they come in?" asked The Hero.

"Six, including azure, that's a new one."

"Azure? Is that a kind of blue?"

"Yes Hero. You're spot on, as usual."

"It's a kind of a bluey greeny Mediterranean hue of a blue I'd say Mr Jones."

"Well Hero, I'd say that's even more spot on."

This was my father's cue. He took Jones by the arm and dragged him out to the back door where he pointed to row upon row of Cushion Soft nesting in the upper shelves of the back store like white doves.

"Be on your way out of here now Jones. And never darken my door again with your con man antics."

"But Liam," replied a shaken Jones, "the brushes are for nothing."

"They're a great bargain," added The Hero.

"Sure we can't even teach the crowd around here to wipe their arses not to mind brush their teeth," countered my Dad.

Jones left a beaten man. The Hero was mortified and never lost an opportunity to remind my Dad of his insensitivity.

I couldn't bear all the fighting and the endless almost-always contradictory advice. I spent most of my time depressed in my room.

* * * * * *

In our house you could stairsdrop a conversation through the gap at the neck of the creaky step on our stairs. All you had to do was unscrew the brass rail that bolted the lino to the second last step. My Dad and Grandad were discussing my future. Your mother was about three months' pregnant by this time. It wasn't too long before she left for good.

The Hero was talking. "He's not the first young fella who got himself into a mess like this. Sure isn't he only nineteen? The poor boy doesn't know what to do."

"I know. I know that Dad," my own father replied.

The funny thing is I can see him now as he said it, even though I only had sound back then. I know his honest, open face is worried and puzzled from wanting to do the right thing whatever the cost. I could always tell by one look whether he was really worried, even when he had the shop face on.

He's addled, walking up and down the kitchen. There are a few shirts, a couple of underpants, and The Hero's long johns drip-drying on the bars above the range. Drops hit the stove underneath every so often and gallop in a mad frenzy until the heat sends them back up as steam.

The Hero was probably stretched out on his big old soft chair near the range with his legs criss-crossed on a small three-legged milking stool with a specially upholstered cushion on top.

Dad - walking up and down fiddling with his braces and straightening pictures - was annoying The Hero.

"Will you leave those shagging pictures alone and sit down. And did anyone ever tell you braces are gone old-fashioned? And, as I'm at it, that suit you bought is like something the Politburo would tog out in."

"Ah, I can't even sleep Dad. I was awake all night trying to figure out what to do. I'm afraid he left us all down."

"Ah sure isn't half the country in the club and the other half lucky they aren't in it. And sure isn't the other thing only human nature. And isn't Sandy human, so what's all the fuss about and sure it mightn't even be his anyway."

"That's an awful thing to say. Mary O is a decent person. And you know it's not the other thing that bothers me but the way he's ignoring that poor girl."

"Sure Liam," Grandad said, "as I was saying and you taking no notice, Sandy's only human. He had it tough with no mother and that sadist beating the shite out of him up in the school for years without us knowing it."

"But she's pregnant," said my Dad in a low, hurt voice. There was no anger there, just a terrible yearning to be fair to everyone.

"She's expecting Sandy's baby. And he won't marry her," Dad went on. "Half the time he's locked up in his room listening to your man, what's his name, Jethro Tull."

"Is Jethro Tull a man or a band?"

"Jesus Christ, Dad, who gives a damn if it's a boiled egg? If a man gets a woman pregnant he has to marry her. I can forgive the act but if a man hasn't his honour he has nothing. She seems like a nice sort of a girl. There's something decent about her. She comes from good stock. The family are mortified and hurt."

"Tom Tie is stock alright," said The Hero. "He's a bullock. I'd say it's a man alright Liam. Although they make enough of noise to be a band."

"Who's a band?"

"Well that's it. That's what I'm saying. You never listen to anyone. Now the best thing is for the adoption to go on ahead and no more about it. My mind is made up. And that's that. Is Jethro Tull a man or a band? That's what I'm asking you."

The Hero could always distract my father when he was complaining about something, but this was too big and Dad wasn't going to be put off this time.

"Stop trying to get me off the point. It wasn't Jethro Tull or his drummer, if he is a band, who got Mary O pregnant. It was my young lad."

"It isn't the end of the world, Liam. And how do we know for sure the baby belongs to Sandy? Were you there at the point of impact? Well, were you? Who's to say she wasn't tipping around with someone else?"

"You know full well that Sandy is the father and that is the worst thing that's ever happened to them. She's a decent girl. Sandy admits he's the father."

"All I'm asking you as your father and as a man of vast experience is were you there at the point of impact?"

My father didn't bother to reply to that.

"I remember when Helen was dying in the maternity hospital," said Dad. "There was a girl of maybe only sixteen or seventeen in the next bed. She had her baby and a day later it was gone. Taken away for adoption by a priest and a nun. Eyes big and hollow with nothing happening at the back of them. I can only picture her in black and white. No visitors. No flowers. No father or mother. No cards. No father of her baby to be with her at the birth to say come on push a bit harder or hold her hand or share the miracle of the first sight of the child with. I felt like buying her a teddy or something. I know it's stupid but that was all I could think of doing."

There was a pause for a while.

"Ah, sure you were going through a terrible time in those days and so is Sandy right now," interrupted The Hero in that gentle voice he only kept for me when I was a small fella.

"The fact Mary O's parents are poor," continued my Dad, as if he never heard Grandad's words, "makes it even worse for them. I know we're not wealthy by city standards but like it or not around here we're seen as the aristocracy. You're a Hero. I own a pub and a shop. Her parents are probably in a state half way between hatred of us for what we have and hatred of themselves for what they don't have."

"Listen," said Grandad, "there's no point in the two of them getting married and being miserable even if he is the father, which he might not be. Women can be devious creatures."

"He has to marry her, Dad, there's no other way around it."

The Hero was trying his best to avoid me marrying. He wasn't a big fan of the institution of matrimony.

"Sandy's career would be badly held back if he was to marry now. No, it's for the best if the baby is put up for adoption. A forced marriage is no marriage. Trust me."

"I offered them money," replied my Dad again, not seeming to have heard a word The Hero said.

"They threw it back at me. Of course I was patronising them. Trying to ease my own conscience. But I wanted to show solidarity but it turned out all wrong. The little girl ran out the door crying. Tom Tie roared, 'Is it how you think a miserable few pounds can make our daughter a virgin again or maybe you want us to send her off to England for an abortion? Shove your money up your arse, Mister Big Shot Landlord'.

"I assured them I only wanted to help. Her mother said nothing. She just sat there as if she was afraid to say anything."

It was the straight way or no way. The Hero always said Dad was a very black and white man. You either did the right thing or you didn't. Everyone was either good or bad. There was only one answer to every question. The truth.

"I'm going back to Mary O's tomorrow and will offer to support the child if they want to keep it. Maybe Sandy will come round in time. I might ask Fr Fitzgerald to help. In years to come Sandy might see sense and at least he'll know where the child is."

"Watch yourself. Bring the priest with you," The Hero said. "That's a good plan. That mad father of hers has no brain. But getting married. Don't make it an immediate issue. If it's to happen later on it'll happen but don't force them into it. Don't say anything to them about whether it's Sandy's or not."

The bell rang from the bar. My Dad left. There was no such thing as long talks in the pub game. I fixed the rail and screwed it into place. I snuck back up to my room and put an Eagles record on the turntable. 'You can check out anytime you like, but you can never leave.'

I hadn't a clue what to do. I just stayed in my room and tried to forget.

The following day I hitched back to college without so much as saying goodbye.

CHAPTER TWELVE

THE BARRING OF THE DREAMTIME CANNIBALS

I HAD TO GET The Dosser in to look after the pub. With so much on my mind, I couldn't face the public, so I escaped to Ballymore for a game of golf. At such short notice, I just couldn't get anyone else to mind the house.

The Dosser is always on the make and if it's possible to be a creative accountant then he's your man. There's always an apology for hitting the wrong buttons on the register. Thousands are cashed up accidentally on purpose thereby making it impossible to gauge the day's takings. He gets paid about half the minimum wage in the certain expectation he'll help himself to the other half.

The Dosser also appointed himself to the post of Quality Controller. There's no doubt the little hoor is helping himself to a few drinks at my expense.

The Dosser isn't a native of Glenlatin. He's 'a Bread and Tay boy'. Bread and tay boys is the name the country people have for the Ballymore lads, meaning the Ballymore boys' main form of sustenance was bread and tea.

The Dosser lives in a one-bedroom cottage situated on the Toreendonal end of the village. He inherited it from his Uncle Dan the

Dauber, the world's worst interior decorator.

The Dosser has a slightly disdainful attitude towards The Glen people. It's as if he considers himself their intellectual superior. He works about one-tenth as much as the small farmers and still manages a higher level of disposable income. He draws the dole and is always doing income-supplementing odd jobs, which usually involve a minimum of hard labour.

Still, he's earned his wages and his fiddle today in spades even though there were only two people in the pub. When I came back from the bit of golf, my heart sank when I saw the pair sitting up at the bar counter.

There is nothing worse than boring company in a pub. Just because they pay you the price of a drink they think that it licences them to go on and on in a way the headwreckers would never be allowed to get away with in their own homes.

Retired Sergeant Brogan's bushy eyebrows give him a sort of a wise old owl look, which is certainly not deserved. He was sitting up at his usual seat, right next to the beer taps where you'd have to talk to him even if you didn't want to.

"When I was married I never laid a finger on herself until the Monday after the wedding. I would not enter into relations on a Sunday," he said.

"The wife was related to you so Sergeant?" I asked.

"Ha," he replied.

The Bore Brogan was in the company of the one and only Sammy Suck, who, despite being barred for life, was served drink by The Dosser. The same man was petrified of Sammy ever since he cut off Houdini's tail just for a bit of fun. Sammy specialised in castrations as a sideline to the illegal dump. He had to keep the belly maintained, he said.

There wasn't a man in Ireland who didn't press his two knees together and grimace when Sammy explained his procedure for castrating sheepdog pups.

"First you hold down their neck with a two-prong pike stuck into the earth so they can't run away or take a bite out of you. Then you catch their two hind legs together like you were catching a handle of a wheelbarrow and then with the free hand you chop off their john tom. And off they run licking theirselves."

"Ah," says The Bore, "there's no taste off the vegetables anymore. When I was a boy we grew carrots and parsnips that were full of goodness manured by our own dung and . . ."

"You mean Sergeant," I interrupted, "ye used your own excrement to manure the carrots?"

That stopped him, for a while anyway.

I made for the kitchen and signalled to The Dosser to follow me in.

"Dosser, you gobdaw, you served Sammy. It'll take me a month to get rid of him and the grief and the begging to be let back. Warn him this is his last chance. Any messing and he's out."

"I'm sorry Sandy, but you'll have to do it yourself. Sure he's a headcase."

"Well, you're supposed to bar headcases."

"And what'll I do if he goes mad?"

"Call the cops"

"But it might take them five minutes to get here at the very best and by then I could be dead."

"You have no bottle Dosser, do you know that?"

"And what about the hitchhikers?"

"What hitchhikers?"

"Well, that's it, there's none around here is there? That lunatic could have them buried under floorboards or stuck in deep freezes. That Tubbermore Torso thing got an awful death. I wouldn't put anything past that gang."

There was no answer to that. It was Halloween and The Dosser's imagination was passing itself out.

"Can I go home now?"

"No Dosser, you're booked until eight."

The Dosser headed back to the pub in a sulk.

"Dead man walking," was his parting remark as he left the sanctuary of the kitchen.

There was no way could I face another second with those two. I went up to bed to get myself a good rest before facing into the night's work.

I woke about two hours later after a succession of horrendous nightmares. In my dream, The Bore and Sammy were barbecuing me. Basting me in my own juices. I was trussed up on a revolving spit a few feet over a roasting fire which reared up every few minutes when bits of my body fat fell on the flames. Sammy was eating slices of me with great relish, contentedly patting the rolls of flesh below his navel, all the time drooling at the mouth. Rivers of spitgrease rolled down the avenues of his jaws, congealing here and there on his unshaven jowls. The run-off created a reservoir in his lower lip, which was the size of a child's paddling pool.

"Is his arse cooked yet, Sergeant? Bags I his Mickey."

Sammy was interfering with himself as he spoke.

"Quick Sergeant Brogan," calls Sammy, "hand me the skewer and carving knife, the tassel is getting singed . . ."

The Bore is, as usual, ignoring whatever anyone else had to say, even when the topic concerned the consumption of my penis.

I didn't know if it was day or night when I woke up, whether I was late for work or not, whether I was alive or dead. There's nothing worse than lying awake in the dark on your own. I felt this overwhelming sense of isolation and loneliness. It's always been the same. There are times when I find it impossible to get up and impossible to stay in bed. Paula says I'm afraid of things that will never happen, that I notice too much.

When I was a small fella I made a cross out of my schoolbooks after a visit to the pictures in Ballymore to see 'The Bride of Dracula'. Sometimes when I wake in the middle of the night I phone far flung cousins in different time zones just to have someone to talk to.

I stumbled down the stairs to the bar. A dendrologist can tell from the number of rings the exact age of the tree. It's the same with a barman. From an inspection of the tidemark rings on the side of the glass I'd swear that miserable bastard of a policeman was still drinking from the same half-pint he had when I took to the bed.

It was probably the cumulative effect of years of his head-wrecking company, or maybe I was still in dream time, but there and then I barred

The Bore as well as Sammy.

"Finish up your drinks and get out of here. I'm sick of this carry-on."

"Ha?" responded a shocked Bore.

"Out now. Come on, get out. Enough is enough."

"Is it just Sammy?" asks The Dosser.

"No, it's the two of them. They're both barred. Out, out, out."

"Go easy," counselled The Dosser, "you sound just like Mrs Thatcher."

The Bore got up from his stool and hauled himself up to his full height of six feet three inches.

"I'm not a man for not staying where he's not wanted. There was always a bit of a want in you my buck, so there was. A bit of a want."

"Well, what kept you here for the last twenty years so?" I replied, raising my voice to take him on.

The Bore and Sammy walked slowly towards the door. I was afraid of my life Sammy would turn on me. My left knee shook uncontrollably as it often does in times of physical danger in the pub. Sammy was well capable of losing the head and dismembering me as easily as you'd tear the wings and legs from a well-cooked chicken.

The Bore must have been aware that Sammy was capable of violence and took him by the arm.

Then it dawned on me that I had barred a guard and I went to the front door to tell The Bore he was welcome back but without Sammy.

It was too late. He was so mad he didn't hear a word I was saying.

"You hypocrite. How dare you insult a man who cherished and

upheld the laws of the Republic of Ireland and you a suspected murderer."

Oh Jesus, I said to myself, what have I done this time?

"Ah I'm sorry Sarge," I said through the half-opened front door, "I must be on tablets or something. Come on back in."

There was no stopping The Bore now.

"The game is up now so it is. Your game is up my bucko. I'll see you in the dock before the year is out. By golly, there's no sorry. You're in my book now."

The sergeant was roaring at the top of his voice. He could be heard in Ballymore. Every now and then Sammy joined in.

"Hear! Hear! Sergeant. He done her in. Oh he definny done her in."

I closed and bolted the front door. Through the big bar window I could see the spits beginning to calcify at the corners of Sammy's mouth.

"If you confess now, we won't put you in with a ladyboy in the cell. We'll get the priest after you . . . make a clean breast of it and he'll give you absolution."

The Bore was playing both roles in the good cop, bad cop routine. It was a trick he learned when he was the only guard in the little village of Owenmore over the border. I suppose he had to improvise.

Sammy took the lead from his companion. He rode in with his tuppence worth. "And you dumped her in my bog and got me into trouble as well."

"Oh yes Sammy, he done her alright. Done her and done her in," agreed The Bore. "He gave her an awful death. He murdered his own sweetheart and cut off her poor head."

At that very moment Minnie May Murphy was passing The Mayo Bar on her way home from pestering the doctor in Ballymore.

Minnie changed direction and hid behind a parked cattle lorry in The Square, near enough to the pub to hear everything but far enough away to be out of danger if Sammy lost the head. She held a hankie to her nose to deaden the smell. Even from where I stood the stench was overwhelming but Minnie would have crawled up a cow's arse if she thought there was a bit of news there.

Minnie didn't hear everything but she heard enough. In ten minutes everyone in the village would know what happened. The story would be twisted and tweaked and misrepresented until it bore no resemblance to the actual event.

Old women who had been house-bound for ten years would hear every detail within a half an hour. Soon the story would reach Ballymore. Before long, Glen emigrants in bars in New York and Sydney will discuss me. The overseas spin on the tale will gallop back to The Glen initially as supposition but will harden into fact when one person in the chain neglects to mention the assumptions are theoretical. The Hero summed it up well: "A pimple on the arse in Ballymore will turn into piles by the time it reaches Glenlatin".

CHAPTER THIRTEEN

LET SLEEPING DOGS LIE

IT WAS EASTER SUNDAY 1980, the year you were born.

I found myself alone in the flat in Cork. My friends were all at home for the holidays. The city boys didn't know I was on my own and I was too embarrassed to tell them I had one of my girls in the family way.

Easter Sunday was always a great day in The Mayo Bar. The Glen Diaspora came back from the cities for the weekend. There was a buzz about the place you only get at Easter, Christmas and long weekends. I always loved Easter Sunday. There was a feeling that the winter was over, even if the weather was winterish.

Easter is the time of rebirth. It gave me great consolation when I was a small boy to know that my mother was capable of rising from the dead. I remember one Easter Sunday morning - I must have been six. The bulbs my Dad and myself planted in November, the month of the dead, were now daffodils dancing on my mother's grave. My indoctrination into the one true faith had just begun and I was greatly impressed by the story of the resurrection.

Master Moran was to spend the year young boys matured into young men, from five to six, telling us all about the devil and hell. Moran felt that by five you were ready for anything, which was mostly verbal abuse and physical punishment. He was very descriptive when it came to hell and didn't spare the pyrotechnics.

Then when the boys and girls of Senior Infants thought they were doomed Moran would lower the fire escape ladders: Confession and Resurrection.

I waited and waited for my mother to come up out of the ground. My father arrived about three that day. He was frantic. I'd say he didn't know whether to wallop me or hug me. When I told him the reason I stayed there he told me I was an eejit and that I wouldn't meet my mother again until I went to heaven. The Snipe was with him. He handed me an Easter Egg. We ate it in the back of the car.

"I had to show them all our secret spots," The Snipe said. "They thought you was stolen." His face was smeared with chocolate from the egg which was well melted from the car window.

There were sweets in the middle of the Easter egg and when I asked my Dad if he'd like one I could see he was crying.

I learned two things that Easter Sunday morning. One was never put a chocolate egg on the back window of a car on a sunny Easter Sunday and two, my mother wasn't coming back.

The Hero told me there was no such place as hell and even if there was it couldn't be worse than watching Ballymore beat The Glen by eighteen or nineteen points in the North Championship. Heaven was a grand spot, he said, with a sweet shop on every corner and toy shops on every street. And my mother would surely have opened one by now, her being well settled and her being such a lovely woman when she was down here, and her being very fond of me and knowing I'd love a toy shop when I'd come up to see her. There were tears in The Hero's eyes too.

My father turned back and said, "Sandy, don't go away anymore or I'll turn into a slapping father. I'm warning you." But even though I disappeared many times afterwards he never laid a hand on me.

I didn't expect to see The Snipe on another Easter Sunday morning. "Your Dad sent me with your dinner," he announced, handing me a tinfoil-wrapped plate. A hundred and ten miles of a potholey drive to bring a bit of my father's famous roast mutton, pandy and marrowfat peas that had to be steeped the night before.

It was the same menu every Sunday in our house except, of course, when Christmas day fell on a Sunday. Then we had turkey. The pandy and the marrowfat peas were a staple though.

Sometimes Dad would forget to steep the pebbly peas in water on Saturday night and he would be forced to open a tin. The Hero used to go into a desperate sulk and refuse to eat at all. He was a traditionalist. He'd storm out of the house and rev the car up several times in a fierce temper and off with him to the Ballymore Park Hotel for Sunday lunch.

The Snipe handed me the tinfoil-covered plate and an envelope from my Dad with a tenner in it.

"About the baby."

"What will I do Snipe? I'm going crazy here on my own. I spent the weekend eating semolina and culling mice just to pass the time."

The Snipe looked around the wreck of a flat. I could see him thinking to himself how does Sandy live in such a kip. He sat down on the edge of the bony sofa. The rest of it was covered with old magazines, chip cartons, books and sundry items of clothing. My bed blankets were bundled up one end. I couldn't bear the thought of sleeping in the bedroom on my own. I left the snowy, rabbit-eared TV on all night for company and as an insurance against nightmares.

"That's what your Dad said. You'd be cracking up. He's fierce worried."

"What would you do?"

"Go to her and tell her you'll back her up."

"You mean marry her?"

"No, not unless you want to but you have a half share in the baby. You'll be sorry when you're old. Facing up to something is the best way to go."

"Jesus Snipe, you sound like my oul' fella. Did he put you up to this?"

The Snipe stood up and went to the oven to put the dinner into it for warming up but after one look he changed his mind and said we'd better eat it cold. We split the mutton into two plates. The Snipe lost his appetite after his inspection of the mushroom factory oven.

The condemned man ate a hearty meal. I took off the jeans I'd been wearing for the last week. Showered. The Hero described showers "as useless except for the freezing cold water preferred by monks and the like who want to take their mind off the other thing". I stood up on a chair to put on my pants. The net curtains on the window were eight inches short and I was anxious to avoid a charge of indecent exposure.

After two and half hours of cautious driving and atrocious country music, we found ourselves outside Tom Tie's. I was terrified.

The cottage was neat and newly whitewashed with an acre of ground at the back. The Tom Tie's planted potatoes and cabbage and carrots. Added on an extension to the house to match the extension in their family. Whitewashed, put down paths and a lawn. Painted and planed. Scrubbed and furnished until they had a home they could be proud of.

"Come on Snipe, let's vamoose. They're probably out visiting. There isn't a sign of life. Not a dicky bird."

The Snipe stopped in his tracks and looked at me for a few seconds as if to say 'what kind of an eejit do you take me for?'

"Faith then there is. There's smoke and I can see movement behind the lace curtains. Come on Sandy. It mightn't be as bad as you think."

"Ah great, Snipe. No bother. I'll just pop in and say a 'Hi Mr and Mrs Tom Tie. I just polled your daughter. Cool for Easter isn't it but sure it won't be long warming up'."

Rover, the border collie, jumped from hind to front feet like a rocking horse and invited me to play. The big old Morris Oxford was parked outside the front door, gleaming and immaculate. Ten years old and as good as new. It was one of the few English habits Tom Tie had picked up from his sojourn across the pond. Car husbandry was about as far as it went though.

There was a little singing glasha flowing by the house. A row of soaking wet clothes dragged down the sagging clothesline. But there were no unisex Wranglers or shirts without collars hanging off the line.

A few Rhode Island Red hens scratched for worms and a high Nelly bike lay up against the wall minding its own business. It belonged to Mary O. The greyhounds in the run behind the house were howling a chorus to the sound of the car pulling in.

The path leading up to the house sunk below the level of the lawn due to the softness of the ground. Rows of late daffodils fluttered on either side. The early ones were fading fast in the cover of the ditch on either side of the house. The clustered clumps of daffodil stems were bound together in elastic bands. No one could ever explain why. Seven Up bottles full of water were spread around the lawn. The idea was dogs and cats would see their own reflection in the bottles. The cats and dogs would run off to avoid a territory dispute and of course would deposit their insides elsewhere. The Hero marvelled at the cunning of it and said, "It's no wonder the English conquered the world."

I was hoping the path would go on forever or lead to nowhere like a mad famine road.

"Do you remember that lovely poem by Wordsworth about the daffodils?"

"Kind of Sandy," replied The Snipe, who no doubt thought it a strange time to be reciting poetry.

'I wandered lonely as a cloud
That floats on high o'er vales and hills
When all at once I heard I shout
Get off the fecking daffodils.'

We laughed at the joke and not for the first time. But the cottage was still in front of us like a suspended sentence. I kept on up the path. The Snipe was at my side. At last I was doing the right thing. On the side of the cottage was a big timber rain barrel. Mary O and I brought frogs from the bog for her little brother Joey to play with. There was only the two of them in the family.

The window of the lopsided extension tacked on to the side of the old cottage was open. This was Mary O's room.

It was built at your grandmother's insistence. She's still alive. Lovely woman. Molly was one of a big family and had to share a room with three other sisters and a couple of baby brothers. She always wanted Mary O to have her own room. Your grandfather built it himself, working all hours to get it finished. The room was spartan but tidy and feminine with teddy bears and pink walls and a poster of a tin of beans.

We opened the front door. There was no such thing as knocking in the country back then. You just opened the door very slowly to give the people inside a chance to settle themselves.

Your grandfather was asleep in the armchair by the turf-fired Stanley number five. His shirt was open. Rosary beads necklaced the top of the armchair. Tom Tie's braces were out of commission down the side of his pants. The tie rose and fell on the swell of his belly. The kitchen was like an oven. The Stanley was revved up to the last to roast the Sunday dinner.

Molly, your grandmother, was cleaning the dishes in the sink at the other side of the kitchen.

"Hello. It's me," I announced in a voice just a few decibels above a whisper at the same time pushing the door in slowly.

Tom Tie woke up with a jump. I remember at the time thinking he reminded me of the giant whose chicken was stolen by Jack of Jack and The Beanstalk fame.

Fee-fi-fo-fum.

I knew instinctively that I should run. But I couldn't. Tom Tie's manic half-asleep, half-awake eyes hypnotised me. His eyeballs looked as if they were attached to springs that were so taut they would snap and send his eyes flying at me. I should have moved off or even moved to one side to break the spell.

The one thing about being reared in a pub is that you can see danger before anyone else; I can walk into a crowded room and scan it in seconds. I think I wanted to be hit. All I could do was stand there. Then he made for me. It was as if he had been dreaming about giving me a good hammering before he woke up and now here I was in front of him.

"Don't Daddy, stop," shouted young Joey who knew only too well what his oul' fella was capable of.

Tom Tie hit me full on the mouth breaking one of my front teeth. My face seemed to be shunted until it hit the front of my brain in a head-on collision. I went backwards but I didn't fall. The blow was intended to break my teeth, not to knock me. My hands were hanging by my side. He body-charged me and slammed me up against the dresser. A flurry of digs followed.

There was blood all over the place. I made no effort to defend myself other than to put my hands up to my face. He threw two or three or four more punches. One caught me in the ribs. It was the hardest blow I ever got in my life. It still comes against me.

Then he ripped my hands from my face and gouged my eyes, temporarily blinding me. It wasn't the first time he did a job on a fella.

Tom Tie knelt on my chest choking me so I couldn't breathe. This was the way the bull suffocated his victims. I gasped and wriggled for breath like a fish on the side of the riverbank. I thought I was going to suffocate. I was so out of breath I couldn't even shout stop. The Snipe jumped on his back. I managed to squirm free. Tom Tie tossed my cousin to one side.

Molly rushed over and threw herself on me. Young Joey was screaming: "Stop Daddy, stop". I was almost choking in my own blood. I had swallowed one of my teeth. I played a bit of rugby in the college that year and I was taught how to protect myself in a loose ruck. Hands over head, I curled myself up in the foetal position. Tom Tie was coming in with kicks. He was screaming: "You bastard, you ruined us. You shamed us. You ruined my little girl's life. Big-shot bollix with your big pub. College boy shit. Smarter than us, is it? Smarter than the navvy thick."

The words he used seemed to justify to himself at least what he was doing to me. He kept shouting as if he needed to hear himself say such things to keep up his fury.

From where I lay I could see his Sunday shoes gleaming black under the armchair. Beside them was a hair slide belonging to Mary O. I was amazingly calm. Almost relieved. He pucked me three or four more times. I felt my arms go numb from the force of the blows which were of such ferocity they went straight to the bone. Years of slavery on the building sites of England and on his own place, as well as the hurt bursting out of him, gave him superhuman strength. And wasn't I the man who abused his hospitality and dishonoured his only daughter, destroyed his dream? He might as well have stayed in England.

Then he stood up and stopped. The man knew he acted like an animal. I could see he wanted to say something, maybe apologise, but the words that flew so freely from his mouth seconds before were all gone. Your grandfather looked around at the kitchen wreckage as if he had just come in. Then he walked out the door without saying a word.

The whole incident lasted no more than a few minutes but it seemed like an hour. If The Snipe, Molly and Joey hadn't intervened he might have killed me. I'll never forget the choking. The panic. The realisation I might die. And then the strange sense of calm as if death might not be such a bad thing. Still, I think he would have stopped at a certain stage. He was just overwhelmed by my theft of the dream he worked so hard to attain.

The Snipe reckoned afterwards if there was ever an old saying that made sense it was 'let sleeping dogs lie'.

Molly put me sitting down on a chair. She dabbed my wounds with cotton wool soaked in iodine. The stinging from the iodine brought me back to the horrible reality of what had happened as the Morris Oxford pulled out of the haggard with a screech.

No doubt your grandfather was off to the pub. Later he would probably confide in a few friends that he gave me a good hiding. A few freeloaders and arse-lickers would agree with him that he did the right thing. After five or six drinks he would feel his honour was restored. Until he woke up the next day, that is.

The kitchen looked as if it was a bomb scene. Blood on the white linen tablecloth. Blood smeared on the sideboard. Blood spots on the mirror of the sideboard. The Sacred Heart must have fallen off the wall in protest and lay in smithereens, bleeding on the floor. The red and green leprechaun who lived in a small, transparent plastic dome was lying on the floor. The little prisoner could make it snow in summer when you turned his house upside down. Mary O's Holy Communion photographs. Six in a white dress. The glass was smashed. Blood on the dress. The happiest day of Mary O's life. She was smiling and excited. There would be a trip to Ballymore for a toy. The neighbours would all call round to the house for the Communion breakfast. It hit me all of a sudden that I was an adult now. Mistakes were punished ruthlessly.

"I'm sorry, Sandy. He's never like this," your grandmother said. "Not since we married. He used to fight a lot after the drink in England but never since."

"I had it coming Molly. I treated Mary O very badly. I'm so sorry. Where is she? I came to see her."

"Gone to have the baby and then to have it adopted, Sandy. We think she's with the nuns. Mary O left on Saturday morning with nothing only as much as her old suitcase would carry. She didn't tell anyone she was going but I'm sure she's in good hands. The priest knows where she is but he can't tell us because he promised Mary O he wouldn't."

Molly looked away from me as she said it, as if to emphasise it was a done thing.

"I need to see her badly."

"Will you marry her?"

"If I have to."

"If you have to? Is it how she isn't good enough for you, is it? Is it because we're not big people? If you made the doctor's daughter pregnant you'd have married her."

"We're not like that Molly. There's no bigness in The Heroes. I'm just too young to get married. I don't know what to do. I must see her. It's my baby too. Even just to talk to her and explain myself."

Molly softened a bit. It wasn't like her to be hard on people and she didn't normally feel in any way inferior. She was one of those mighty women who just got on with things and kept the family in one piece with hard work and sacrifice. Now her years of extraordinary effort were all for nothing.

"I'm sorry Sandy. It's hard for you too. It's such a mess. I had such high hopes for Mary O. She'd have been the first of our crowd to go to university."

Molly started to cry. Joey helped her sit down on a sugan chair by the Stanley.

"Fr Fitzgerald advised us not to tell where Mary is and sure doesn't he know best? Anyway we don't know where she is?"

"I'm the father of that baby and I love Mary O. I know I was selfish but I didn't know what to do. Please ring up Fr Fitzgerald and tell him I'm on my way as soon as I get cleaned up. Please Molly, I have to see Mary O."

"It's none of my business Missus, but it might be nice if Sandy and Mary O got the chance to talk." The Snipe as usual kept his mouth shut until what needed to be said was said. People took notice of him when he talked.

"Alright so Snipe, if Fr Fitzgerald gives the alright we'll let Sandy see Mary O. I can tell you this though, she mightn't even marry you now. That's what she was saying before she left . . . Her father wants nothing more to do with her . . . He hit her again the other night . . . I'm afraid she might never come back . . ."

We left the poor woman crying in her broken kitchen.

CHAPTER FOURTEEN
SPAGHETTI BOLOGNAISE

THE BAR WAS QUIET tonight. I'm reminded of the boycott around the time you were born. I hope it's nothing more than the November abstinence. If it isn't, I'm in big trouble. There's no Hero or Dad to help me out this time. Paula has to be put through college. I make a living here in the pub but no more than that. And the village, like most country places, is very much in decline. People are drinking at home more. The Hero always advocated home drinking should be banned as it led to secret alcoholics. Especially the women whom he said were genetically addicted to wine.

I spend most of my spare cash paying for Paula in Dublin. But I have an overdraft and a car loan. I'm not as bad as The Hero with money but I'm not as good as my father with it either.

If people in a small village turn against you, that's that. You have to lease or sell out altogether. I have been lucky, I suppose, I don't have any opposition. But the worst thing of all is that my own people would even think I was capable of murdering a girl I loved - or loved for a while anyway. Not just any girl but your mother. My good name is at the mercy of The Rumour Factory. And what if Paula hears about the whole carry on? Some drunk or a "friend" might blab it out, dying to see her reaction.

Paula is thinking of moving in with her boyfriend. I am opposed to it but there isn't much you can do other than point out the pitfalls. She's a bit young for getting tied down with the same man and I feel her focus should be on getting herself qualified and not on a relationship. I also want her to see a bit of the world before she has a job and kids. Nobody travelled much in my time except maybe to the States looking for work. Times were bad and there were no jobs at home. For many it was a one-way trip. It's not that I want to live her life for her but I want her to make the best possible use out of her youth. I told her as much. As usual when told something she doesn't want to hear, she flew into a rage.

"What would you know about it?" she snapped. "You're a confirmed bachelor. Do you think I should deny myself the pleasure of living with someone I care about just because of your old-fashioned Catholic prejudices? Get a life."

At least it was better than the endless and extremely annoying 'whatevers' she threw back when I gave out or advised her over the last few years.

I reminded her of the financial aspect of our relationship. I was putting her through college and how dare she lecture me when she was getting into a commitment with someone she hardly knew. I shouldn't have said anything about my being her sponsor. It actually gives me comfort and pride to pay for her. Paula's a hard worker and if occasionally she comes home pissed out of her head she always gets herself back on track the next day. Before I could retract she flew off the handle.

"I'm nearly done in college and I can get a loan to go to America for the summer. In fact, I would go on the game before I would take another penny from you. Shove your cash up your arse."

And then as usual she slammed down the phone - if such a thing is possible with a mobile.

I was upset, not so much for myself but for her. There should be a law passed that no one should get into a serious relationship until they are thirty-five for women and about seventy for men. Anyway, I knew we'd sort things out between us in a few days.

Liam felt it was only a matter of time before The Bugle got hold of the story of the barring. If the concerned citizens were capable of writing to the Superintendent, they were capable of writing to a newspaper.

Paula called back to apologise an hour later. We compromised. Danny, her boyfriend, would move in for weekends and Paula promised not to get pregnant but we didn't get into specifics. About whether or not she was taking proper precautions. I just couldn't bring myself to talk to her about that kind of stuff. The promise not to get pregnant covered the lot. The Hero would have been proud of the accommodation.

I was about to arrange to go to see her and tell her the whole story but as usual I chickened out.

"You'll love Danny. He's a dote but not a softie or anything. He plays football and stuff. You know he really cares for me. He even cooked for me last night."

"Spaghetti Bolognaise, I suppose?"

"How did you know?"

"I just know."

CHAPTER FIFTEEN
GOLF LESSONS

THE SNIPE TOOK ME to my Auntie Annie's after the beating in your mother's kitchen. I surveyed my face in the hall mirror. My bruises were starting to change colour. Purpley-blue and reddish, like a threatening evening sky. I wondered how would I explain the state of my face to Rachel, if she ever decided to talk to me again. It wasn't easy being in love with two women at the same time.

Auntie Annie cleaned me up and put more iodine on my cuts. The missing teeth were the worst part. My father had false teeth, as did The Hero. My father was self-conscious about his teeth. He had dentures top and bottom.

"Promise me one thing little fella, always brush your teeth," he'd say. He must have said it to me a thousand times. I promised and I kept my promise but now I would have to wear a plate. It would be a terrible blow to him after all his years of teeth husbandry. There would have been glory and reason if I lost them playing football but this was crazy.

How could I ever explain what happened? I could tell him I was mugged in Cork but then he'd follow up with the Guards. If I told him I had a car accident he'd want to meet the driver. My father always had to see things through to the finish. He had an unquenchable thirst for truth.

Auntie Annie was very upset when she saw the state of me. She was a very kind woman but could get into a temper if she saw someone wronged. Auntie Annie wanted to call a policeman but only after I spoke to my Dad. I wouldn't hear of it. I had to get to see Fr Fitzgerald at all costs. Auntie Annie finally persuaded me to stay the night and to put off seeing Fr Fitzgerald until after eleven Mass the next morning, Easter Monday.

We finally agreed that if my Dad and The Hero saw the state of us they would lose all reason and maybe The Hero might have Tom Tie kneecapped. The Provos hadn't yet developed the technique of shooting people through hands joined in prayer. This was of course years before The Hero told me the true story of The Mayo Job.

Auntie Annie said my Dad was a much more dangerous man.

"We must keep you out of sight tomorrow at all costs," she said. "Go back to college and I'll talk to your Dad in due course. He won't let things lie. Your Dad is a moral man and will see things through whatever the cost."

I remember waking the next morning and for the first minute all my troubles were forgotten. There was always a great sleep in Auntie Annie's. Then a terrible feeling hit me, a feeling of having to face up to things. I buried my head under the blankets and tried to go back to sleep but I couldn't. Then I tried my menage-a-trois fantasy but even that stalwart left me down.

My tongue felt the raw holes where my front teeth used to be. The injured ribs were affecting my breathing and my arms were so sore I couldn't lift them without feeling a wrenching pain. I was tempted to sneak out the front door and leg it to Ballymore where I could get a bus back to Cork. The two-hour wait until the rest of the house stirred was an eternity.

I knew The Snipe was feeling very guilty, blaming himself for pushing me to meet the Mary O's.

Auntie Annie arranged for Taxi Tony to collect me and bring me to meet with Fr Fitzgerald. Auntie Annie took down a tenner from the chocolate box with the pusheen in front of it and told me to give it to the parish priest to say a Mass for my mother. There was a tenner for myself which I promised to pay back later in the summer when the exams were over.

I wore The Snipe's duffel coat. The sleeves ended above my wrists but it had a big hood like a monk's cowl, which I pulled over my head and held with my two hands as if I was keeping curtains closed.

Taxi Tony as usual regaled me with tales of the antics of lovers in the back seat. The five miles slipped by quickly. Too quickly. Again I almost funked it but after a chat with myself I slipped quietly in by the side of the church to the presbytery at the back.

The Canon's housekeeper led me into a big room full of polished mahogany furniture. The centrepiece was a huge dresser with carvings of nymphs and Greek gods and a mirror which I tried to avoid looking at. A silver tea-set, polished until the silver was almost blue, sat on top of the dresser. I could see the reflection of my bashed face on an urn. It was almost comical, as if I was looking at one of those trick mirrors you see in funfairs. The bookcase was full of the most vapid books you could imagine.

'Gardening for Seaside Gardeners'. 'The Life of St Malachi the Merciful'. At the time I was reading 'Catcher in the Rye' and a smuggled in copy of 'Lesbian Lovers 3: Unplugged'.

The dining table was so long that if you were asked to pass the salt you would have to slide it down the shining wood like the bartenders in the cowboy movies.

Our sitting room at home was my favourite room. The wallpaper was torn here and there and the carpet was threadbare. The Hero's chair had enough room for two small boys and himself to watch Tombstone Territory. There was always a dicethrow of Lego scattered around. Then when Paula came along she girlied up the place a bit with pink Teddies and Barbies and little heart-shaped picture frames. But this room was neither masculine nor feminine. It was sterile and cold.

I started to leaf through a book on the smaller of the two tables, 'Fashion in Florence in the Sixteenth Century'.

For a big man, Fr Fitzgerald was light on his feet. I was only alerted of his presence by the whisper of his cassock.

"So you have an interest in the Renaissance, Sandy . . . and fashion?"

"Not really, Father," I replied.

He looked disappointed so I immediately handed him Auntie Annie's tenner, which seemed to cheer him up no end. He finessed the note into what seemed like a secret pocket in his soutane.

"You must have had a bad fall, Sandy, or maybe it may have been football?"

"It was neither Father. I was in a fight with Tom Tie."

"Oh my gosh, Sandy. These things do happen."

"I'm afraid I deserved it Father, over not standing by Mary O."

The priest sat down on a high-hoisted, throne-like armchair and pointed to an antiquey-looking, narrow-arsed, thin-legged mahogany chair well away from him over on the other side of the room. He spoke as if he was reading from a script.

"No road is without a pothole, my boy. The initial act or series of acts which caused the pregnancy is of course a very serious transgression but provided you have resolved not to re-offend you can put the matter to rest and move on to a life of fulfilment within the Catholic tradition."

It was the first time it dawned on me since I knocked up Mary O that Confession could wipe the slate clean. It was a far more practical concept than the resurrection. I resolved there and then to go to Confession immediately and to abstain from any act or series of acts until I was married. But all the Confessions in the world couldn't alter the fact that the act or series of acts had your mother pregnant. I said as much to Fr Fitzgerald.

"Sandy, your concern is gratifying and exactly what I would expect of a young man of your breeding and education."

I explained my case to the priest. I wanted to find Mary O and help her in any way I could.

"Can I take it you will marry her, the young woman?"

"I don't know what to do. I'll marry her I suppose . . . if I have to."

"My dear boy, the Mary O's are a good family but the girl in question took advantage of a temporary flaw in your character."

"Ah no Father, it wasn't like that at all. It was nearly all my fault."

He stirred himself in the throne, sat up and leaned forward.

"It would have been a feather in her gap (I swear he said gap and not cap) to have married into a prestigious family. You can by all means marry her if you wish but I promised the young lady I would not reveal her whereabouts."

"Father, I just want to meet her and tell her I will support her and the baby and then in a few years we can see if we want to get married."

"That would be totally unacceptable, Sandy. The female in the matter has resolved to put the child up for adoption. This is the best for all concerned. I promise you the child will be well cared for and the mother will also be seen after. It's for the best. People who are experienced in these matters have taken control of the situation. People who have your best interests at heart, I might add."

"But Father she disappeared only on Saturday. Do you mind me asking Father if you have any idea where she is?"

The priest dismounted his seat and stood up, indicating our little chat was now over by holding his hand out flat and then waving it in the direction of the door.

"Tell me now Sandy are you still at the golf? Is the putting any better? We must play sometime soon."

He was moving away.

"Could you ask her to let me visit her, Father? I promise it will be for only a few minutes."

"I wish I had your power and accuracy off the tee. I'm good around the greens though. Doctor Dan said to me the other day, 'Padre you are some man on the dance floor,' meaning the green. He calls me Padre and I let him. 'Padre,' he said, 'you're the best high handicap putter in the world.' Can you imagine such a thing? Ah, he's a card. The best high handicap putter in the world. By golly."

"But Father. Please can I see her? Please?"

I gasped for breath from the pain in my ribs as I rose up from the bony old chair.

"Now I have other duties to attend to, if you don't mind."

With that he walked towards the door. I made one last plea.

"I have to see her. Please help me. I know you can persuade the family into allowing me to see her. They'll listen to you. Please Father."

The priest spoke to me sideways from the doorway.

"Sandy, believe me when I say this to you. I am on your side. I know the exact nature and scope of the conflict that is going on in your head. There are forces and dynamics at work here beyond the scope of my intervention. I too am subject to constraints and while I would like to help I just cannot do any more than offer my sympathy and condolences and reiterate I fully understand the dilemma you find yourself in. I can of course offer forgiveness and if it is convenient I will even hear your Confession here and now.

"The Hero knows what is best. I beseech you to take his advice. You have to. You have to. Trust me please. It is best for all of us if the baby is placed for adoption. I will personally ensure the child is placed with a good family. I promise you that. You must do as The Hero says. He has great influence and will use it to suit his purposes - or should I say for your benefit.

"Keep at your bit of golf, Sandy. It's a great way to take your mind off things. You have a natural swing and a bit of work with your short game will play rich dividends."

He put his hand on my shoulder for a second and walked off quickly.

The Reverend Father was gone through another door at the far end of the hall before I could get in another plea to see your mother. He was fast with those twinkle-toed feet of his and I was directed out the front door by his housekeeper. It was like an illusionist's trick. Both the priest and myself seemed to leave the room without my noticing.

CHAPTER SIXTEEN
We Manufacture a New Rumour

THE BALLYMORE SQUAD CAR had been parked out in the Square just opposite the presbytery for about half an hour. Liam was chatting with the driver and the front seat passenger. I waited for it to drive away.

It was four in the morning, and I couldn't sleep. Too tired from recounting the past to write anymore about it. The emotion of it all has left me drained. Since I started writing I spend half the morning in bed but it has to be done. Still, the worst is almost over. Almost. I had hoped getting all this down on paper would be in some way therapeutic but it doesn't feel like it. I'm driving and something hits me and it's back home to cut and paste. I wish I could edit my life. Wouldn't it be very handy?

Liam spotted me standing inside the big window of the bar. He tapped at the window when the squad car drove off. The collar of his pyjamas was sticking out up over the blue police shirt. Dried red wine stains circled the rim of his lips like badly-applied lipstick.

"You're up late, Sandy. Is everything alright?"

I told Liam I was fine.

A car was stolen in Ballymore and was heading towards The Glen. The squad car roused him. He had company back in the station, "a woman from over the water". Whether that was from the other side of Ballymore Bridge or England I couldn't tell you. He had time for a quick nightcap, though. I'd say he knew I was addled.

I asked him if there was any word on the torso.

"I was going to call to tell you tomorrow, Sandy. It's not official yet but the corpse dates back to the time of the Famine. She was murdered alright, but I think you can take it we won't be investigating this one."

I thanked Liam for the good news but it wasn't anything we didn't already know. The policeman tucked the collar of his pyjamas inside his Garda shirt. I slagged him for wearing pyjamas while he was in bed with a woman.

"Ah I'm old-fashioned, Sandy. I'm not into this foreplay lark either. It's wearing."

"You know The Glen definition of foreplay don't you?"

"No Sandy, but I'd say you're going to tell me."

"Pull across the curtains, Brigid."

"Don't get that one, Sandy."

I left him be for a while as he sat at the bar counter trying to figure out the joke. While he was sitting there I forwarded the gag to Paula who was a compulsive collector and disseminator of prurient text humour.

"Liam not a word about it. Let's keep it quiet."

"About the foreplay and the PJs?"

"No, you bollix. About the corpse. Let's send out a few stories that the corpse was beheaded by an axe. I suppose they hardly had chainsaws back then. The Tubbermore Axe Massacre. Coming soon to a cinema near you."

"Sandy, The Hero will never be dead as long as you're around," smiled Liam. "I'll keep it quiet as long as I can, Sandy. Let's give The Rumour Factory plenty of rope. I'm looking forward to seeing them making absolute eejits out of themselves."

He headed for the door. "And I don't get that axe murder remark either."

CHAPTER SEVENTEEN

MY FATHER PROPOSES MARRIAGE

I LEFT THE PRESBYTERY after the talk with Fr Fitz and walked straight out through the coiffured grounds of St Teresa's with its monkey-puzzle tree, gazebos, trellises, garden seats and the well-tended, pebbly graves of former parish priests. A peacock picked at worms upscuttled on the lawn. A thrush gave himself a good wash in a birdbath and a raiding party of crows dropped in uninvited in search of anything that was going. Over on the wall separating the garden from the square was a tromp d'oeuil. I tried to open the false door plastered on to the cut stone wall. I felt like an even bigger fool than I already was. I imagined there were hundreds of people sitting up on the wall clicking their shoe heels together with their delight at my stupidity, sneering and pointing at me, falling off with all the laughing. A crow caw was a guffaw. Their hoarse chorus was mocking me.

It seems so long ago and so far away, even though the church grounds are exactly the same today.

I see myself now, standing in the Square, with the duffel coat and the black eyes peeping out from under the cowl. It's as if I'm viewing a clip from a movie. I'm not even looking at the Sandy who is writing this but at a different person, like maybe my son or someone very close to me. The little boy who waited at his mother's grave on Easter Sunday isn't me either. I feel so sorry for him. I want to help him, hug him, and bring his mother back. I want to avenge the student lost in the Square in his own village. I want the me who is tip-tapping here tonight to fight his corner. I know the road the boy is about to take and I know which paths to avoid but I can't tell him.

It reminds me of the night Mary O and myself were kissing and messing about in the back seats of the Plaza Picturedome in Ballymore. John Wayne rode into an ambush and some fella who had seen the film the night before roared out: "Fuck sake John, you gom. Don't be going back into that shagging gulch again."

The whole thing is like a movie where different persons play the main character at different stages of his life. Sandy the boy. Sandy the man boy. Sandy the man. But there's only the one take. There isn't the luxury of a director's cut years after.

The Square was empty save for the tractors of a few stragglers who were either doing a bit of shopping or having a few drinks on their way home from delivering milk to the creamery or just playing down the clock until it was time to do something.

A stranger asked me for directions. His sunglasses were skyfacing on his head and he had a nice girl parked in the front seat of the car. I was tempted to run and leave him there when I saw my Dad's black Cortina, KIN 954, drive past.

But The Glen was a place where courtesy was a sacrosanct duty.

My father jumped out of the car while I was trying to tell the stranger he had to get up and over Fat Arse first before he saw the sprawl of Ballymore before him on the other side. These directions confused him no end. I was explaining Fat Arse was a hill and not a person when my father pulled up. He jumped out of the car leaving the engine running and the door open.

"Jesus Christ, what happened to you? Who did this to you?"

The priest's car flashed by almost subliminally. He didn't even look in our direction.

The stranger moved away without turning his back. His sunglasses were pulled down from the top to cover up his eyes as if it would make him invisible to the two lunatics in The Square. He got into his snazzy car and kissed his dolly girl. How I envied him.

I told my Dad that boot boys in the city attacked me on my way home from late night study in college.

"I was just in the church to say a prayer about the exams and they jumped me on my way out."

I was always a great man to come up with a spontaneous lie in times of trouble but this was my father and he always knew when I was fibbing.

"Where did you say the prayer?"

"That big cathedral at the bottom of College Road. I forget the name of it."

"St Finbarre's is it?"

"Yes Dad. St Finbarre's. That's the one."

"Sandy, first of all St Finbarre's is a Protestant cathedral; and secondly, churches are not left open late at night. I don't suppose you even went into a Catholic church since you went to Cork not to mind a Protestant one."

"I got mixed up, Dad."

"You're as mixed up a man as I've ever met. You're a man who lives his life in a cement mixer, you're that feckin well mixed up. Get in."

I was in no position to argue.

"What happened? And no shite about boot boys or prayers."

"Jesus Dad, I'm telling the truth there was three of them. I had no chance, they jumped me."

My father didn't believe a word. He just knew. When I was a small fella and he was trying vainly to get me into the habit of telling the truth he'd say, "Sandy, stick out your tongue 'til I see if it's black". I would keep my lips sealed and pressed so tight together the colour drained out of them. Eventually out would come the tongue.

"I thought as much," he would say in a grave voice. Then I would spill it all out. The truth.

"That's The Snipe's jumper you're wearing and where did you get that coat and there's no way that shirt is yours?"

It was easy enough to pick out The Snipe's jumpers - they were knitted by Auntie Annie from patterns straight out of the 1958 Woman's Realm Christmas Annual. In the summer, The Snipe wore parcel-from-America shirts. You'd want sunglasses to look at them. These were shirts sent by our cousin Tony who left home when he was sixteen and subsequently turned native.

Tony thought we were badly in need of clothing and sent home enormous parcels packed with the worst excesses of gaudy American fashion. Tom Tie had torn my denim Wrangler shirt to pieces in his rage. I was wearing a rayon puce shirt with Waikiki written on the front, pointy collars and a terrible smell of mothballs. The American moths must be the size of blackbirds. Dad was right - if I had a choice I wouldn't be seen dead in such a rig-out.

"You stayed in your aunt's last night didn't you? I won't be hard on you. All I want is the truth so I'll now how best to help you."

I told him the whole story. If I learned anything from my audience with the priest it was that for the second day in-a-row I was boxing well above my weight.

I can see myself sitting in the car with your Grandad in another scene from The Sandy of Easter Past. The me of today is there too. I'm standing around like a narrator in a play observing and commenting.

My father was calm. He just listened to what I had to say. He didn't interrupt or give out. I thought he'd lose the head and go after Tom Tie. He didn't. I suppose he couldn't afford the luxury of losing his temper even if he was seething inside.

Dad asked me if I would be prepared to take whatever action was necessary to see Mary O and keep the child from being sent for adoption. The way he asked only allowed for one answer. He fiddled impatiently with the keys and tapped at the dash as if he was dying to rev up and go off somewhere.

"I do Dad," I replied almost in a whisper.

"Will you marry her? I think you should."

"I just want to see her and ask her to keep the baby. I might marry her in a few years. I love Rachel."

My father almost jumped out of the seat and through the roof of the car.

"Jesus Christ, who's Rachel? But you're some man to complicate things. Rachel. Don't tell me she's pregnant by you as well."

He seemed greatly relieved when he I told him Rachel wasn't pregnant. I told him I was too young to get married but that I would support the child and Mary O.

"I'll quit college and get a job Dad. I'm not sure what to do. Tony always said he'd give me a job in New Jersey."

"You probably are too young to marry but it's the only honourable course of action open to you," said Dad.

"I'm proud you decided to come back and take responsibility. There's no question of giving up the university. I would have killed to go to university but the chance just wasn't there in my time. It was your mother's dream for you to get a degree, you know."

He always dipped his head and lowered his voice when he spoke of my mother. The mention of her seemed to calm us a bit.

"You told me Dad, but I just can't do it anymore. Maybe if I took a couple of years out?"

Dad told me it would break his heart and Grandad's if I gave up college. The two of them thought that once you had a degree you were on the way to everlasting prosperity and happiness.

"I have enough to look after Mary O and the baby and still put you through college. The one thing about being tied up behind the bar day and night is that you don't get a chance to spend any money and most of your own drinking is done at cost." He smiled at his little joke.

He was trying to cheer me up. I look at the two of us sitting in the car now and I want to put my arms around him and tell him I love him and what a fine man he is. But the car is a glass case with two exhibits and I can't get in.

"We'll go straight to Tom O'Reilly's house. There must be some legal right for a father to have say in the destiny of his own child."

Tom was a solicitor in Ballymore and a friend of my father's.

"A solicitor? What has a solicitor got to do with it? I don't want to go near any solicitors."

Dad ignored me, as he usually did when he was thinking aloud and not conversing. His mind was made up.

"We'll have to go as far as we can to get fair play. We might be in the High Court by tomorrow morning looking for an injunction or something. Right is surely on our side."

"Will we get Grandad?" I was afraid of my life of facing a solicitor without him.

"No. He'll be two hours getting ready. Shagging about trying on different jackets and plastering himself with after-shave and waiting a week until the bits of newspaper stuck onto his shaving cuts falls off. I want to know where we stand straight away. I can't handle all this waiting around."

In minutes we were outside Tom O'Reilly's Georgian bungalow in

Ballymore. Dad apologised for bothering him on his day off.

O'Reilly was in his slippers but didn't seem to be too put out by our intrusion. The Hero sent more clients his way than showers of rain in April. Dad told the whole story. O'Reilly listened attentively. For the first few minutes he took down notes only interrupting to clarify a few points. When Dad explained the purpose of our visit was primarily for me to seek some form of legal redress regarding the future of my unborn child, I knew from his demeanour the news wasn't going to be good. He stopped taking notes. It reminded me of a surgeon opening someone up only to close the person seconds later because there was nothing to be done.

"Sandy, your Dad and yourself have my greatest sympathy but I'm afraid the law doesn't offer you any solace on this occasion," he began. "Whatever my personal feelings, and believe me when I say morally you hold all the cards, legally you have no rights whatsoever."

My father jumped up from the sofa. He was furious.

"That's a disgrace. Can we fight that law somehow, Tom?"

The solicitor took a minute to compose himself. He seemed to be taken aback by my father's temper. Dad was normally a quiet man.

"I'm afraid not Liam. The highest court in the land has already ruled on the matter. The Supreme Court decided on a vote of 3 to 2 that a Greek Cypriot gentleman by the name of Nicolau had no rights over his unborn child due to the fact the child was conceived out of wedlock and the parties did not subsequently marry.

"The only way for you to have a say in the adoption of the child would be for Sandy to marry his child's mother. If the child were not to be put up for adoption you would have visiting rights in the event the marriage did not work out and could make an application to the courts regarding the child's welfare. The unmarried father of the child has no more standing than a stranger. I'm very sorry. There is nothing I can do. You could mount a constitutional action, but it would cost a fortune and there would be little hope of success in the current climate."

Three to two. It was like being pipped in a five-goal thriller in a soccer match. Beaten by the odd judge in five. I couldn't believe what I was hearing. I knew what was coming next. My Dad wasn't as quick to take things in as The Hero or myself. I could see his brain cranking up.

"Am I right in thinking," he asked the solicitor, "that my grandchild can be put up for adoption without my permission?"

"Yes."

"But if Sandy marries the girl we have rights."

"Yes."

My father gave me his 'you must do the right thing at all costs' look. I could see the expectation in his face when he used the word 'we'. It wasn't my child but our child as far as he was concerned. The 'we' meant go on son, marry her. Go on Sandy, take your medicine like a man. Sacrifice yourself at the altar of decency.

I see a young boy buried in the soft dip in the middle of the sofa with his knees drawn up to his belly button. The Sandy of Easter past is spotted with 'acene' as Sammy Suck calls it and is picking his nose with the nerves. He's pale and thin with a big mop of blond hair and the black and purple forlorn face of a defeated boxer.

All he wants to do is escape. The Sandy writing away here now wants to come in and solve everything retrospectively.

O'Reilly suggested I shouldn't make any decision for a while. Think things through, he said. Talk to The Hero, a man of great savoir faire. The child couldn't be put up for adoption until it was born and Mary O still had five or six months to go.

Then the solicitor in him took over.

"Unless of course the child is born prematurely. In such case time may be of the essence."

I thought of Rachel and how much I loved her.

Mary O was a nice girl but I had changed a lot from the time when we were kids. I knew enough about women even then to figure out the Rachel thing would always be hanging over us. With my Dad and the Mary O's piling on the pressure it would be a firing squad marriage.

I also knew from a practical point of view that The Hero was right. We were too young to get married. I was hardly out of adolescence and Mary O was doing the Leaving. She had never even spent a night away from home.

We were attracted to each other as much as anything by the fact that there was no one else around to go with. The marriage might work out and we might live happy ever after but the odds were against us.

I wanted to travel, see a bit of life. I wanted most of all to find myself, be my own man. I couldn't fathom being married, looking after a child when I was almost a child myself.

"I suggest you write to the Mary O's straight away with an offer of marriage. It's the only way forward, the honourable thing to do." My father had made up his mind. I was getting married and that was that.

"Hold on a minute," I said, speaking from the depths of the sofa. It was the first time I spoke since I entered the room.

"Who's going to marry her, you, is it?" I stood up. "Because I'm not. I have my life to live and here you are proposing marriage for me."

O'Reilly was very uneasy and stood up himself. "I don't think proposing marriage by solicitor's letter is a very good idea." Matchmaking obviously wasn't on the curriculum at law school. The solicitor suggested another visit to the Mary O's house by a third party such as the local parish priest. He began to shuffle the pages of blank paper in front of him.

"No, I wouldn't trust that fella as far as I could throw him," said Dad.

I nodded. At least we agreed on something.

"What about The Hero then, Liam?" suggested O'Reilly.

"He could be the man to broker some sort of arrangement, say whereby the young people could at least talk things through. He's a great diplomat and with his background in the War of Independence, The Hero is welcome in every house in the county. He has a keen brain and has undoubtedly Sandy's best interests at heart."

"My Dad could be the key," said my father, who brightened up a bit at the thought of the old wheeler-dealer getting involved. He looked relieved as if everything would be nicely squared away once the great man worked his magic.

The solicitor warmed to his own suggestion.

"I have been his solicitor for many years and am well aware of his tact and discretion. He's a man who has acted as an intermediary with some success in several turbary skirmishes. Any man who can solve a dispute between two Glen men over a turf boundary could run the UN. Savoir faire."

O'Reilly had a little laugh at his joke but neither my Dad nor I joined in.

"Savoir faire, Tom? Is it a legal term?" asked my Dad.

"Savoir faire means The Hero knows what he's at," I said.

My Dad looked pleased that I knew what savoir faire meant.

He agreed that The Mary O's wouldn't resent The Hero.

"I'm sure of it. Yes, my father's the man. Fr Fitzgerald is a great friend of his as well. Sure isn't he in there every week with him drinking whiskey and yapping? The Hero can bring the two sides together if anyone can. Who knows maybe if Mary O and yourself got to talk we might broker a marriage after all?"

"Well, you can't force a marriage on people," interrupted O'Reilly. "It has serious consequences for the validity of the marriage and may well lead to subsequent proceedings for nullity leading, inter alia, to the children of the union becoming illegitimate, retrospectively. Perhaps Sandy might be able to persuade her to keep the child. You would of course be responsible for maintenance in accordance with your means and the needs of the child."

"Marriage is the right way forward. That's that, then. We'll run with your idea of getting The Hero in as an honest broker." Dad thanked O'Reilly.

Your Grandad was like a ferret down a rabbit warren; when he got hold of something, he'd never let it go. The Hero said my father should have been a detective hunting the same man for twenty years. He was still at it as we left the solicitor's sitting room.

"Anything else is only a cop-out Sandy. Marry the girl. I'll give ye a few quid to get ye set up. I'll see you through college and after until you get fixed up with a job. We can sell that bit of ground we have at the back of the church to get you a few pounds towards a house."

The whole thing was too much for me.

"Jesus Christ, Dad, will you shut the fuck up about getting married. I don't know what to do. Just shut up and let me alone."

I ran towards the door. I always bolted when I couldn't handle the pressure. Dad caught up with me.

"That's nice language to use in front of a solicitor."

My father had great respect for professional men. He followed their advice unflinchingly without a quibble or a question. He was shocked and embarrassed by my carry-on.

He thanked O'Reilly and asked him how much he owed him.

"Nothing," replied the solicitor.

My father threw a twenty up on the hall table. He hated to owe any money to anyone. Tight, but honest. That was your Grandad.

He started at it again in the car.

"I'm only trying to do my best for you. I always found that sometimes the hard option might really be the easiest in the finish. I have this terrible vision of you lying in bed when you're my age wondering what your child was like. Was he married? Is there grandchildren? Did his new parents look after him? Is he in trouble?"

"Dad, I know you might be right but I have to think of myself too. I had so many plans."

"I know the sacrifice you would have to make but think of the thrill when you'd see him kicking a ball for the first time or going off fishing with you in his little wellingtons and walking as fast as he can to get to the Ballymore all the quicker. Making his First Communion in his shiny new suit and he missing half his teeth. Funny things he'd say. All the questions. Looking at you like you were the greatest man in the world. Asking like, 'Dad are you stronger than Superman?' Do you remember asking me that, Sandy?"

"Did I ask you that Dad?"

"Every day. You'll be his hero. Until he's fourteen or fifteen. And then when he gets a bit older he'll see you as just a human kind of a fella who maybe tried to do his best as a father and you'll be his hero again. I don't mean like The Hero but a real hero. It's what this whole merry-go-round is all about."

"But Dad I'm only a teenager. I can't think that far ahead."

"It won't be long coming. Life is only like a day but there's a load more to look forward to. The first pint together. Getting a good result in the Leaving or helping if the results were bad. Giving him a few quid when he's going out."

"That's rich - you never seemed to get much pleasure out of that." We laughed a bit at that.

MY FATHER PROPOSES MARRIAGE

"Ah sure Sand, I was afraid you'd turn out like my father. Ah there are hundreds of other things. I got a great kick out of the time you started noticing women and tried to grow a 'tache. Do you remember the day you scored two points off play on Dargan, the county minor from Ballymore? And when he started shoving it on to you, you gave him buckets of it back."

I never knew he thought I did well on Dargan.

He really was a seriously decent man. It's only now that I'm at his age that I realise he offered himself up for me. Body and soul. He never messed about with women. I know he could have had plenty from watching them coming on to him in the bar but he just stuck to his duty no matter what. Maybe fathers know that there will come a day when their children see clearly all he did for them, even if he isn't around to be told. This can't be too easy for you either knowing I was so close to keeping you. You're reading how I let you slip away. It must be agonisingly painful.

I tried The Hero's distraction stratagem.

"I played well that day, Dad. Dargan is getting a run with the seniors in the league Sunday week."

"Is he then? Ah I was so proud when you were born Sandy. I wasn't allowed in to the birth. It's a great regret but that's the way it was in those times. But when I saw you first I said to myself this is it now boy. This is it. The greatest moment of your life. I thought I was going to burst with the excitement. I was dying to get you home to have a good look at you. But then your Mam . . ."

"I know Dad."

I could see the pain in his face before the head dipped into his chest.

But he quickly got back to the point.

"Think of yourself by all means but this is what will be best for you. Mary O is a fine girl. If I thought she was some falbo who would make your life a misery I wouldn't be saying these things to you. It's not myself I'm thinking about. I know you. You have a conscience Sandy. It's the worst kind of conscience in that it's a kind of a conscience somewhere in between the totally righteous and the kind of fella who doesn't give a damn about anyone.

"I suspect as you get a bit older you will go one way or the other and it's my certain guess you will go the righteous road even if it is via the scenic route. A bad decision now will eat at you like a cancer when you get older. Sandy I don't give a damn about the moral side of it. I never once gave out to you about what happened. It's dealing with the consequences of what happened in the right way that really matters.

"There are some roads you can take where you can turn back but once those adoption papers are signed, there's no turning back. You'll have no more rights over your child's future than a black stranger."

He didn't say anymore other than to praise Dargan and comment that in his opinion Dargan was sure to start in the championship.

I think it was the longest conversation I ever had with him. We never seemed to get to the core of things after that. I would go into the sitting room. He'd be reading the paper. I'd ask him for a tenner and he'd say 'didn't I give you a tenner yesterday' and that would be that. We might mumble something to each other about football or he'd send me on a message for milk or a paper if he saw me stretching out on the sofa. He was like his mother in that he hated to see anyone sitting down.

Small things got in the way. It drove him mad if I read the paper before he did. It was as if my scanning would rip the print from the page. We seemed to be embarrassed by intimacy. I'd say we had both had opportunities to settle this but neither of us seemed to take them. I always thought that I'd maybe sort it out in time but it was really only on his deathbed that we found the closeness we had when I was a small boy.

Still he knew I loved him and even though we had only the one father-son chat I realised that he had such love for me that he would die for me. As I said, he was a bit tight with the money but when I'd be leaving the room he'd put his hand in his pocket and say 'here's a fiver'.

CHAPTER EIGHTEEN
A RAID BY MY UNCLE

THE FORCES OF LAW and order are moving in on me.

The Bore, still smarting from his barring, has been in to the station in Ballymore every second day canvassing for a raid on the pub for after hours. Liam was instructed by the Super to carry out the operation.

He called tonight at half twelve in the company of two gardai from Ballymore. The pub was well cleared by then. Liam even told me the exact time he would call so we could still do a bit of after hours. He searched every bit of the pub in the full knowledge that at least one of his colleagues would tell all to that bollix Brogan who is still an ex-cop.

Liam called in by appointment after the cops left. "Sandy, there's something else I have to tell you."

"Let me guess. You wear your socks in bed?"

"You trust me, don't you? Even though I'm a guard?"

"Yeah I do. I was warned to talk to no one about the so-called murder but I trust you. Liam you've gone well beyond the call of duty on my behalf. I don't know how I can ever thank you. If there's anything I can ever do for you, anything. I'll do all in my power to do it."

"Ah sure, I know that. Thanks."

Liam finished his drink and started to make for the door.

"Ah, it can wait or maybe I'll never tell you Sandy. I'm afraid to tell you."

I was getting a bit worried. For some reason it went through my head that something happened to Paula. Maybe she was in some kind of trouble. The country was full of drugs. Even though I trust Paula you always have to be vigilant. She was drinking for two years before I found out.

"Better out than in Liam."

"No Sandy, the time isn't right."

"Go on Liam, tell me. It's Paula isn't it?"

"No, it's not Paula . . . It's to do with you and me."

"You're gay and you love me Liam. I always knew dem wimmin you smuggles inta de barracks is only a front!"

"Jesus, Sandy, will you stop always taking the piss outa me. I'm bewildered enough as it is. I'm still trying to figure out jokes you told me twelve months ago."

Liam stood up, took a deep breath, exhaled to let his belly out before pulling it in again.

"I'm your uncle."

I didn't know what to say to that one. Could you blame me? Anyone else and you might think it was a wind-up but, as they say in America, Liam didn't do humour. He twiddled nervously with the silver-plated button on his uniform until it was so loose it almost came off. I was trying to think of something to say.

"What?" was the best I could manage.

"Sandy, I'm The Hero's son. I'm your uncle."

"The Hero's son? That would make you my uncle."

"That's what I just said. Are you thick or something?"

The button was now completely off and Liam started at the one above it.

"The Hero and my mother were . . . well close, Sandy."

"Well they must have been. Babies don't get conceived by people unless there's some bit of contact. Uncle Liam, that's incredible. Welcome to the Heroes."

I was shocked but genuinely pleased. And nothing surprised me where The Hero was concerned. Liam finally left the buttons alone.

"Ah Sandy, you don't know how happy I am to hear you say that. I'm deadly happy. Ah it's brilliant Sandy. Ah brilliant. Fierce happy. Ah Sandy thanks. It's strange I know because your Dad was Liam too. The Hero had two sons by the name of Liam. Your Dad was my brother. I have the same name as my own brother. But don't just take my word on it."

He sat down, relieved he was rid of his secret and delighted he was received into the family with good grace. The effort left him slumped in the chair but there were formalities. The guard broke out in him in spite of himself.

"I'd like to get it confirmed by DNA all the same," he said. "My mother told me and it's true but I want you to know it for a fact."

"I believe you Liam, but I'll do the test anyway. Why did you tell me now?"

"Well, I wanted The Hero's estate to be all finished up in case you thought it was money I was after or something. I'd like to get The Snipe to do the test as well. I'm his uncle too. I always wanted a family and I can't think of two better nephews to have than yourself and The Snipe."

Liam told me his mother loved The Hero until the day she died and how he was very generous financially, which of course was probably the main reason he was fiddling the till.

"So The Hero is your oul' fella. Did you know all along?"

"No Sandy, I didn't. The mother told me not long before she died. I always had a suspicion but I didn't want to insult the mother by asking her straight out."

I was curious. "But aside from the time you were stationed here did The Hero ever come to see you?"

"The Hero was always coming to see me when I was small. He was very good to us but I never knew he was my father. Did you know he got me into the guards even though I was an inch at least under the minimum height and he made sure I was transferred to The Glen from the city? He gave me a hundred pounds the day I was going to Templemore to take my course. He hugged me and said I must never turn my back on my own. And the tears came down his eyes. I suppose he felt guilty over maybe not acknowledging me."

"That man had some clout alright."

I started to fill two more pints to celebrate the arrival of my new uncle.

"He called every Christmas Day with presents and every other chance he got. And I'd say he loved my mother very much and I'd say me too judging by the way he used to put me up on his lap and tell me stories."

"But Liam he never told you he was your father."

"I suppose he should have but he was a big man and it would have drawn all the wrong kind of attention to myself and the mother, what with your grandmother being in the picture as well. The mother was just as happy she said. If it came out half the country would be talking about us. The Hero got it put out my father was killed in England on the buildings when a trench collapsed on him and that himself and the mother were married over in Camden Town on the quiet because his people who were loaded didn't think my mother was good enough for him."

"Will I have to call you Uncle Liam so?"

"Ah stop Sandy with the jokes. We'll keep it to ourselves for the moment. If we go public they'll take me off your case or maybe even transfer me to some place where I'll have to work for a living."

Before he left, Liam told me the cops had leaked it to The Bugle that the Tubbermore Torso was in fact murdered and was decapitated when the head was hacked off her and didn't fall off by natural means.

The Rumour Factory will put their own spin on the news. Hatchets will be left on bedside lockers, dogs will be asked to increase levels of alertness, the television will be turned up to the top and left on until the snow falls and crackles across its face.

CHAPTER NINETEEN

NANA, JOHN WAYNE AND THE EASTER LILY

THE HERO HAD TO marry my grandmother when she became pregnant. There was no escaping in those days. It was marry or else. Even War of Independence heroes were forced to march up to the altar. That was the way it was, not even The Hero could scheme his way out of that one.

The thing about grandparents is they never seem to have ferocious fights. It's hard to say whether they loved each other years ago. They seem to develop an accommodation, realising neither is going to win the war. It's a type of armchair armistice.

This was not the case in our house. Hostilities were ongoing with frequent skirmishes and the occasional pitched battle. Nana and The Hero hated each other. My grandmother was a waspish, malicious woman who liked nothing better than to tear strips off The Hero and was best avoided in the morning when her temper was particularly vile. The Hero referred to his extensive research of women's mags and put the whole thing down to hormones. For a while he even doctored Nana's tea with primrose oil.

Nana used to hide the dentures to stop The Hero from gallivanting off all over the country spending money, or to punish him when they had a row. Sometimes The Hero would offer a reward for the recapture of the teeth.

"Search the places you'd least expect to find a set of teeth like in a flower vase with flowers in it or in the hollow of a holy statue."

"But Grandad," I'd say, "we don't have a flower vase."

"Isn't that what I'm saying to you? Does anyone listen to me? They're the places to search. The unexpected places."

Most of time the errant teeth would be taking a dip in a glass of water by The Hero's bed or lying around on the flank of his armchair trying their best not to fall off and get stood on by some one of us.

Nana's idea of a good night out was a gossip and gamble session at the St Vincent de Paul Golden Ball Bingo in Ballymore. The Hero hated Bingo. I spent most of the night running errands for herself and her friends and checking how many cards the Ballymore crowd were playing at the one time. I always had a sore throat the morning after bingo from inhaling Nana's cigarette smoke. At the age of ten I'd say I was smoking a pack a day even though I never had a cigarette in my mouth.

Nana was always giving out to The Hero. Nagging. Mondays were the worst. There would be no Bingo or fagfest for four more days. Aside from Mondays, your great grandparents didn't see very much of each other. They had separate rooms because Nana said she couldn't sleep with The Hero's snoring.

The tips of Nana's fingers were tanned brown from the fags and her teeth matched. She wore slippers on the street and often wore a sock around her neck when her throat was sore.

Nana was a very hairy woman. She had tentacles of ear hair and nose hair sticking out like one of those insect-eating plants. The toilet bowl always had huge disgusting clumps of hair clinging to the bowl with the static electricity. I think it would be fair to say that she had let herself go. A lot of women of her age did that in those days. She lost interest in the other thing a few years after the child was born and ate like there was a famine forecast.

She'd look into our room and we'd both pretend to be asleep. I always knew her form from the way she used to clatter around. If she was in fair form she'd just look in and maybe have a scrounge through The Hero's pockets. He always hid his money in my Meccano box but sometimes he'd leave a little a bit of change just to throw her off the scent. I think she resented the fact The Hero was still in bed while she was up and about working. The two of us just lay in bed there pretending to be comatose until she went away and then we'd continue our chat in whispers. The Hero maintained women hated to see a man stretched out doing nothing.

"Even if there was nothing much to be done it still annoyed them no end."

The Hero pleaded with my Nana not to take me to the Bingo. The odd night he succeeded and we'd go to the pictures in Ballymore. I once overheard him say to his pal Turpentine Twomey of The Mayo Marauders that they were married "to two fierce horrors" after they watched Rita Hayworth at the Picturedome.

But I was handy as an errand boy for Nana Fags, Grandad's name for her, and her pals. Most of them weren't talking to their daughters-in-law so it was the motherless boy who became their slave. I enjoyed the bad language most of all. If you ever want to get an eighty-year-old daily Holy Communicant to say "fuck" just get another eighty-year-old to shout "check".

The Bingo Hall in Ballymore was cordoned off into sections like the fans at soccer matches. The Glen women with my grandmother were downstairs just in front of the balcony. The various Ballymore factions were at the front. The Tooreendonallers - being from the hilliest parish in the county - naturally enough sought refuge in the balcony.

If one of the Tooreendonallers shouted "check" the winning Bingo card would be lowered down for examination by the 'scrutineers'. The tenner prize was then attached to a clothes peg which was in turn tied to a piece of string and hoisted up again. This was all done to spare the feet of the upstairs bingo people.

The best night was the time one of the Tooreendonallers won the spot prize of the twenty seven pound free-range turkey. The Glenlatin women put their hands over their heads and curled into the foetal position in case the turkey would fall down on them. But sure all that was inserted in the peg was a voucher from Molloy's Family Butchers in Ballymore.

The Hero roared with laughter when I told him the story in bed the next morning. He couldn't wait, he said, to tell the boys in the bar that night.

Maybe Ted the Dead, the village undertaker, was right. When he saw the great time Grandad had after he buried Nana, his comment was: "Anyone should bury the wife."

The Hero didn't seem that upset when she died. My father was very traumatised. He loved Nana, which I suppose was fair enough because she always took his side in arguments with Grandad. She idolised him and was never done boasting about him.

I have no doubt my Grandad acted out of the best of motives but as in his nicknaming he was always trying to mould life to suit his own agenda. He longed for popularity more than anything else. He was even neutral in the Civil War.

I know though he had great time for me. I was his favourite other person in the world. His humour and love of company were his great gifts but he was a Celtic Machiavelli. He'd buy and sell the Borgias.

* * * * * *

When The Hero arrived back from his 'savoir faire' mission to the Mary O's, there was something not quite right. He was hunched and weary. He took off his hat and placed it on the corner of the chair. A man beaten and exhausted having fought the good fight against forces and people he could not control.

"I'd kill for a mug of tea," he said, and he grimaced as he pulled his slip-on off the bad leg. I put on the kettle.

"Is the one on the range boiled?" asked The Hero.

"No, it's shagging well not," replied my Dad. "Do you think timber grows on trees?"

The Hero and myself burst into laughter but my father didn't. He was, as they say, focused.

But I wonder how hard The Hero tried? I remember the time the local IRA called to the bar for a donation. The father ran them. He would have been even more Republican than the grandfather but he hated violence. He also had a fair idea most of the money would go on administration, in other words drinks and commission for the collectors. The prisoners' kids would be lucky to see a lick of a lollipop out of the collecting. It was like the time of the hunger strikes when brave men were starving themselves to death in Long Kesh, the local desperadoes were drinking pint bottles of porter under blankets in their new underpants outside the Post Office over in Ballymore.

The father said: "Hero, don't be giving them gangsters money now do you hear."

"The hell I will," he replied.

It was straight from 'True Grit'. The Hero said it with such conviction you could see him galloping headlong at the baddies, reins between his teeth, firing thirty or forty shots from his six-gun, his left eye patched, the horse sweating shaving foam, no shave by himself for two days and a Woodbine vice-gripped between his teeth.

"I have a good one for you, Hero," the IRA collector said, "not like the olden days, but a good one all the same. One of the lads done a bank job up above in Dublin. The Owl. You know who I'm talking about? Well, The Owl was asked by a young lad who was a look-out if he should count the money they robbed. 'No need,' replied The Owl, 'won't we hear how much it is on the radio?'"

There was a big fit of laughing by The Hero. I spotted him palming a pound to the collector. He slipped their symbol, a tricoloured paper Easter Lily, out of sight into his top pocket. He did it in such a way that he gave the impression he was pinning it on his lapel. It was three-card trick standard sleight-of-hand.

And he walked away across the Square back to the pub with one hand behind his back military-style, carrying his exaggerated limp along with him.

"Them fellas weren't fit to lace our boots," The Hero said to Dad, referring to the current IRA. (Sometimes, but not very often, The Hero seemed to forget he wasn't a bona fide hero).

The Hero probably didn't give the Mary O visit his best shot. I think The Hero took a pull at the reins in a way a jockey does when he wants to stop a horse in a race. You can give the impression you're doing your best to win but if you are a good enough jockey you can still make sure the horse doesn't win even if ostensibly you are putting up a good show.

He told us he was well received by the Mary O's. Tom Tie was most apologetic about beating me up and was most appreciative of the fact that I kept the incident in the family, so to speak, and didn't call in the police. Bygones would be bygones and life would move on. He would salute me if we passed in the street and in the fullness of time would be seen to take a drink with me after a match. Tom Tie even offered to pay for my new dentures. Or maybe a second set for good wear if I already had a pair.

They made tea for The Hero and gave him a slice of a fresh cream cake imported from Ballymore especially for the occasion. Molly told him if he ever ran for the Dail he'd walk in.

"He'd walk in and all," agreed Tom Tie.

Tom Tie admired The Hero's tie. The Hero said a man he did a small turn for purchased the tie in the city for a small fortune. A turn which, though it was small for The Hero, was big for the man. It was pure silk. Grandad, as a gesture of friendship, took the tie from his neck and placed it around Tom Tie, who wore the two ties together and stroked at the silk for the rest of the visit as if it was a cat sitting up on his lap.

We thought he'd never get to the result of the meeting. My father was ready to strangle him when he started on about how he advised young Joey, Mary O's brother, to stretch his legs and hands from one end of the bed to the other if he wanted to be long enough to be a goalie. Then he started on about how he gave Tom Tie an old cure made from nettles for the red water in cattle. Your grandmother complimented him again and said he was in fine fettle and "how he never left himself go".

For the first time in my life, I lost the head with my Grandad.

"Jesus Christ Hero, will you tell us what they said about the baby?"

"Dead right. But watch your language," agreed my Dad.

The Hero was genuinely surprised at my intrusion. It was the way of the old people to give background. They had plenty of time then, you see.

The Hero pleaded his case.

"If I say so myself, John F Kennedy himself, God be good to him, couldn't have done better. I told Tom Tie and Molly the house was like a palace."

Then Grandad said Tom Tie nearly burst with the joy of being praised by a man whose bravery he had often heard sung of in pubs from

Doncaster to Truro. The only famous person he ever met.

"And I told them that the lino they put down was as nice as you could get and presented them with a vase for flowers or for just doing nothing if there was no flower in the garden, which there wasn't being the time of the year that was in it. Molly complimented me on it and said the vase could stand on its own two feet if it needed to.

"And of course I made no reference to the fact that it was a replacement for some of the finery broken up on the Sunday he gave you the hiding. By the way, I couldn't let it go but to mention to Tom Tie that if I was a younger man his attack on you would not have gone unpunished."

Tom Tie, apparently, seemed a bit put-out by this remark and stirred himself in his chair but The Hero stared him out, guessing correctly Tom Tie was half-afraid of him and was of course a bully, which meant he was automatically a coward. There were people out there who thought The Hero was capable of having them kneecapped or tarred and feathered. The mixture of praise and threat didn't work.

Tom Tie announced the family, meaning himself, felt adoption was the only solution. Mary O would never get a husband, he maintained, if she was an unmarried mother.

Who would have her with a past like hers? No, she would be better off in England where she could make a new life for herself. She was bound to have hit off for England.

Nobody would know her there and she might get herself a husband in good time. It was the best thing and the worst thing about England, he said, not being known but at the same time no one knowing your business.

Mary O was still young and there was no mad hurry about getting married. She could do the English Leaving or get fixed up doing the books for her cousin Mossy the Merc, who had graduated to being a builder with sixty men working under him. With only five of them on the books he would need a good bookkeeper. Someone he could trust.

And the Catholic hospitals were always looking for Irish girls to train on as nurses and Mary O was always very soft and very fond of small children and would make a great nurse. Fr Fitz would give her a top reference and no mention of her bit of misfortune. And would The Hero put pen to paper on her behalf?

"With a heart and a half," The Hero replied, "and we can even say she worked in The Mayo Bar and did secretarial work for me. On and off."

"And the matron might probably be Irish and have heard of you then," added Tom Tie. Sometimes Tom Tie put the word 'then' at the end of his sentences. The Hero said it was an affliction he picked up in England.

Tom Tie would look after her financially in the meantime. Under no circumstances would any assistance be accepted. No offence intended and greatly was the offer appreciated. And the existence of the offer and its sincerity would be communicated to Mary O in due course and in the fullness of time, even though they had not heard from her since she left four days earlier. And Sandy's heartfelt apology and his best wishes for her future would be made known to Mary O.

Tom Tie's greyhound Ballyloughbeg Boy had a right chance in the seventh at Ballymore, but not to go too mad on him as he was drawn in trap two and would prefer the six box as he had a habit of cutting out at the first bend.

And was The Hero interested in buying a pup then?

Fr Fitzgerald, The Hero said, took a similar view. Heartfelt sympathy. Decent young man. Glenlatin's first family. Put the matter behind me. Keep up the golf. A future leader of the community. And The Hero was a fine man who never shirked his duty to his country, his family or his church. I could almost hear 'Faith of Our Fathers' in the background as The Hero spoke.

My father put his hands through his hair. He was almost grey and it made him look very old. It was the first time I realised he was getting on a bit. I think it was around then he got the cancer. I know it sounds crazy but he looked worn out, drained and dry. His skull was exposed on the balding side by his tossing of his hair with his hands. Something he always did when life was getting the better of him. A blue vein throbbed on the exposed side of his head.

I put Dad's hair back into place a hundred times the night he died. It was then that I realised the precise moment the cancer incubated inside him. It was the night of the 'savoir faire' conference in our back kitchen over twenty years ago. I suppose you could say it was the night I killed my father.

I wasn't as upset as you might think at The Hero's news. In a way I was relieved. My conscience would be easier on me and I was beginning to forgive myself. I knew The Hero was a schemer. I saw through him in a way my father could never have done, being the straightforward man that he was. I kept my suspicions to myself and let the matter rest. After all, I did all I could. Or so I managed to convince myself. A solution had been brokered. Conscience appeased, I was able to put up with myself.

A few weeks passed and I was back in college. Dad gave me a pep talk and at the same time said he had every sympathy for me trying to do exams in such circumstances. The examiners took a different view and I failed every one of them in spectacular fashion.

.

CHAPTER TWENTY

Two New First Names For People I Knew Well

THE LITTLE BIT OF weight Mrs Moran, the teacher's wife, put on in her forties made most of her clothes too small for her. Her skirt is tweedy tartan and faded from multiple washing. It has a big pin tied on to it at the bottom. Mrs Moran never wears make up. Too dear, her husband says. Women are desperate eejits, he maintains. Victims of cosmetic company scams and their own vanity.

Still, her skin is without a wrinkle but she has a sudsy grey complexion as if someone sponged dishwater on her face. Mrs Moran doesn't put a great deal of effort into her appearance.

Her hair is as uneven as a lawn cut for the first time in spring. Coarse grey straws run through it. For the most part she keeps her head in a tea cosy woollen hat. She hasn't been to the hairdresser since the morning she married.

I like her. She is unfailingly polite and hardly ever raises her voice above a library whisper. She must have an awful life with your man. It's always the same order. She asks for a pint to go on the pretext of making a porter cake. The pint is really for her husband, who hates pubs and mine in particular.

Sometimes I stand Mrs Moran a glass of sherry. She drinks it in quick, furtive sips like a little animal who sneaks down to a waterhole at night.

Moran only gives her enough money for the pint. But for hand-me-downs from her own family the poor woman would have to go around naked. She has no income of her own. She doesn't even have the bulwark of the children's allowance. Mrs Moran is childless but not infertile. Moran harboured a deep-seated antipathy towards children, which manifested itself in his treatment of the inmates in his school. He also considered children an unnecessary expense.

The teacher read an article about bringing up kids. It cost as much £150,000, the journalist made out. Moran was so shocked at the enormous expenditure involved it is said he remained celibate ever after, contraception being an anathema to him on religious grounds.

His poor wife slaved away for Moran without ever a word of thanks. The teacher barely acknowledged her in public.

When we were kids we used to capture small birds by placing a cut of bread inside a cardboard box supported by a stick. A piece of string would be tied to the stick. We'd hide under cover of a tree or a bush, maybe forty feet away. When the little bird walked into the box to collect his food we would pull the string. The box collapsed and the bird was trapped. This was the stratagem Moran used. He lured Mrs Moran with a promise of comfort and safety and then when he had her where he wanted her, the string was tugged and down came the box.

Her mother encouraged her to marry Moran because he was a teacher, a job which carried status and security. She was years younger than

Moran, naive and anxious to get away from her strict Catholic home. She yearned to be the mistress of her own house. Instead she swapped authoritarianism for slavery.

Moran had a way of breaking people by taking away their confidence. His wife was one of his many victims. She was just as trapped as us schoolkids.

"I can't leave. I have nowhere to go. Who'd have me. All I'm fit for is doing the odd bit of cooking and cleaning," a tearful Mrs Moran confided in her sister in England, who confided in an old flame of mine who confided in me. There are few secrets in a small village like Glenlatin. People who live in London are very open about everything. It's what comes from living in a city of millions. Everything gets back to The Glen.

I poured out a pint from the slop tray under the beer dispenser into the enamel half-gallon porter transporter and topped it up with a fresh drop to give the Guinness a nice, creamy, frothy head. I double-checked as I placed the blue lid on the white enamel bucket.

"You're sure you're not drinking any of this yourself, Mrs Moran?"

"Oh no Sandy, I tried it once but I didn't like the taste."

Mrs Moran took a quick sip from her sherry. She took off her hat. The sherry must have heated her up. Her face was rosier than usual and her hair was nicely combed.

"Could you tell Arthur he's needed. If it's no trouble, Sandy."

"Who am I to tell?" I asked, not knowing of anyone by the name of Arthur.

"Arthur."

"You have me there Mrs Moran."

"Everybody calls him The Dosser."

In all the years it never dawned on me The Dosser's real name was Arthur. There are families in The Glen and Ballymore who don't know their siblings' real names. It's all nicknames around here.

"Oh right. I'll tell Arthur."

"Thank you Sandy."

And she looked happy with herself that she managed to organise the gardening without recourse to her spouse.

"And Mrs Moran, if I might be so bold, could I enquire as to your own first name?"

She paused for a minute as if she was trying to remember it. Her husband always referred to her as Mrs Moran.

"It's Sally, Sandy, and you can call me Sally Sandy. I mean you can call me Sally, not Sally Sandy. Sally Sandy that would be a strange name for a girl wouldn't it?"

She giggled. It was the first time I had ever seen Mrs Moran laugh and it never dawned on me before now that she was a woman. She put the glass gently down on the counter and went as red as a beetroot.

"Oops . . . I almost forgot. There's a letter here for you from my husband. Thanks for the sherry. It was lovely. Don't forget to tell Arthur he's wanted, if it's no trouble."

She donned her tea cosy hat, slipped a Silvermint in her mouth and put down the pint container into a deep message bag.

Then, like a performer waiting to go on stage, she took a second or two to get back into character before the bird steps back to her cardboard box.

The letter was a photocopied invitation to the AGM of The Glen Development Association in two weeks' time. The PS at the end was in Moran's own handwriting. 'I presume in the circumstances you will not be seeking re-election.'

THE LAST OF THE HEROES

CHAPTER TWENTY-ONE
Break Glass In Case Of Emergency

I TRIED TO GET Rachel to talk things through but she refused. I apologised and apologised. She just walked off and left me where I stood. I even started going to lectures in the hope of running into her accidentally on purpose, if you know what I mean.

Eventually, she agreed to meet me in a cafe in a laneway off Patrick Street. Rachel made absolutely no effort to dress herself up. Her hair was tied up in an austere bun and she swapped her usual bright colours for greys and blacks. She wore corduroy baggy pants I had never seen before. I always told her she had the best jeans arse in college.

Our relationship was over, she said. I could never be trusted again. What's more I didn't treat her with respect. All I wanted to do was to get her into bed. Mary O was a nice girl who was blackguarded abysmally. She told Daddy and Mammy everything and they advised her she'd be crazy to have anything to do with me. Her brother, who was a second row with College, threatened to disembowel me.

"Sandy, I know you have good points but this mess is just too much to handle and I have exams to pass. I cannot fall out with my family. I have to admit I still have strong feelings for you. We had a lot of fun and I thought we had something very special. I feel sorry for you in some ways but I just can't let myself forget you were sleeping with someone else while you were still seeing me."

She put her hands on mine and looked me straight in the eye.

"I always meant to tell you, Rachel."

"And why didn't you? Why didn't you? I would have been very, very upset but we could have sorted it out."

That statement went through me. If only. It should be my epitaph.

"I hated telling Mary O it was all over. I just couldn't face up to it. I had no idea she was pregnant until that night in the flat and anyway I only slept with her once while I was going with you and that was after about a gallon of beer and a couple of shots."

"Once. Oh that's fine Sandy. A guy is allowed one fla when he's going out with someone. Is that it? I trusted you with my innermost secrets and all the time you were screwing your childhood sweetheart."

I didn't know what to say. I deepened the hole I was digging myself into.

"Is it coming up to your period, Rachel."

I didn't know why I said it. It drove her crazy. She stood up and grabbed her bag. She stormed off but was back a couple of minutes later for her coat. I told her what I did was wrong and that was that. I had already apologised a hundred times.

Now that I understand women better, I know that she wanted to talk for hours about the bloody thing. And then make up her mind. And then more than likely she would put off the decision again and there would be more talk. I just didn't have the patience for it.

There was a punishment element to the discussions as well. I'd have to serve my time and then she might forgive me even though the odds were against it.

In a way getting the hiding from Tom Tie was easier. There was finality. I felt that even if I made it up with Rachel this endless discussing would go on forever or at least every now and then, whenever she had a touch of a period or for no reason at all. PMT had just been invented by the women's magazines and it was the way of us young bucks to blame everything on what The Hero termed "a dose of initials".

I just stood there waiting for Rachel to say something else. She just looked away from me and then around the cafe a couple of times and then out the window. All I could manage was my seventeen-thousandth 'I'm sorry'.

She zoomed in on me again.

"Do you think 'sorry' is going to make that poor girl okay or make things okay between us? It's easy to say sorry. It's just a word."

"Well, it's all I can say. And Rachel if you take me back I'll never cheat again. I can promise you that on my mother's grave."

"Don't try to get me all weepy over your mammy dying when you were born. I nearly slept with you that night if I remember correctly. And that's probably another lie."

This time I walked off, sick to the death of discussing the whole affair and very hurt Rachel didn't believe me about my mother. Rachel was flighty and I knew we would always have turbulence but I still loved her.

I came back after a couple of minutes but she was gone.

A month later when the exams were over I phoned Rachel and asked her out for a drink but it was too late.

She was thinking of seeing someone else, she said. The guy who took her to her debs was back in town. He was a med student in Surgeons and his exams were finished early. She didn't want to do anything behind my back.

I was upset but not as devastated as you might think. I was young and thought the world was full of Rachels and Mary O's.

I ran into her in college most days after that. She would mime a 'hi' and shuffle on in a hurry.

Then, near the start of what should have been my third year had I passed the exams, I asked her to come back to the flat with me. I was drunk and she was out with the Debs Man.

"No Sandy, I could never go back with you, I'm sorry."

Her escort came over and the two of them just gathered up their stuff and moved away. He was big shouldered, wore nice clothes, had a wavy head of immaculate hair parted precisely, expensive shoes and a set of car keys dangled from his right hand.

"Why don't you hang a fucking stethoscope out of your fucking arse pocket as you're at it, show-off dickhead?" I bawled at him as I staggered over towards where they were sitting.

I grabbed Rachel by the sleeve and tried to pull her up out of her seat. Her boyfriend pushed me back and I fell back on to a table full of drinks, spilling most of them. Glasses broke and the bar owner came out from behind the counter.

I followed the two out the door.

"Come on you fucking nancy boy, fight. Fight, you fucking coward,"
I roared.

A few pals held me back. There was no need for anyone to restrain
the Debs Man. He was in total control and very mature and superior
looking. Rachel was crying. The Debs Man took Rachel by the hand and
said, "Come on Rache. Let's get out of here," in a measured, calm voice.

I used to call her Rache.

Rachel looked over her shoulder at me as he ushered her into the car.
The look she had said this guy is a mess and I'm getting out of his life
before he messes mine up.

I just sat there on the frozen footpath propping up my jaws with
my palms and watched the car drive out from the front of the bar towards
the city.

I went back into The Wheel and put my fist through a window in
the toilet. The owner, who had never seen me like this before, took my
previous good record into consideration and drove me to hospital. He put
my hand in a plastic bag to keep the blood from ruining the car. A med
student fixed up a tourniquet. I didn't feel a thing, only self-loathing.

The car stopped at the lights on the way back. There was some
mention about more fish in the sea. Rachel and the Debs Man were
walking along Washington Street holding hands. She craned her neck
upward. He bent his head. She pulled his scarf down by the ends and
kissed him the way she used to kiss me.

CHAPTER TWENTY-TWO
The Origin Of The House Of Suck

WHILE THE RUMOUR FACTORY went into overdrive on the subject of the axe murder after another exclusive in today's Bugle, Liam (I have to resist the temptation to call him Uncle Liam) dropped in with a request for background information. Sammy was due to be charged over the dump and resisting arrest, and The Super was anxious to discover the origin of the House of Suck.

The Hero, of course, had told me the whole story here in The Mayo Bar many years ago.

"Sandy, it was in the old days. Times were bad. The women hadn't much so there was a communal dress code called the shawl. It was a type of purdah. The priests were all for it because it covered up every bit of a woman the same as the poor Arab women of today. It was hard on the men as well. A glimpse of a nicely turned ankle was as much as you could hope for. I was two years married before I saw a woman completely naked and that was by accident when I walked in unannounced to your Nana's room. And she nearly lost the head over it, refusing to speak to me for weeks."

"You're joking me, Hero."

"No, it's true. And I wouldn't mind but that was after your father was born. Half the men around here never saw a naked woman even though they might have ten or eleven children."

"The Sucks?"

"Oh right, Sandy. Well breastfeeding was very popular. The children were at the breast in many cases until they were five or six years of age. Young lads were knocking their mothers over such was their rush for a drink when they came home from school. There was even talk that the Breasteen Boyle slipped off for a feed from his mammy at half-time in the 1943 North U14 football final. It might be true because when he came back he refused a drink out of the communal bottle of lemonade. In those days you only got a drink of lemonade on Christmas Day. What's more, the Breasteen played a blinder in the second half having only been fit to be taken off in the first. It was probably the first case of milk doping."

"Grandad were you breastfed?"

"I was but I'd say I finished up early. Maybe I was only five when closing time was called. We had a close call. When I was about five and I arrived at the bottom of the lane where our house was situated before I bought the pub I used to roar 'mammy rip' meaning my mother was to rip open her blouse so I could have my supper. For a while we were known as The Rips but luckily it fell into disuse after The Mayo Job."

"Go on about The Sucks Grandad."

"Anyway Sandy, poor Mrs Suck was a misfortune and could you blame her being married into that crowd of lunatics?"

"Wasn't she a bit touched herself?"

"She was all that Sandy. You see that's the thing about savage families. They get worse from generation to generation. No one will marry into them only other mad families and so the blood gets worse and worse. Sure that was the cause of the First World War with all the royal families falling out with each other with the inbreeding."

"What was the cause of the Sucks, Grandad?"

"What's with this Grandad thing?"

"What was the cause of the Sucks' name Hero?"

"Missus Suck . . . She was a customer in the days when the shop at the front of the pub was thriving. Do you remember that, Sandy?"

"I do."

"Well, that bit of a shop was there for eighty years before the supermarkets closed us down. It was more than a shop. It was a drop-in centre for the women of the parish. A bit like the cafes of today. My poor mother was always advising people and trying to sort them out. 'Nonie,' she counselled Mrs Suck one day, 'you're getting very pale and worn out lookin' from nursing that young lad. Isn't it about time you weaned him off?' With that, Jereen Suck stuck his head out from under his mammy's shawl and shouted, 'Missus Sullivan, will you fuck off and mind your own business.'

"Two members of the ad hoc village nicknaming committee were on their way in to the Upper House for a drink and overheard the exchange. Jereen Looby became Jereen Suck."

Liam said I would have to meet The Super for a drink to tell him the story myself. It was vital to keep him on our side. The Bore had the Sergeant's ear and was trying to get him to raid the bar again. This time there might not be a tip-off.

If a Garda took a set on you, he could ruin your business. They would call every night on the dot of closing and leave all the other pubs serve away into the early hours, giving them a trading advantage. Your customers would be stopped on their way home. One or two might be breathalysed on country roads where the only activity would be a fox running across the road after his prey. The Super told Liam he was trying for years to get the Sarge transferred to a posting as far away from Ballymore as possible. The Sergeant's wife was the Minister for Justice's first cousin so there was no hope of sending the Sarge off to the tip-top of Donegal.

The Bore problem would have to be solved, The Super said. For everyone's sake. And fast.

CHAPTER TWENTY-THREE

MURDER IN THE CATHEDRAL

I LOST CONTROL TODAY. Fr Fitzgerald was the celebrant at Auntie Annie's month's mind Mass at eleven o'clock in St Teresa's of The Shingles. From the parish that brought the world midnight Mass at seven o'clock, a month's mind a fortnight after a burial was nothing unusual.

I loitered near the back of the church. Master Moran was togged out in his best three-piece suit. Moran has the shiniest, cleanest, reddest face I have ever seen. It's as if he was scrubbed with a wire brush. He was wearing the white socks which The Hero always maintained was a sure sign of a bollix. Moran, he said, "had the face of a zealot and a black heart".

His shiny shoes reflected the light from the huge stained glass windows donated by big farmers and the families of American emigrants. "Fire escapes," The Hero called them.

"Pray for the Soul of Thomas Mullaghatawney whose family generously contributed to the erection of this window. And starved his servant boys and rode the servant girls whether they wanted to or not."

Everything and everyone bothered me today. I wouldn't have gone to the Mass at all if it weren't out of respect for The Snipe and Auntie Annie. That pompous bastard Moran bound up the church to

Communion with that permanent 'I'm a great man amn't I?' smirk. He was as usual stinking of that shagging stinkysweet aftershave and his jaunty spring-sprong step announced at every footfall that he was the fit bucko for his age without an ache or a pain because he was such a holy good living conformist yes man Catholic who showered twice a day like an American even though he wasn't even dirty and fuck everyone else for being bent and crippled and imperfect and pulling their wire.

I wasn't in the best of form. I'm not making excuses for what will unfold but I was tired from being up all night writing and drinking. And I was spending too much time thinking. The past and the realisation of the hurt I had caused to so many people had stirred up almost uncontrollable bitterness towards myself mainly but a few others as well.

I wasn't looking in from the outside any more. It was me who did those things and it was me who had to accept responsibility.

The school tour to Knock. That was the great day for the resistance. With a sweet shop full of sugar and a couple of pints of tepid holy water inside me I vomited over Moran on the bus. I deliberately swivelled myself in his direction when I felt the vomit coming on but of course pretended it was an accident. Moran was probably the only teacher in Ireland who carried the cane on the school tour. He walloped me through five counties and for a month afterwards but it was worth every belt. I was a Hero, my classmates said, just like my Grandad. Still I was even more afraid of Moran ever after and developed a bit of a stutter when I was asked to read aloud in class. That was until The Hero put the squeeze on him .

* * * * * *

It was an airy day with a big dome of a blue sky encasing the village like one of those glass covers in a cake shop. I decided I would be much closer to God if I moved outside the church.

Fr Fitzgerald was conducting the congregation of the living dead. For the most part the attendance comprised of befuddled mantra repeaters desperate to ingratiate themselves with the Man Above before the final grading.

I peeped through one of the transparent squares of the stained glass window set in the high double bishop's hat front door. Mass was nearly over. The Rumour Factory snapped the last of the Communion from Fitz's fingers. Holy Communion is the fodder for their gossip.

"Body of Christ."

Snap.

"Amen."

There was no one outside to talk to. I saw the ghost of Brainy Boyle before me as Fr Fitz dropped the Hosts on the Rumour Factory's stiffened tongues and criss-crossed palms.

Moran and the Host, the body and blood of our Lord Jesus Christ. It was a black Mass.

There's blood on Moran's hands.

Moran murdered poor old Brainy Boyle.

The people in these parts throw prepositions into their day-to-day speech like a chef sprinkles spices on dishes to embellish the flavour of the food. I suppose it's a throwback to a hundred years ago when everyone here spoke the Irish language.

For example, we say 'are you going over to Ballymore' or 'across to Cork' or 'beyond to Toreendonal' or 'up to Gleannaphooka' even though it's in a valley and 'down to Garryantannavalla' even though it's in a valley as well.

It drove Moran mad, not so much because he was a language purist but because he could never quite figure out which preposition to place before which place. He was always saying stuff like 'down to Shanballymore' which of course being on a hill was an up, even though hills were almost always ups but sometimes they could be downs.

Like 'down to Cool Na Greige' even though it was even further above sea level than Shanballymore. And if you were going down to a lower hill from a higher hill that too was an up because you would of course still finish up on top of a hill even if you had to go down to get there. You just had to know your vernacular and topography.

One day Moran asked a pupil if he was 'down in Toreendonal' at the football game and who won it. Brainy Boyle was a boy who was so bad at school Moran had given up teaching him, which really meant he gave up beating him as it was a waste of time and totally exhausting. Moran also realised that while it's possible to beat brains out of a child it's impossible to beat brains into a child.

Brainy always put his hand up when Moran asked a question but he never succeeded in answering a question correctly. The very seldom time he knew the answer Moran wouldn't ask him. Moran had a gift for knowing which boy to pick from the sapling forest of small hands. He'd never ask you if you knew the answer. He called every bluff and always won. Nowadays Brainy would receive help from a special skills teacher but back then in the time of Moran's reign of terror Brainy was left to fend for himself.

He was odds-on anyway to finish up in England labouring, drinking and signing the back of his cheques with an X in pubs. Crafty gangermen would tell him what a great worker he was and nickname him Horse, so much so Brainy would think he was a horse and slave accordingly. Then when his strength was stolen by hard work and drink he would be sent on his way. There was no pension for working off the books. Life was as simple and complicated as getting pissed up on Chateau Monday all year round, living in a hostel for the down and outs in winter and a park in summer.

"It's 'beyond in Toreendonal', sir."

"What's that Boyle?" snapped the teacher.

"Toreendonal is a 'beyond' sir and not a 'down'."

Brainy was delighted. He was smiling and looking around at his classmates for approbation but we kept our heads down and the smile soon disappeared. Brainy should have realised how lucky he was and kept his mouth shut because Moran decided to start teaching him again.

His fingertips were well reddened from then on. Brainy used to close his fists and wring his hands like a woman squeezing out a heavy, wet towel. His red eyes danced in his bowl haircut head as if they wanted to jump out and escape. You'd think he was going to explode with the pain of never being able to learn. His nails were bitten back so far you could see he was waiting for them to grow a bit so he could start the pruning all over

THE LAST OF THE HEROES

again. Brainy kept looking at the raw fingertips as if the biting of the nails was in some way a relief. Jesus you'd feel like screaming the answers out for him. We laughed initially when Brainy stuttered and stammered and made a total mess out of the easiest sums.

He was a nice little lad. Harmless and innocent. After a while we just kept our heads down. We would have shoved them under blankets if we had them. We just didn't want to see his face. It would embarrass him if we saw him crying.

Brainy never looked at a book. His parents were illiterate and couldn't help him even if they wanted to which they didn't.

Anyway it would suit them a lot better if Brainy shagged off to England out of their way. It would mean a plate less on the table and in the beginning anyway he'd send home a few bob to help out with the six or seven left behind. He obliged Mammy and Daddy Boyle by leaving on a big ship when he was fifteen. He didn't come back again until he was forty in a small urn.

"Ah look at Brainy Boyle, wearing the sister's jumper and the family heirloom trousers. Ha ha ha, hee hee ha. And did you cut the hair yourself Boyle. Hee hee ha, ha ha hee hee."

Then Moran would beat his thighs to emphasise the hilarity of it all. This was the signal for the rest of us to laugh and I'm ashamed to say I joined in. Brainy was an easy target and Moran knew once he started the thigh-slapping the boys would taunt and tease poor old Brainy.

Moran knew if Brainy complained to his parents they would beat him as well. That rotten evil bastard Moran heaped scorn on a world he could never understand and to which he would never be allowed enter because he was a horrible man.

There was another day. The day The Snipe peed in his pants. I spilled my milk over him to cover it up. We were both flaked unmercifully, but at least The Snipe escaped detection and further humiliation from Moran and the big boys in the class. I always said that some day I would get revenge on him. But how? I resolved to wait for my chance on The Hero's advice. He was a keen student of 'The Godfather' and was very much in favour of taking the long view.

* * * * * *

There was something bothering The Dosser as he darted across The Square towards the church and to where I was standing. He's always looking for lodgers for the worry rooms in his head. That man's mind offers no block to incoming junk mail. The Dosser violin-bowed his steel combs through his hair. You could fry a basket of chips and sausages if you refined the oil out of his head.

I always look forward to his bits of news. Possibly someone was knocking off someone's wife over in Ballymore. Maybe his news is international. An expatriate Glenlatino gone from the husband in England.

His last big scoop was "an outbreak of lesbianism beyond in Toreendonal".

"I came as fast as I could. My bit of news Sandy, it's not good. In fact it's bad, very bad."

THE LAST OF THE HEROES

"Better tell me so Dosser."

"Sandy, it's in The Bugle."

"What's in The Bugle?"

The Dosser danced from foot to foot as if he couldn't make up his mind which direction he should face.

"Fr Fitzgerald and Master Moran and The Bore Brogan, they've collected seventeen signatures."

He gasped for breath and shoved his asthma inhaler in his mouth almost choking himself.

"Slow down Dosser, get your news out."

"They're calling for a murder investigation into Mary O's death."

"Mary O's death?"

"Well Sandy, she must be dead if they're calling for a murder investigation? I never heard of a murder investigation into the death of a live person."

"Is all this in The Bugle, give us a look?"

I took the paper from The Dosser and sure enough it was all there on page one. I was in shock. It was beyond belief.

The headline read: 'Glenlatin Murder Probe'.

My left knee started to shake uncontrollably with the fright of it. Everybody around here reads The Bugle. Even though my name wasn't mentioned, the paper reported that "a local businessman may be the prime suspect in the disappearance of a young girl almost twenty years ago. The discovery of The Tubbermore Torso has reignited the suspicions that the girl, who was pregnant at the time of her disappearance, may have been abducted and murdered."

I was near enough the only local businessman in the village. Liam's plan backfired on me.

The first person I thought about was Paula.

I walked back into the church to find The Snipe on his way out. The Snipe took the paper from me and rolled it up tightly. "I heard the news," he said. "Keep the cool Sandy. Don't show them you're upset. Shop face Sandy. Shop face. Give yourself a chance to think this through. You were late as usual. I waited outside but I had go in when it was the mother's Mass and all that. Please keep the cool Sandy. Please."

I was beginning to boil over.

"That's right Sandy. Smile at them Sandy. Smile at them like you was a prostitute," buzzed The Dosser into my left ear.

I grabbed The Bugle back from The Snipe.

'Missing for twenty years . . . seventeen signatures calling for the reopening of the file.'

There was another headline: 'STILL MISSING'.

There was a list of murdered and missing girls going back over thirty years and none of the poor girls had even the remotest connection with this part of the country.

The list of signatories was on the letters' page. The letter called for "a thorough investigation into the disappearance of Mary O". That shagging word 'closure' was used about six times. The letter was signed en bloc by The Rumour Factory. Fr Fitzgerald and Moran were the first two signatures on it. There was no sign of any of the Tom Ties on the list.

There was no doubt Moran masterminded the coup and bullied his sidekick Fr Fitz into signing. Fr Fitz knew the real story but Moran didn't give a damn about your mother's family or the community. It was me he was after. It was a power thing. An excuse to act the big man. Get his own back on The Heroes. He was after closure alright. Moran wanted to close me down or see me closed up in a box.

Fr Fitzgerald made his way towards The Rumour Factory. He removed a tasselled purple hat, the shape of the Pentagon in America. It's as if he's trying to show the faithful he's almost an ordinary person with a real head. He's all small talk and big smiles. But then again, didn't every one of the bitches in The Rumour Factory pews sign the petition?

"Ah sure, isn't that a lovely coat Nora?" saluted Fr Fitzgerald, standing well back to avoid the permanent stench of stale sweat and fresh sweat and inner juices Nora carries around with her.

"Ah sure Father, I have it for a dog's age."

"Oh it's a lovely coat Nora, all the same."

"Ah Father, you're only saying that."

"Ah Nora, sure I wouldn't say it if it wasn't true now, would I? Would I now Nora? Ha?"

Lovely coat my bollix. That woman will need an operation by a Siamese twin surgeon to get that shagging coat off her back.

"Ah lads, isn't it a pet day and tell me now did ye hear every word of the ceremony out of doors?" Fr Fitzgerald walked in my direction with a big wide smile. He seemed to have hundreds of teeth. He carries the Pentagon in his left hand and the Bible in his right just like George Bush.

"And how are you Sandy? It's only like yesterday since we buried your poor Auntie Annie?"

I could see Moran, a step behind, sneering in that way he did when we were small.

"Sullivan," he said, "doesn't time fly as the man said when he threw the clock out the window. Ha ha ha, hee hee hee." Moran laughed at his own joke, as was his custom.

The trigger was pulled by his laughter. Murder in the cathedral. I walked quickly up to Moran and kicked him in the testicles. I reasoned in that millisecond he wasn't worthy of a proper belt. He doubled over like a continental soccer player and started rolling around the ground holding his private parts as if someone was trying to steal them. It was his turn now to scream and roar. I gave him another kick for good measure when he was on the ground. And then I pulled his hair so hard a clump of it came off in my hand. Then I pulled hard at his ear.

"Wig wig wig. Do you remember this trick Master Moran, Master Bater?"

He squealed like a pig. I'd say it was the first time anyone called him Master Bater to his face.

The Rumour Factory operatives were screeching as well. Nora threw a Rosary beads at me. Minnie May sent the 'Lives of the Saints' flying in my direction. There followed a shoe and a barrage of penny candles taken from the candleholder up at the front seat. You could see Minnie May's elasticated-at-the-knee baby blue knickers as she threw herself over the front pew to grab more candles. Minnie May couldn't quite reach the brass candleholder so she see-sawed herself back and forth, reaching out unsuccessfully at the candle carousel with her tiny mittened hands. She swung back and forth like a trapeze artist trying to build up momentum until she finally made the candle catch and fulcrummed herself back into her pew. Then she launched the candles.

I went for Fitzgerald next but The Snipe and The Dosser jumped me.

"It's my mother's month's mind Sandy. It's your Auntie Annie's Mass. My mother, Sandy. You can't dishonour her memory."

"You'll get jail for this you thug you," roared Moran, guarding his testicles with the one hand and rubbing his head in a circular motion with the other. "You pup. By God, the guards will put manners on you yet."

But I was the big man now. I tried to break free and almost succeeded. Moran ran towards the annex at the back of the altar. He peeped out from behind a huge replica statue of The Infant de Prague. Fitz kept rubbing the underside of the orb in a semi-circular motion. I stopped trying to get free. When Fitz saw me calming a bit, and securely held by my friends, he tended to the stricken teacher.

I told The Snipe and The Dosser I was fine and to let me go.

"You're sure you won't do anything, Sandy?"

"I promise Snipe."

"Promise Sandy. Promise."

"I promise. I promise. I'm calm now. I'm fine. I'm sorry Snipe, I just don't know what came over me."

But it was a lie.

I ran after Moran again. I landed a kick on his arse, which almost lifted him off the ground. Fr Fitz bolted. He can move very fast for a man of his years but I rugby-tackled him just before the try line. I held onto his ankles as he tried to crawl into the sanctuary of the Sacristy. He started to whimper and was so feeble I left him go. I could swear I heard him say "help mammy" but maybe he was mumbling some kind of martyr's invocation.

The priest disappeared out the door of the sacristy and then on towards the presbytery.

That was it. I was calm. I was back in total control. The priest's reaction stopped my madness. It was all over that quickly. Violence only takes seconds but it seems to last forever.

The Snipe suggested we get out of the church before the police came. Liam was off duty until later and you'd never know who would be investigating.

In minutes we were out of the Square and half way up Fat Arse.

"I'm going to go on down to my mam's grave."

"I'll come with you."

"No Sandy, you stay up here and calm down. Maybe Fr Fitzgerald might appear or something. You're in big trouble Sandy."

"It's worth it Snipe."

We marched on for a while up the hill at a fast pace and The Snipe was out of breath. He stopped for a second.

"No it's not worth it, Sandy for fuck's sake. You were wrong. Fighting is wrong. And Sandy he's gone the seventy. And anyway what was the point? Nobody takes any notice of the church anymore. And Moran, sure there's no more Morans. I don't really give a fuck about Moran or the church. No one does."

It was the first time ever I heard The Snipe curse. He was livid, which again was very unusual for him.

"Yeah Snipe and he was the man who had you pissing in your pants."

The Snipe regained his composure.

"I have enough. Will you just move on. I'm going to the grave Sandy. You'll have to get a solicitor. Even Liam can't stroke this one. It's very serious Sandy. Jail serious."

The Snipe disappeared in a dip at the graveyard side of the hill. I turned round to view The Glen down below me, sleepy and slow like a cat in the sun. My village. Treacherous as a cat. How could they sign against me? I was devastated. My own people. How could they believe I would murder someone, let alone Mary O? I was tried in my absence and found guilty. I should have let Liam release the news of the forensic tests. We were too smart.

By the time The Snipe came back up the hill from the cemetery I'd swung from calm to depression.

"How could they do this Snipe?"

My cousin would always tell the truth no matter what.

"On top of being fine and thick and unfair Sandy, some of them in the village are a small bit jealous. A big bit jealous."

"Jesus how could they be jealous of me?"

"You buy a new car every other year. You have a permanent suntan from all the holidays. There's rumours you're knocking off the doctor's wife over in Ballymore. You're up to Limerick once a month tipping a widow as well."

"I never touched the doctor's wife. Ah what am I doing taking any notice of The Rumour Factory anyway? You let them win if you take any notice."

"I wouldn't ignore them, Sandy. People want to believe rumours. It makes them feel better about themselves if everyone else is up to their eyes in trouble, especially a man who's going well."

"Going well? All I want to do is find my child and help people out."

By now we were over the ditch at Molloy's meadows and taking the descent into the village as fast as we could along the fields. Our shoes were wet and the bottoms of our pants were drowned from the flow of the water down Fat Arse. I was cold and miserable.

Bouquets of inedible rushes stuck out all over the land like a bad haircut. Green knives of useless fellistrims filled the wet fields. The trees were scantily dressed for the time of the year. A dozen chattering starlings gathered in low branch conclave while more sat silently on the sagging electricity wires.

"Sandy, when you help people in trouble they block you out because it only keeps reminding them of the trouble they got themselves into in the first place. It would be fine if you were up to your eyes in it yourself. But you're flying as far as they're are concerned. Do you remember The Hero always telling us to put on the poor mouth and say we were going for tests or that the tax man was after us?"

We walked on a while laughing at The Hero.

"The bar is throbbing every Saturday night and you have a great life of it. You have the bit of golf or a day's racing when the mood hits you and plenty of folding money. Looks and brains. Paula and your friends. Sandy, the problem with you is you don't know how good you have it."

We climbed over iron gates and straddled barbed wire on our way down. It was like when were young lads. The ground was drier and we warmed a bit as we picked up pace.

"I was addled from writing that journal. It brought everything back. I thought I was alright about it but it brought out the worst in me. Then I got to thinking of Brainy and when I heard Moran laugh it set something off in my head."

"Well Sandy, you have a new chapter now that's for sure. You're in fierce trouble. I'm thinking you should go to Tommy Junior's. Get advice. This is the biggest mess you were ever in."

"No Snipe, it's the second biggest."

Later in the day I seconded The Dosser from his sometime task of marking the prices of the horses on the board in the betting shop in Ballymore and threw him in behind the bar.

I knew he'd take the job of Quality Controller on himself the minute he saw my car leave The Square. But I had to get to the ocean.

Paula phoned just as I was taking a tenner out of the cash register. I just couldn't answer the mobile when I saw her name come up. I was almost gone out the door when The Snipe picked up the bar phone. He told Paula I was right beside him.

"Guess where we are?"

I got it into my head she was at Ballymore railway station with the boyfriend, what's his name, for the purpose of having it out with me. I told her as much.

"Having what out with me. Ah the living together thing is sorted. We're just doing it and that's that. The living together thing I mean." There was a big giggle. "We're in Prague. Just got a mad fit to go for the weekend. Cost us a fiver each and taxes."

"Great, what's it like?" I asked, greatly relieved she took the bargain.

"Incredible city. Saw the statue of the Infant today. Class city. Cheap as well. Had a bottle of wine and an excellent dinner for a tenner. This is costing a bomb. Almost outa credit. Love you lots. Bye bye. Love you. . ."

Thank God The Bugle isn't on sale in the Czech Republic.

CHAPTER TWENTY-FOUR

A Paddle

THE GLEN IS SO near the sea, the salty southwest winds burn all the conifers on one side while the eastern half of the tree remains green and thriving. Sometimes you can smell the salt in the air but you are still inland and might as well be a million miles from the ocean.

Ten minutes in the car and you're in a different world. The ocean is the only place to be when there's a storm in the head. The breeze and the pounding of the waves on the rocks are the most therapeutic remedies on earth. I love the notion that there is nothing between me and America save for maybe a freighter crawling up to the neck of the estuary. I got a mad fit to take off my shoes and socks. I turned my ankle jumping off a stone wall on the way down the hill with The Snipe. The salt water is supposed to be a great cure for aches and pains. The last trickling of the waves licks my toes like a little puppy. On a stormy day the wave-endings turn into a jelly foam that wobbles and shivers at the frontier of the tide's jurisdiction. The waves rise up on each other's backs, leapfrogging each other in their rush to the foreshore. The spray gushes up a hundred and fifty metres on a stormy day and curls in an arch until it passes over the top of the cliff.

I feel privileged to be part of creation. It fills me full of appreciation for just being able to go there and see and hear and smell and feel the power and the glory.

The Snipe was right. I have Paula and so much more.

I paddle around the little rock pools looking up every now and then in case someone sees me. Small crabs scurry under stones when I put my hand down in the water. Tiny almost transparent fish shoot out from under rock ledges. Periwinkles soak and stay moist under seaweed. Barnacles glue themselves higher upon the rocks where the splash of the tide will find them without causing them to move home. The rock pool dwellers live in fear of predators. The gulls get them when the tide is in and the crabs when it goes out.

High up in the ice-age sculpted coal black cliffs, sea birds rest for a while on ledges and shelves. Then they descend and soar and swoop and glide on the magic carpet air currents. They know where they are going but they can't go the direct route. First they fly west and low, then an upcurrent sweeps them here and there and maybe even further away from their destination than they intended. They are phlegmatic when each gust sends them backwards knowing they can hitch a ride on another squall. Even when they are sent backwards their eyes still face out in front. Then suddenly they drop beneath the gust, almost touching the shore itself as if they pressed a button in an elevator. Sometimes they dock for a while, nose down, eyes trained for the slightest disturbance. Three toe claw marks signpost the gulls' awkward trot. Then the arrows stop. 'Here lies buried treasure'.

The Snipe and myself were always looking for pieces of eight on the beach when we were small fellas. If you added the two of our ages together we were eighteen. We'd get the bus from Ballymore all on our own to the strand. Different times. Small boys left home at nine o'clock and only returned for dinner and at nightfall. And no one worried.

The Snipe had to rely on my say-so as to the location of the treasure. When he was tired I would tell him to keep on digging, swearing that if we didn't find pieces of eight we'd surely spot a kangaroo or a dingo or two at the end of our shovelling. While all the other boys and girls were building castles, we were digging holes.

I went straight from the sea to his farm. It was a small, well-tended oasis in the desert of monotonous forestry. I found him feeding cattle in a shed at dusk. The cattle were bellowing loudly. I had to raise my voice.

"Will you back me Snipe?"

"That goes without saying Sandy but we're up against it. Did you go to the solicitor?"

"No. I'm going to talk to Liam first."

"He says you're not to talk to the Ballymore Sergeant whatever happens. He's a Bore supporter and will do you if he gets a chance. What came over you anyway, Sandy? Talking about making a total eejit out of yourself?"

I hate myself when I lose all reason. It's as if I'm a puppet blown by a gale. The fury seems to control my brain, my limbs and my tongue.

I asked The Snipe to get our friends to call to the pub that night to see if we could get some sort of rival petition together. I couldn't let them get the better of me.

The Snipe was delighted I was going to put up a fight. He suggested we get Turpentine Twomey to back us.

"Have you any idea why they have it in for you?"

"No. Not for sure. I think it might be a power thing or maybe the two of them fancy themselves as amateur sleuths or maybe they're just bonkers. I have a plan. Tell our gang it's code-named Operation Seagull."

I wasn't back from The Snipe's a half an hour when Liam walked straight into the kitchen. He turned on the lights.

I'd say it was his intention to go back to bed when our discussion was concluded and judging by the wrinkled condition of his shirt and the tossed state of what was left of his hair he was only just out of it.

"It's bad for you to be sitting in the dark."

Liam picked a sausage from my plate, buttered two slices of bread, daubed one end with mayonnaise, plastered the other end with mustard and took a big bite.

I pointed to a splash of sauce and crumb on the corner of his mouth and after failing to lick it off he used the sleeve of his Garda shirt.

"Sandy, even I can't solve this one."

I gave him my side of the story and he showed me Moran and the priest's statements even though he wasn't supposed to. They didn't spare me.

"Make no statement about the actual assault. It's you against the two. The Rumour Factory are in living dread of you."

"Did you tell them I went off killing people for The Holy Souls?"

Liam looked at me for a minute to assess my mental health.

"You're not cracking up on me now, are you?"

"It's a joke Liam."

"You'll have to say the teacher and the priest abused you. That's your way out. Make statements to that effect and I'll politely imply that if you withdraw your charges they should do the same. And I'll give them a donkeyload of shite about Christianity and forgiveness so they won't feel they've been backed into a corner."

I told Liam that Moran was a sadist but the priest never laid a hand on us schoolboys and girls. He was actually nice to us when he came to school and Moran was all jolly and friendly during the priest's visits.

"I'll tell them your abuse charges might well stick in the current climate," Liam continued. "I was half the day trying to figure it out after I heard. The Christianity angle will be their way out. They will say they never laid a hand on you. But I will persuade them if they are Christian and drop the assault cases we will drop the abuse allegations. That's it Sandy. The only way of keeping you out of the hotel with no carpets."

"But Liam, they never abused me."

Liam was beginning to get annoyed. He told me I was losing my marbles. A man saw me paddling around the beach on the coldest day of the year. He stood up which was unusual as he normally stretched out on the sofa when he was talking to me and sometimes even fell asleep in mid conversation.

"I'm not talking about sex abuse. I'm talking about mental and physical abuse. It'll be hard to pin on the priest but we have the teacher and he's the one making the running on this. The priest is pretending to be all Christian and forgiving saying he'll pray for you and that there's a want there."

"A want?"

"A want is right. You're not the full shilling, he's saying. Another expression he used was the elevator doesn't go to the top floor. Moran said you were strange even as a boy and you were always on his shortlist to come to a bad end. He said years ago he forecasted you were a prime candidate to be stabbed outside a chipper in Birmingham."

"Why Birmingham?"

"Ah how would I know? There's just as good a chance you could be stabbed outside the chipper in Ballymore the way things are going over there. Fr Fitz makes out he's going to pray for you while at the same time in private he's driving on Moran and passing remarks about rendering unto the Minister for Justice what's the Minister for Justice's."

"Which means what?" I was confused.

"It means go ahead and crucify Sandy. I'm washing my hands of the whole thing. Do you know I'd say he's afraid of Moran."

I began to think that maybe I was a bit touched. I wasn't proud of beating two old men and said as much to Liam. And I resolved never to go to Birmingham.

"Touched my arse," said Liam. "Sure half the country wants to wallop violent teachers and dodgy priests. Did you know I was nearly adopted myself over one of them?"

"No Liam, I didn't."

He lay down on the sofa again and stretched his legs out to the full, closing his eyes as he spoke.

"Only for the mother digging in her heels before a priest I was gone. The mother had that gang of con artists well copped. She used to work as a servant girl in the presbytery when she was young. The priests had the only radio in the parish and when a sunny day was forecast by the weatherman they'd pray for fine weather at Mass that Sunday."

Then he opened his eyes and turned towards me as if he had to open his eyes when talking about the present.

"Have you a solicitor?"

"I was going to go to Tommy Junior. His father was my oul' fella's solicitor and his father before him."

"He's a top brief all right but he won't make up a story for you. Go with the mental torture one from the priest and the physical one from the teacher and hopefully it'll keep you out of the slammer. Oh yeah, and by all accounts there's a letter in the post from Moran's solicitors already. He's suing you. The cratur is suffering nightmares and headaches and has an appointment to see a shrink."

"Jesus that'll break me."

"Ah it mightn't be that bad."

"How much do you think he'll get?"

"I haven't a clue. Go to Tommy Junior. He's a smart boy. But give him the ammo. You might as well throw in the bit of paedophile dirt as well. Tell him the Padre put his hand on your willie while he was asking you who made the world or he was playing with himself while you were at Confession. What with the way things are going now and the amount of them that were at young fellas and the cover-upping that went on, no one will believe him anyway. Or at the very worst it'll delay things for three or four years and who knows with a bit of luck the two of them could have snuffed it by then."

"No Liam, I couldn't do that. Bad as they are, they're not that bad."

"Fine Sandy, do what you like but you're being set up here. And if you don't do what I say Moran's name will be over the door of this place. Moran's Bar and Grill. It has a nice ring to it . . ."

"No Liam but I'll use the violence bit. That's true and half The Glen will back me on that. But the priest was never violent. I'm not going to run with that one."

Liam just looked at me, threw his head up in the air and then shook it as if to indicate there maybe was a bit of a want in me. He changed tack. The Super, he said, enjoyed the story of the origin of the House of Suck but he would have to go public on the Tubbermore Torso. The Chief was on to him and said we were lucky the national papers didn't pick up on it. I suppose they were too busy with all the other murders. Twenty years ago there were only about three or four homicides a year and it was big news. Now there's one every couple of days and the day after the murder is publicised you forget it ever even happened.

"The Super is cracking up Sandy. The Bore is in to him about six times a week. Walks straight into the office without even a knock. The Super has to hide in the jacks until he's gone. He's on your side because of his friendship with The Hero but his heart is broken. And the Sarge is against you because you barred a guard.

"Believe me when I say this, the Sarge is a bad bastard if he takes a set against someone. The Super therefore would be grateful if you made the peace with The Bore."

I promised Liam I would sort the matter out. That 'the Super would be grateful' was in fact an indirect way of issuing a direct order.

"Have you any other dirt on the Dynamic Duo? Something we can use as leverage?"

"No Liam. Not aside from the beatings. The Hero had something years ago and he used it to get Moran off The Snipe and myself but he never told me what it was."

"You can be certain it was something weighty. A pity he didn't tell you."

* * * * * *

There was a missed call from Paula on my mobile. I thought she must have heard the news for sure. I called her back immediately. It was late. She had a few in. Paula told me she was going to try to find her real parents. Have one more try. Her mother always refused to see her in the past. It was something that caused Paula terrible distress. I told her I had someone with me and I couldn't really talk. It was the first time I ever lied to her. Ten minutes later the phone rang again. It was Paula. I didn't answer the mobile and took the house phone off the hook.

I just didn't have a clue what to say so I phoned Sr Maura.

Sr Maura was the nun who brought Paula to The Glen when her parents died. She was like a mother to Paula after that. Maura told Paula women's things and was only a phone call away if help was needed.

She was getting on a bit now but was still full of energy. Maura advised me to tell everything to Paula before someone in a pub told her the whole story. It wasn't as if I didn't know that already.

Paula was like that, very trusting. She always believed me and took everything I said as being true, which ordinarily it was. I never lied to her and the only secret I kept from her was the story of your adoption. I made it my business to always tell her what I thought even if it sometimes drove her into a fit.

Five minutes later Liam phoned me from the station in Ballymore. He had a habit of shouting into the phone as if the distance between us necessitated it. I had to put the receiver about six inches away from my year.

"A woman purporting to be Mary O made contact with us," he roared.

"We're checking it out. It might be a hoax you'd never know. But the lads think it might not be."

CHAPTER TWENTY-FIVE

CAUGHT IN THE NET

I HARDLY SLEPT. A million possibilities teemed through the weir in my head and all of them were negative. The irrational worries of the night, as is their way, disappeared with the day. The phone rang at eight in the morning just after I dozed off. The battery ran out as Liam was about to talk. I plugged it in and the very second it repowered Liam was back to me before I even had a chance to dial.

"She's in London," he roared. "She phoned her mother as well. Read the report of her death in The Bugle over the Internet and said it was greatly exaggerated. The Super is here as well; he wants to talk to you."

"Great news, Sandy. I never doubted you mind, but it's some blow to my tormentors. Look, can you do anything about The Bore? I had to be handcuffed the other day and taken out of the station with a coat over my head just to throw him off."

I promised him I would sort out The Bore issue. I had no choice. The barring order will have to be rescinded.

An hour later Liam arrived in the kitchen. He embraced me.

"The priest and the teacher and The Rumour Factory are all bollixed now. We bate 'em Sandy. We bate 'em."

He hugged me and kissed me and told me to get my number ones on. We were heading to Ballymore to go on the rip with The Super to celebrate.

"Did you ask her about the child, Liam?"

"The Super is delighted and so am I. It's a catastrophic embarrassment for The Committee for Doing in Peeler's Heads. I could wallpaper the station with the amount of letters they've been sending in about the shagging bones in the bog. If today was yesterday I'd feed the whole frigging lot to Houdini."

"Did you ask her about the child? Did you ask her about my child?"

Liam sat down on the sofa. You could see from his hunched-up posture he was disappointed with himself. He hushed down his tone a gear or two.

"Sorry Sandy, but I wasn't talking to her personally. I'll get the detectives to ask her what happened to it, him, her. I only have skimpy details. I should have realised the finding of the kid was all that mattered to you. Sorry Sandy."

Liam did have some information.

Mary O was married and had three kids. She was living in London and was very distressed when she read the report on the net. She didn't intend for her disappearance to develop into "a full-blown murder investigation for her mother and brother's sake".

The Ballymore detectives had the English police check her out. Her husband was an Englishman. Older than her, apparently, a decent type, the principal in a grammar school in Surrey. Mary O worked part time as an administrator in an artists' co-op. They were well enough off and seemed to be just a normal couple living in a four-bedroom semi in suburban London. Her eldest girl was sixteen, which, of course, meant she wasn't mine.

Oh sweet Jesus, how I've longed for this day. I've never allowed myself to visualise this moment but it's so near now, so near. It's a day I thought would never come to pass. I'm so close to kissing you, my child. How often I've dreamt of that when I saw parents hug their kids in a park. I just had to leave Glenlatin on the days you were due to have made your Holy Communion and Confirmation. Christmas morning was the worst until Paula came to me.

I just wish my Dad was here. This day was all he ever wanted, not so much for himself but for me. I have an image of my hands pushing back the last strands of grey hair and rubbing them and combing them into place with my fingers as he lay dying and I'm telling him 'we have the baby, we have the baby'.

Soon I might have a chance to make amends. Oh God, thank you, and thank you Dad. I'd say somewhere over the rainbow you interceded and pleaded on my behalf. He has to know I'm going to be alright. I'm sure he does know. All this can't be just pure chance. There has to be a director and a screenwriter working on this plot at God's right hand side. There just has to be. There's no other way of explaining it all.

I was overcome and had to ask Liam to give me a little time to myself. I couldn't hold back the emotion. Tears flowed as if a tap was turned on. A whole lifetime of sorrow was lanced from my heart.

And then after a while there was a sense of anti-climax.

At least everything is almost squared away and in its rightful place at last. I love packing the empty bottles into their cases in the yard at the back of The Mayo Bar. It has a finality to it. The bottles are in their places in the crates and the job is done to everyone's satisfaction – from the barman to the man collecting them, to the manufacturer. Life never worked out as well for me. I kind of thought 'why me' for this miracle? What did I do to deserve it? A Suck takes biscuits to bed, a mummy gets found in a dump, and I finish up finding my child.

Paula always says I think too much and I know she's right but I can't help it. This thing is too big for me but I'll take it and embrace it with open arms. Surely Mary O would agree to put me in touch with my own child? I couldn't imagine her refusing me now. There was always something decent and honourable about her. She could be a bit distant at times but was honest and would never cause harm to anyone.

Mary O, your mother, was a romantic at heart and I suppose getting pregnant and rejected didn't fit into her plan. She detached herself when the going got rough. I'm sure that's a throwback to having a father who was a perpetual roarer and bully. There were times when she seemed to be almost unworldly. She could stare into space for hours on end or just lie in her room playing with the strands of her hair.

The night she lost the head with me in the flat was brought on by extreme stress and was a bit out of character in some ways. She never went absolutely berserk with the temper; the switch never tripped. It was always a gradual thing with her. Mary O even found it hard to criticise her father, saying that but for him they would never have had their own place. He had it tough, she'd say, heading off at sixteen for the hydroelectric stations being built in Scotland. He had no childhood or fun, which was why he was so strict.

This is the nearest I have ever been to finding you in all these years. By this time next week we could be sitting here having a drink.

I am certain I can get around Mary O. She'll surely understand that I am a different man now. I will apologise to her. Tell her the whole story, the honest truth. I will give her these pages to read. Definitely. And, as for me, the baby bobbing about in the Thames will finally be brought ashore.

CHAPTER TWENTY-SIX
THE KITCHEN DÁIL AND LIFTING THE VEIL

IT'S FUNNY BUT I'M a different man when I spend time in my room. The gloom of the room permeates my thinking. I just hate being on my own.

I'm a different Sandy again on the soft shush of a beach or in the bee buzz of the bar. The bedroom is my worry room. It has always been so. I worried if my mother made it to heaven when I was small. I'd worry about school, especially on Sunday nights but then I'd have less rational worries about things like the concept of infinity. The thought of something going on forever without end made no sense to me. I wondered about wherever it would finish up and that place scared me. Thousands of screaming numbers looking for an end to their never-ending miseries. I always fell asleep with the light on and the cross made from my schoolbooks guarded the fringes of my bed against vampires and werewolves.

I'd worry about Dad and The Hero dying and who would look after me when they were gone. Then I'd sit on the stairs so I could hear the voices rising from The Upper House. I could hear some of what was said and it always cheered me up. Sometimes there might even be a song.

The hum of the talk and the loud laughing was enough to keep me from being lonely. Dad often found me asleep at the top of the stairs. He was guilty he couldn't stay with me at night, but the bar is a tough taskmaster and he just had to keep at it to earn a living.

If only I treated Mary O with respect I would be more confident she might be better disposed towards me now.

The detectives said she was very upset when they spoke to her. She could have changed. Mary O might well be a tough woman who would just pitch me to hell.

I'm going through a terrible dose of 'the poor Sandy's'. Ah well, I have only myself to blame. I was arrogant and blind to what was going on around me. I indulged myself in a cowardly attack on two old men. The thought of jail scares me half to death but the worst thing is the effect a prison sentence might have on Paula.

The pounding of the hot shower on my head eased the torment a bit. I looked at myself in the mirror as I shaved. Seventeen signatures think you're a murderer, I thought.

Sad Sandy. It has a bit of alliteration and even a resonance of assonance. Hair licked up to cover the bald spot, stomach sucked in to hide the soft underbelly. Off to Limerick once a month to see the widow, no strings attached, and that was that.

There's no chance of my forming a relationship on a permanent basis. I always said I'd marry if I could find one couple who were happy and never had a cross word between them. I know I'll never find that couple. I just don't have the stomach for the kind of battle and sacrifice marriage entails. I'm afraid the woman I meet will turn into my Nana.

There's no happy-ever-afters in relationships, only happy-sometimes and sad-sometimes and something in between the two most of the time. Even though I never read one of the shagging things, I was always looking for a Mills and Boon woman with no corners to her and no danger of a row.

The Hero told me once that if things are at their worst a fella should always throw on his good suit.

So I polished my leather shoes which were still caked with sanctified mud from Auntie Annie's graveside and said a prayer to her.

My friends were in the kitchen for a meeting in support of me. It was part of Operation Seagull, with The Snipe the main organiser. The plan is to get a counter-petition together for The Bugle protesting my innocence.

The Hero said you'd always know the inside man in a three-card trick operation by his shoes. The card dealer would look disgusted when the inside man, who would be wearing a nice suit, would win for the fourth time in a row. It was the shoes that gave the game away. The inside men's shoes were always worn with the soles flapping like a window left open in the wind.

"It's no good having a big car, Sandy, if the tyres are worn," The Hero would say. The Hero always knew when I was down and cracked a joke or two to help me get right.

As I polished the shoes I said a little prayer to my Dad and my Mam. I always prayed to my mother when I was in trouble at school. Lately, I've taken to praying to my Dad. As I get nearer to him in age I begin to understand him better. He was always good and honest. Who better to pray to than the righteous?

Even now with well over half my life over I still seek the protection of my parents. I've heard people say you're never done rearing your children. In my case it goes on even after my parents are dead. In a strange way I kind of feel they're with me sometimes. I'd say I'm on speaking terms with them now rather than just straight out praying. It takes a while to get to that stage. At the start you just go into automatic pilot and say the formula prayers.

Gradually you ask them about things and later on again you bring them bits of news. The next thing is that you start to talk to them as if they're right there beside you.

What would The Hero do next?

I splashed a few drops from his last bottle of Hubris aftershave and donned the shop face. I skipped the creaky step.

But I turned back and opened up the gap on the stairs for the first time in two decades. The one thing about a bachelor's house is it doesn't change much with the years.

I peeped through the spy hole. The coat stand was full with the coats piled on top of each other like bodies in a rugby ruck. I thought of my Dad. Or maybe he thought of me and I thought of the last time I stairs-dropped. Grandad and Dad were in the kitchen. It wasn't long after the Mary O affair.

"He didn't set out to leave anyone down. He's not a bad lad," Dad said.

"Ah, you're right, Sandy is a good lad," agreed The Hero.

"He's all that. He's all that."

It must have been the first time ever they agreed on anything. The Hero then made a suggestion.

"We'll give him a score and send him off somewhere with The Snipe. Listowel Races."

"We will."

That was the second time my Dad agreed with The Hero in one day. A record.

"And we'll give The Snipe a score as well," said The Hero

"We will."

"We might even give them a pony. Porter's gone up."

"Tell me, how much is a pony, Hero?"

"It's bookie talk for twenty five."

"Right."

"Will a pony be enough?"

"Loads," replied my Dad.

* * * * *

I could barely hear the voices in the kitchen. I pulled back the carpet further to hear and see all the better. The coat stand tumbled from the weight of the coats. The Dosser righted it. A draught coming from the open kitchen windows just below tunnelled into my earhole. The Dosser looked up instinctively towards the peephole. I lay still on the stairs. All sound then and no pictures. The sickle moon looked like an ear listening in the frame of the skylight above me. A satellite pretending to be a star looked over me. The meeting was in full flow.

"He was always loyal to his friends and treats everyone the same behind the bar, rich or poor. Sandy's no saint, I know, and he doesn't hate drink or women. He's the only one trying to keep The Glen from turning into one of those deserted villages you see in cowboy pictures, with the swinging doors of the saloon shrieking in the wind like banshees and hay sheds of tumbleweed cartwheeling up and down the main street."

There was a pause as everyone tried to transpose Turpentine Twomey's widescreen image of economic depravation in the Wild West to The Hero Square in the editing suites in their head. It took a minute at least. Old Turps was in very poor health, but his mind was still sharp. The old boy started to cough a bit and there was a further silence until he continued.

"This man is The Hero's grandson and would never lay a hand on a woman. He's not bred to blackguarding."

Poor Old Turps was frail and thin beyond belief. There wasn't much left in him. He had lung cancer from years of chain-smoking Woodbines. When he finished talking, he got a terrible fit of coughing and shook so much you'd think he was going to fall apart.

"I agree with Turps. I have known Sandy man and boy and there is no way he is capable of doing such a thing. I know he lost all reason in the church but maybe he had a good excuse."

That was the way of Sr Maura. To the point and fearless. The two most respected of the parish elders were on my side. Then The Snipe made a contribution.

"I was there in the thick of it. This is a ganging up on Sandy," he said. "He did all he could to find Mary O. My uncle and himself even went to solicitors to see if they could force her to come forward."

When a shy man like The Snipe spoke in public everyone listened. There was a long, generous round of applause.

Someone else started to speak. It was my cue to scamper down the stairs, almost falling in my haste. I ran back up again to cover the spy hole. Back down again, taking two steps at a time like a young lad. I made my entrance and thanked my friends.

There was a raucous cheer. Someone said there were seventy-three people crushed into the little kitchen. The biggest crowd since we waked The Hero. There was another twenty or thirty listening in from the bar. Old Turpentine spoke for everyone present.

"Sandy, we're here to gather up a petition to send into The Bugle to say we believe in your innocence."

"Thanks Turps, but there's no need. You'll have to wait for next week's paper. But the body in the bog is some hapless, starving Famine victim."

I told the assembly Mary O was still alive and well and living in England. There was a cheer loud enough to rattle the bottles on their shelves. People started to chatter excitedly amongst themselves. My friends came over to congratulate me. More dashed out to make phone calls. Text messages were flying. My back was well clattered and my fingers were sore from the squeezing. I was overwhelmed.

I thought of the letter delivered by Sally Moran. And in an instant I formulated a plan to turn the convocation in the kitchen into a positive force for The Glen. The AGM of The Glen Development Association to be held in The Ballymore Park Hotel on November 19th.

Fr Fitz was the honorary president and Moran was chairman. The whole set-up was just an excuse for the two of them to spend Government money on trips to Dublin, purportedly for rural development conferences.

The Development Association's sole contribution to the betterment of the village was to paint the perimeter wall of St Teresa's green for St Patrick's Day having painted it Papal yellow the year before. This well-maintained wall would show prospective factory builders what a progressive village we had, full of vitality and 'entrepenooooors' as Moran called them.

Fr Fitz began the painting every year. He wore an old Pringle golf sweater and put his heart and soul into the daubing.

One of The Rumour Factory would then offer to take over the painting, or rather she would have her husband take the brush. The Hero said once "it was probably the only time the poor oul' husbands would ever get to handle their missuses' brushes". Fitzgerald would refuse to hand over the paint brush at first. The old Tom Sawyer trick. Then he would do the Christian thing and give it over to the acolyte's arthritic spouse who would barely be able to grab it due to his gnarled, frozen fingers and anti-clockwise ball and socket shoulder joint.

For years I have wanted to do more than just talk about the future of the village. I don't know why but I decided to speak out. It wasn't planned or anything. It just happened. I suppose it's something that has always annoyed the arse off me. The people who were running things were left to do as they wanted because the rest of us just couldn't be bothered.

I stood up on a chair and shook a bell my father kept for calling time. It took a few minutes. The confederation in the kitchen were still yapping away excitedly about my revelations. At last there was silence and then I spoke out. I thanked them, of course, for their support. It was a noble gesture and typical of the Glenlatinos to rally round a man in trouble.

"All bar seventeen," interrupted The Dosser to loud laughter.

Maura took a note of what I said. I'll quote it back to you:

"We have to harness the community spirit and sense of goodness that is so obvious here tonight. I am putting my name forward for the post of chairman of the Development Association. I am going to oppose Moran. He and his ilk have failed the people miserably. The Glen must not be allowed to die. We have to take our future into our own hands. The authorities are refusing planning permission for sons and daughters of Glen people who want to do no more than build on their own lands. The plan is to make cities and big towns bigger and to leave the countryside to ramblers and sheep. The cost of a mile of motorway in Dublin would revitalise the whole county. The price of a hundred metres would mean The Glen would live on, strong and resourceful. But there is no hope for us with those people. They do not understand us or comprehend how important it is to society to keep the small towns, the little villages and rural communities strong and vibrant. We are the source but no one will help us unless we help ourselves. We have to start here in the community and build from the bottom up. We live in a time of dangerous vacuum. Apathy reigns. Every man looks after himself but it hasn't spread to The

Glen and it never will. We will look to ourselves to fight our own cause. Our own just cause.

"I am no saint and I am no man to say I am better than anyone here. I might even be in jail before long but I hope in spite of my shortcomings you will join with me in the fight to save The Glen. Fr Fitz and the politicians spoke of bringing a factory for years but they never did anything about it. Maybe they could build a suitcase factory for all the emigrants. (Laughter and applause.)

"We as a community must stand up and fight. These people have taken over from the English. The Government only bothers with us when they want our cash or our votes. They shut our school, they are trying to shut the Post Office, they shut the creamery but, by Jesus, I swear they won't shut our mouths. The big people will lose. They will never close down The Glen. Let it start here tonight."

I didn't get to finish. There was another huge round of applause. I was shouldered out to the bar.

Poor old Turps was crying, saying The Hero would never be dead while I was alive.

Maura called me aside when I dismounted and said, "Sandy, today is the day you have grown into a fine man. I am so proud of you. So proud of you."

And she hugged me. Handshakes and more hugs followed. I never realised how desperate the people were for a bit of leadership. It was the proudest moment of my life. Easily.

The Hero once framed a print of a boat sailing out of a marina. The caption on the boat print was a quote from Thomas Aquinas. "Men, like ships, are built to leave the harbour." I finally know what it meant.

The talk and the camaraderie continued long into the night but it was Tuesday and people had children to get to school and work the next day.

The bar cleared without any call of time up. Maura stayed on for a chat. She was high on the success of the night. As usual, she was full of energy, picking her little steps as she tidied up the kitchen. Maura must be nearly eighty but she drives her car and is well up to speed with all that is going on in and out of The Glen. She never allowed herself to grow old.

It was Maura who helped Paula with the girl's things, like periods, the first bra rigmarole and all that kind of carry-on. All the women's stuff I wasn't equipped for, or was too embarrassed to handle.

"And Mary O might be coming home. It'll give you a chance to talk to her and find out what happened to the child. And you can speak to her honestly about the circumstances surrounding the adoption."

Maura knew only too well that I had a habit of putting things off.

I told my friend of my fear Mary O would not help me. I told of my shame and my fears for my relationship with Paula. The speech in the kitchen was spontaneous. Was I a fit person for these people to look up to?

"Sandy, I can tell you there are things I did that I too am thoroughly ashamed of. People I hurt, sins of commission and sins of neglect. For many years I ignored terrible things that were going on all around me," she said.

"But I forgive myself. It's the hardest thing of all to do but you must do it. The thing is to first acknowledge you did wrong. You have done this many times. The next step is to forgive yourself. People know you are not perfect, but you don't pretend to be. For the first time in a long time I felt hope surging in my chest. The Glen lives, I said to myself, The Glen will never die."

Sr Maura spoke in a soft, gentle voice.

"Jesus himself wasn't perfect. He became depressed and went off up a mountain. He barred the moneylenders from the temple in a ferocious fit of temper. You have the temper and the barring in common with Him, Sandy," Maura joked.

I knew I should retain every word; Maura's counsel was always worth listening to.

"Sandy, remember there were only seventeen signatures out of an adult population of about three hundred. Sandy, you know you're going to have to talk to Paula."

"What if she discovers I was responsible for putting my own child up for adoption, Maura? She's like my father, you know, the only way is the straight way."

"She loves you, Sandy. You were always a father to her. She will never turn against you. I will go to see her with you, if you wish."

"Thanks, but I'll have to tell her myself."

"That is the best way, Sandy. Will you fix on a date to tell her?"

"She's due home at the weekend for the pony races."

"Good. Please tell her then. I arranged a Mass for The Hero's anniversary. I hope you didn't mind."

Maura and The Hero were great friends. If Maura ever needed

anything for a poor person in the village, like say a hand out at Holy Communion or Confirmation, she always went to The Hero.

"No, it's fine. I should have looked after it myself. Fr Fitz isn't saying it?"

"Fr Ryan from Ballymore is the celebrant."

"He's one sound man. Thanks Maura. I forgot all about it."

"After all these years, Sandy, I still miss him very much, you know."

Then she paused for a minute. She had let go of my hands and had a strange, faraway look in her eyes.

"The Hero was the first human being who saw me as a woman rather than as nun but he was a schemer. You could never really get to the core of him because of that. Sandy, I'm fairly sure The Hero schemed your child's adoption."

I asked her to explain, even though it didn't come as any great shock to me. It was something I always suspected.

"I'm not quite sure how he was involved. I just know he did. It was something he let slip when we were together. He said, 'I'll find that girl and make sure the child goes to the right place. I know the child is ours and I will not see a Hero go through life without our support. I'm afraid I conspired to send the poor girl away. I had to do it. I had my reasons and believe me when I say this. I had everyone's interest at heart, even the poor girl's and her child but it's a time I don't look back on with any great pride'."

Maura had no idea who adopted my child, but she was certain The Hero was up to his eyes in it. He would have to be stuck in the middle of the whole thing, wheeling and dealing.

"You know what he was like, Sandy."

"Are you thinking what I'm thinking, Maura?"

"Paula? Could The Hero have manipulated the adoption process to ensure his own daughter adopted Paula?"

"It's not such a long shot, is it Maura? Are you're sure he wasn't spinning a yarn? You'd never know what would be going on inside that man's head."

"That's the reason I didn't tell you before now, Sandy."

"Tell me what?"

"I hope you will not think ill of me."

"Never Maura. You know that." And I held her two hands in mine again and squeezed them as if to help her squeeze whatever it was bothering her out into the open.

"Sandy, The Hero changed my whole way of thinking. I was brainwashed and he taught me how to think for myself. Not all at once but over a period of time. He was my teacher."

"The reason you didn't tell me, Maura?"

"Sandy, it was pillow talk."

CHAPTER TWENTY-SEVEN

A HERO LIES IN YOU

THE HERO'S HIDDEN DEPTHS were murkier than I thought. My God, did that man hold anything or anyone sacred? It was hard to put the image of him and Sr Maura together out of my mind but the thought that Paula could be you, my daughter, soon had me addled again.

I felt the odds that The Hero had pulled another famous stroke were very good indeed. After all, Paula is the right age. And The Hero told Maura he was going to make sure the little girl remained a Hero. How better to do that than to ensure his own daughter adopted the child?

I looked at the photos of Paula on the mantelpiece from Holy Communion to her debs. She had The Hero nose but it looked well on her. There was no mistaking she was a little bit like me anyway, and she had those clear, blue, high resolution, multi-pixel eyes of The Hero. I couldn't see any of the Tom Tie in her which, I suppose, had to be a good thing in one sense but in another way it meant Paula might not be my daughter.

I tried to weigh up the evidence and I just couldn't be sure. Could The Hero have stroked an adoption? I knew adoptions were very shady in the fifties, with private adoption agencies sending kids off to the States to good Catholic homes without any documentation or tracing procedures.

But surely the seventies were different?

I have a notion of The Hero sweet-talking a nun in an orphanage. He was obviously good with nuns. The Hero would persuade the sister to put Paula in the front row of adoptees where my sister and her husband would see her or maybe he would tell them some lie like he knew for a fact the child was the daughter of a Nobel Prize winner. Anything was possible with that man. But then again this was a child we were talking about, not an item for sale on a supermarket shelf.

I was exhausted beyond belief. Fell asleep with my clothes on. Woke up to finish this off. So much has happened in just a few hours and at the end of it all I'm as near to jail as I am to finding my child. Still, if I was offered that result at the beginning of yesterday I would have taken it without a moment's dithering.

THE BALLY BUGLE

TRUTH WILL OUT   November 13 • Edition 31

EDITORIAL

IT may have escaped many of us that our relentless quest for finality, or as they now call it, closure, may lead at times to short cuts. In other words, the time-honoured maxim that a man is innocent until proven guilty may well be a thing of the past if recent events in Glenlatin are to be our guide.

The Tubbermore Torso controversy serves to illustrate the conundrum between the proper and correct investigation of a crime and the jumping of the gap between the what and the maybe. The police are to be congratulated for their professionalism and their refusal to bend to the will of the amateur sleuths. They carried out their investigations without fear or favour, as is their remit.

A hastily assembled lynch mob incorrectly deduced that the discovery of a 150-year-old corpse was an invitation to rake up private grief of twenty or more years ago. The Bugle has been inundated with letters and phonecalls asking for us to name and shame an innocent man. This newspaper is steadfast in its adherence to the highest journalistic principles of due process and balanced and fair reporting, irrespective of the public clamour for a head, if you pardon the pun.

A man of high standing was the victim of scurrilous rumour and innuendo. Why this should be the case we cannot but imagine. The parish elders, namely Fr Aonghus Fitzgerald and Mr Mortimer Moran, appear to have misled many of the more vulnerable and easily influenced inhabitants of Glenlatin into the mistaken belief there was a murderer in their midst. Murderer indeed! If it is a question of murder, which it surely is, how can you arraign an innocent man in the court of rumour for a crime committed over a century before his birth?

The chairperson of the self-styled Glen Committee for Public Safety, Mr Mortimer Moran, gave credence to the lie that the discovery of the so-called Tubbermore Torso was an event of cataclysmic importance in the life of the residents of the county's hilliest parish. McCarthyism is alive and well and living in The Glen.

Shame. An innocent man has been put through what we can only imagine is intolerable stress from within the very community of which he is an integral part. This newspaper is steadfast in its defence of the rights of the individual while at the same time reflecting the concerns and necessities of the public good.

Let us now put The Tubbermore Torso to rest along with the innuendo that condemned an innocent man.

CHAPTER TWENTY-EIGHT

MINNIE MAY AND THE IRA

THE DAY AFTER THE Bugle's change of tune I met Minnie May outside the post office and she apologised for signing the petition. Moran put it in front of her, she said, and asked her to sign "for everyone's safety".

She was walking towards the church with angular, arthritic Alfie on a lead. I lifted the little dog in my arms. We were old enemies. Alfie took a snap at me one time after I intervened in a turf war between himself and Houdini, but I had long since forgiven him. I carried Alfie in my arms across the Square. It was cold and the wind was blowing from the north east. Minnie spoke through a scarf wrapped around her mouth.

"Who were the Lynches The Bugle was on about?" Minnie muffled, eyes darting to and fro in case she was being observed fishing for information. She couldn't think of any Lynches in The Glen. And would I know when Mary O was coming home?

"It's cold," I replied, handing her Alfie just outside the church.

Minnie then wondered who the McCarthys were. "There were no McCarthys in Glenlatin either," she mused.

It was a rout. Fr Fitz was unavailable for comment. He was away on business in the city. Moran was missing as well.

The editorial didn't hold back. I'll give The Bugle that much. The last line read like an audition for the Pulitzer Prize.

Still, I felt like ringing up the editor and asking how it was he managed to reopen a murder file that had been closed since Black '47.

It wasn't all good news. Poor old Turpentine Twomey was carried over the hill yesterday. Ninety-seven. He went quickly in the end. Lasted only a few days after the kitchen Dáil. Turps was given a full State funeral with military honours. The Taoiseach even sent a representative and a volley of shots was fired over the grave by the Irish army. He was the last of the Mayo Marauders.

There were the usual references to the bridge at Athlone and Thermopylae at the graveside oration. The Bugle described him as "The Hero Sullivan's most trusted soldier when the battle raged at its fiercest".

I could picture The Hero sitting high up on the curve of a ten-foot Celtic cross, legs dangling, almost falling off from the shoulder-shaking laughter.

The Hero was very fond of Turps. I'll never forget him for showing up at the meeting the other night. He had a decent streak in him and didn't know how to say no. Sure Shot remained a militant pacifist in the armed struggle. He passed on the flame to his son Oisin who is involved in the new IRA as some kind of theorist, even though he has never been north of Navan in his life. A so-called hawk where the 'struggle' is concerned, he is also a staunch member of the anti-contraception, anti-divorce and anti-abortion-in-any-circumstances lobby. Oisin is a pro-life Provo.

Sure Shot and Turpentine, Turps to his closest friends, always acknowledged The Hero was the main man in The Mayo job.

The Hero, of course, had added to his legend when he told his fellow desperadoes that he forced two Tans to jump off the sheer cliff on the western boundary of the barracks.

This was never to be revealed. It leaked out, of course, but was never spoken of openly. Fathers passed the secret of Mayo on to their sons with the addendum that The Hero was a ruthless man but that the times needed ruthless men.

Turps and Sure Shot spent the rest of their lives in awe, and maybe even a small bit afraid, of The Hero. Still, the secret cemented their friendship and as the years went on the two other members of the Mayo Marauders began to believe in their own legend.

The Hero had told me the true history yet again. Grandad gave the boys the impression the Tans did actually jump off the cliff when he met up with the two itchy desperadoes outside Thunder Thighs' pitch in Limerick.

"I whispered an Act of Contrition in their ears even though they were Protestants and were going to go to hell anyway. Sure Shot started to cry. 'Jump into the arms of yer makers,' I said, and the two of them leapt into the Atlantic flapping their arms like mad as if they were trying to fly and pumping their legs up and down as if they were riding a bicycle. They were screaming like gannets until they disappeared under the waves, never to be seen again."

The Hero recalled the frightened look on Sure Shot's face. His lip stared to quiver, he said, and he started saying the Hail Mary to himself in a whisper. He managed to talk through the sniffling.

"Shooting them was fair enough, Joe Joe (Grandad was yet to be named The Hero) but making them jump off cliffs was going a bit over the top."

The Hero told me it gave him all he could do to hold in the laughter.

"I thought I heard screams alright," added Turps.

"And he could well have done," explained The Hero, "for sure wasn't the place black with the gannets!"

When The Hero asked Sure Shot to climb up to the headland where the RIC barracks was gradually falling over a cliff, he declined.

"I has no head for heights, Joe Joe. I'll guard the van. Go on you and don't be worrying yourself about the van."

"What's a van?" interrupted Turps, feeling a bit left out. "I think we should go home. We left the bikes all by themselves and they only borrowed. Will I go back and guard them instead, seeing as I don't know what a van is?"

The Hero explained that in guerrilla warfare the van was either the rear or the front of the squadron. He wasn't sure which. But he was certain the flanks were the side. Sure Shot thought it wouldn't be fair to let Turpentine go on his own and volunteered to mind the van with him, provided van meant the back and not the front. If he could get up a bit of courage, he'd try to do a bit of time on the flank later on but not to depend on him too much.

When Sure Shot was the first of the three to be carried over the Hill, The Hero was the star turn at the funeral.

"Keep an eye on the coffin because Sure Shot will kick the top off and run away," he joked to me at the time.

The Hero stood in front of the coffin as it was being lowered into the grave and saluted his old van-guarder by holding his hand up to his temple in the semi-formal, limp kind of a way effected by John Wayne in 'The Green Berets'.

There wasn't a dry eye in Tooreenbawn. Old comrades saying their last goodbyes. A local sympathiser dressed in a black beret and dark sunglasses played 'The Last Post' on a gleaming gold trumpet. Everyone knew who he was, of course.

Mary O's brother Joey (after The Hero) helped place a huge laurel-garlanded wreath at the side of the grave. His eyes were popping out of his head with the emotion of the moment. The young lad's hands were trembling with the excitement of the bugler, the cordite and the glorification of death and killing. If they asked Joey there and then, he'd have jumped on a plane and blown up half of London that very night.

Joey and I had remained friends in spite of all that happened with his sister and father. I had to call him aside in the pub and explain the reality. It took me months to talk him out of joining up. He was already half in at the time of the Sure Shot funeral, running errands, selling Republican newspapers and firing shots at cans on the tops of mountains. It wouldn't be long before Oisin would volunteer him to go up north. Eventually, The Hero sorted it all out. He paid a visit to the local IRA chief and asked that Joey be released from his duties.

The Hero told The Chief that he felt "the young fellow was a loose

MINNIE MAY AND THE IRA

cannon, and was best left to himself as he could jeopardise the smooth running of the organisation".

The Hero said this "as an old soldier who knew the danger signs. The young fella should be informed he wasn't suited but was not to be harmed in anyway on account of his grandmother hiding a Webley for The Hero during the Troubles".

This, of course, was a lie.

"What swung it, Sandy," The Hero recalled, "was when I cracked a joke about the knickers long ago being so wide and long and the arses being so big you could stash a Vickers machine gun in there. They loved listening to the great deeds of long ago. Joey was lucky. Once that lot get a hold of you, there's no getting out. They're worse than them religious cults."

"That's nice language, Grandad," I said.

"It was cults, I said Sandy. Cults."

"I was only joking, Grandad."

"I know that well, Sandy. Always keep up the old jokes. And will you stop calling me Grandad."

* * * * * *

Joey, your uncle, was a nice lad and suffered his share under Tom Tie's roof. His father found it hard to accept his son was a sensitive boy. He thought him to be too soft and too close to his mother so Tom Tie resolved to harden him up.

On one occasion, when Joey left a gate open on the farm, Tom Tie remarked, "Joey, you little ball of shit you, you wouldn't know your thumb from your prick, only there's a nail on it."

Joey wanted to join up to show his father he was a real man. In time, he was smart enough to distance himself from the IRA. He carried on the family tradition of emigrating to London where he became a project manager with an IT company.

Joey was at Turps' funeral even though he had no paramilitary connections anymore. They were related and anyway everyone loved old Turps. We walked home from the cemetery together. Joey was well groomed. There was a confidence in him. He was home from London every couple of weeks to see his mother. Joey always came into the bar and never lost touch with his school pals or The Glen. He was like his mother. Neither he nor Mary O took after their father.

Joey had become a cultured man who loved to go to the West End and to the ballet at Covent Garden. Mary O was a tall, lithe girl but Joey was small-framed like his mother. He only came out after his father died. No one in The Glen took any notice anyway. Even The Rumour Factory. For some reason, the old people had no homophobic tendencies.

I made it my business to meet with him. There was no movement of any consequence since the disclosure that Mary O was still alive. I asked Liam to pass on that I was anxious to meet with her but he said there was no response. The English detective (with whom Liam had struck up a good relationship) said Mary O just smiled and looked out the window. The English policeman said she was distant, cold even. She did indicate she might come home to see her mother but "she didn't get specific".

"Joey, I hear she might be coming home," I ventured. "Is it true?"

"I hope so. Even if she isn't, I will do my utmost to arrange a meeting in London. At least they know now she wasn't murdered."

Joey explained that hardly a day went by that he didn't think of Mary O. I empathised, and he seemed surprised when I told him she was in my thoughts all the time too. Joey was very upset by the allegations against me in The Bugle and phoned the police to tell them I could never have harmed his sister. But I already knew that from Liam.

"Sandy, she put it up for adoption. Did you know that? I presume you did."

"Were you talking to her?"

"I haven't spoken to her since the day she left all those years ago. She called my mother . . . They didn't talk for very long. My mother was so excited she wasn't able to speak. I guess I'm bitter over the fact she never made contact. There was only the two of us. She must have hardness in her like the old man."

"Different times, Joey, different times."

Joey promised he would do all he could to help me track down my child. It was the least he could do, he said. As he said his goodbyes, he invited me to the old cottage. His mother, Molly O, wanted to tell me that she too phoned the police to say I was not capable of murder. But, of course, I knew that also.

* * * * *

The Turpentine funeral party showed up in the bar after the burial for tea, sandwiches and cocktail sausages – or pygmy penises as The Hero used to call them. Knowing how messy with drink the afternoon would soon become, I desperately tried to escape before seventy-one-year old Mickey Turpentine Junior sang the thirty-seven verse War of Independence epic, 'The Hero of The Glen'.

I prayed for Fat Arse to erupt and vomit up lava over the three sides of The Hero Square. I must have heard that song a thousand times. Unfortunately for me, there was no escape. Trapped.

There was a new verse or two, Mickey explained, composed by himself. That was the problem with 'The Hero of The Glen'. Every half-cracked songwriter and doggerel poet added his or her own verses.

'Sure Shot Shine and Turpentine Tom
Willingly did their Lugers strap on
And out of the mists of Tooreen bog
Strode The Hero with Shep the dog.'

In this new verse, the eleven Tans would shoot Shep just for the craic. This was historically inaccurate on two counts. Firstly, The Hero never had a dog and, secondly, if he had, the Tans would shoot a man before they'd shoot a dog, as they were very fond of animals. But I wasn't going to point that out to Mickey Junior, who kept on with his turgid drone.

'He knelt and prayed at his noble
father's lonely, hilly cairn
As his ancient mother bade farewell
to her brave, wee bairn.'

Again, there were some inaccuracies here. The Hero's mother was only thirty-nine at the time of the raid and was to go on to have two more children and his father, of course, was alive and well which he would have to be if he was to father the children.

The word 'cairn' was used because it rhymed with 'bairn'.

This was known as the Scottish verse. There is another version where the words 'tomb' and 'womb' are used but this has now fallen into disuse as it was considered bad form in the old days to mention the word 'womb' in public. It also gave off an impression that The Hero was human and not a god.

For an instant, I was sorely tempted to stand up on the counter and tell the true history of The Mayo Marauders. Still, Turps wasn't a bad fella and I gave The Hero my word.

The more I thought about the whole thing the more it dawned on me that nothing is as it seems and that very often the people to the forefront are only there because they can control events from a position of leadership.

And as I listened to the unending dirge, I let my thoughts slip away. Had Mary O changed?

It was the staring out the window bit that reminded me of her tendency to switch off as if she was in a state of some kind of meditation. She could sit in her room for hours, drawing huge, dark skulls in ink on long sheets of brown paper and then when the piece was completed she would tear the paper up into little pieces.

CHAPTER TWENTY-NINE
STOLEN BISCUITS

THE MONDAY AFTER THE annual running of The Glen Pony Races is the most depressing day of the year, bar none.

The hordes of freewheeling, big-spending visitors have vanished as quickly as they arrived. The only clue of their presence is the litter blowing around the street.

The Hero Square is deserted except for Houdini peeing morosely against a frontier lamppost, barely going to the trouble of lifting his leg. I would say he suffers from a touch of Seasonal Affective Disorder. In summer, Houdini is full of his fun. He is constantly twirling in an impossible attempt catch his own tail and disappears for days in search of bitches.

Today, he walks off in no great hurry to survey the far reaches of his dominion by way of nasal investigation. A plane passes overhead, leaving two long parallel cloud tracks of a sky road as it races out over the ocean for America. I wish in one way I was on it. I get a fit to get up and go every time I see an aeroplane flying west. But there's my child, there's Paula, there's my hope that they might be one and the same and there's the saving of Glenlatin.

The weatherman has sent a north-easter in from Iceland where it has been kept in cold storage until today.

Over on the other side of Hero Square, the lanky birch trees, scantily dressed for the weather that's in it, genuflect before the gale and catapult elastically back into shape again when the storm drops or gusts.

The Dosser's hand-painted sign 'Poney Races 300 yds' has been ripped from its moorings and is lying wanly at the bottom of an ivy-covered timber telephone pole trying vainly to pass itself off as a tree. A plastic bag masquerading as a hot air balloon blows up into the sky. Crows splash around in a stagnant pothole big enough to bathe a child in.

Houdini pees against the ivy telephone pole and continues his border patrol.

A chip van revs into gear and drives off. The dry rectangle is spotted in seconds from the beginnings of the rain. Soon, if the sky is our guide, there will be squalls and hailstones throwing themselves about indiscriminately from every direction.

I check for the origin of a slate smashed around the street. It's from a falling down, long uninhabited house just down from The Mayo Bar. A grey net curtain twisted and dampened into the shape of a rope is blowing out of the front window. A bonsai-sized sycamore, sired and nourished by a starling colony, grows out of the chimney pot.

The crows emerge from their dip and walk in urgent, inefficient steps towards a chip bag. They are too late. Houdini has beaten them to it. The bag is stuck to his jaws like a muzzle as he extracts the last morsel of burger.

It's a short day for the crows. They only scavenge in daylight. It'll be dusk by six and then it's off home at the same time every evening like commuters in a city to the great rookery in the naked trees on the swollen banks of the Ballymore. Bested by Houdini, they flap away noisily in the direction of the dump. They might get lucky, a careless digger driver might leave dinner exposed. Their raucous caws break the quietness.

The year in The Glen is divided into two, before and after the Pony Races. It goes back to a time when the Pony Races were the social highlight of the year but now while it's still a big enough day, it's nothing like it used to be. The races mark time.

Today is the day for the opening of letters with Government harps embossed on the top left-hand corner and marked private and confidential. Today is the day for freeing blocked sewers by hand, neutering cats, fixing ingrown toenails, force-feeding on five helpings of broccoli and tripping to the doctor for that rectal examination you've postponed until after the races. It's decision time.

* * * * *

Moran's solicitors have served a Civil Bill claiming huge damages against me. The file on the criminal side of the case still hasn't been sent to the Director of Public Prosecutions. The only statements on record are from Moran and Fr Fitzgerald. The Rumour Factory declined to get involved after Liam warned them that every aspect of their lives could be put under scrutiny in the witness box. The murder fiasco severely dented their confidence and Liam said it was bound to come up in cross-examination.

It would be all over The Bugle.

"People are more afraid of The Bugle than even jail or a couple of digs from the guards in the days when guards could give digs," Liam said. "There was no bother in paying fines once the neighbours didn't read about it in The Bugle. And Sandy, will you please go to the shagging solicitors. Once this file goes off to the DPP it's their call whether to prosecute or not. There's no getting at those lads."

It was a struggle to open the front door this afternoon. I'm exhausted, as well as depressed. There will be no customers. I feel like Raftery, the blind poet, playing music to people with empty pockets.

Maura phoned a few times since our 'confession'. She wants me to tell Paula about the Mary O story as she feels I'll never face up to it if I don't do it now. She suggested we should look at the possibility of a DNA test to establish if Paula is indeed my daughter. Oh yes, Liam is my uncle alright, and The Snipe's too. The tests proved that.

Maura said she would help.

Would she go to Mary O? Act as an intermediary. She felt terrible she didn't do more to persuade The Hero to see my father's side of the adoption all those years ago. She was submissive back then, she said. "Submissive and obedient."

Wasn't The Hero a hard man all the same? Himself and Maura. Who could blame them, I suppose? I'd say she was the perfect antidote to Nana Fags.

* * * * *

Well, today is the day. The facing-up-to-things day. The possibility that Paula might be my daughter has occupied my thoughts, morning and evening. I've hardly thought about anything else. I've tipped ashtrays into the grated cheese, gave out wrong change, upsidedowned orders and forgot the names of regulars all through one of the busiest weekends of the year. I'm excited at the thought Paula might be my child but very apprehensive as to how she will react to the news.

Paula came downstairs about noon after a long lie-in. She deserved it; she was worn out after working day and night during the Pony Races. She rolled up her sleeves and got on with it. No airs or graces. Always in good form. A word for everyone. She's a great woman to put on the shop face but she loves people and the life of the bar.

"You gave me far too much pay last night. I only need about half that."

"Don't worry, Pauls, you'll find a way of spending it."

Paula would spend every penny in her pocket without thinking of such mundane matters as rent and food.

"Have you a dose of PRD?"

"PRD Pauls?"

"Post-Races Depression. That's what The Dosser called it last night. Is there something wrong?"

And then I told her about the row in the church.

"Will you go to jail?"

"Not a hope, Paula," I lied.

"But why did you do it?"

"I just lost it."

Paula took on the stance she takes when she's about to straighten things out on my behalf. It's been the same since she was a small girl. One hand on a hip, the other on her side like the handle of a tea pot, her head turned and lowered slightly to get a different camera angle. Then she would place her next-to-front tooth over her lip, straighten her head and look you in the eye before speaking.

"I know Moran used to terrorise you and the other kids but what about the priest? I thought he was harmless and anyway who takes any notice of old guys like him?"

I looked over at her and I was happy in a strange way that she was worried about me.

It's nice to have someone to worry about you, even if you'd prefer he or she didn't have anything to worry about. Her hair was tossed and she was in an old dressing gown with tatty slippers but Paula had grown into a beautiful young woman. I said a silent prayer she would never come to any harm.

"What time is your train?" I asked.

"Two fifteen. The church fight thing sounds really serious, Sandy. You're sure there's absolutely no danger of jail?"

She looked me straight in the eyes again and I looked at her full on. Every liar knows that if you break eye contact you give the game away immediately.

"Certain Paula. Didn't I tell you I'd be alright? I'll drive you to Ballymore."

"There is something else bothering you, isn't there? It's the adoption."

"The adoption?" I could feel myself going weak. Then I had a spasm in my tummy. It always happened to me when I was stressed or was about to hear bad news. I sat on the flank of The Hero's kitchen armchair.

"I'm waiting on a reply from my mother."

"They've traced her so."

"Yes, but she didn't exactly jump for joy when she heard I wanted to see her."

"She probably needs a bit of time to get used to the idea."

"She just can't make up her mind whether she wants to see me or not but I'll know for sure in a couple of days."

"Paula, we'll check it further. I'm sure if we found out who your mother was we could persuade her to see you. Don't give up hope yet."

"Why do you think she doesn't want to see me?"

"Well Paula, it's not you because she doesn't even know you. If she did, she'd be here in a shot."

"My father must have raped her or something. Maybe that's it."

"Paula, that's rubbish. There has to be a logical reason. Nearly all children born out of wedlock were sent for adoption in those days."

It was hard for her to understand that was just the way things were. I looked at her again and this time Paula reminded me of no one I knew.

"I just hope she gets in touch, Uncle Sandy. Maura said I should reassure you that I will always call The Mayo Bar my home and that whatever happens you will always be the same as a dad to me. Not just the same as a dad but a dad, my Dad. But you know that. I should have told you earlier, but I thought you knew."

And she put her arms around me.

"I always knew, Pauls."

Paula went upstairs to pack but she was back down a few minutes later looking for a hairbrush, something she can never seem to find.

"Will you say a prayer for me, that everything will work out?"

It was funny that with all her self-confidence, education and handy talk, she was still a little girl in many ways. Bringing up Paula helped my understanding of women after everything that happened with your mother. I just wish I knew back then what I know now.

"I will Paula. Sure a prayer from a sinner like me will be as good as a month of Rumour Factory novenas. You'll be fine, Pauls. You're a sound woman."

I always liked to give her a bit of confidence. I really meant it.

It seemed like a good time. I was just about to tell Paula there and then but I balked at the last second for the second time that day just as the words were about to come out of my mouth.

I dropped her at the station. She asked if I was sure I wasn't going to jail. I promised her I'd see the solicitor.

I watched her find a seat on the train. She had a great big smile and blew me a kiss. She mimed the words "go to the solicitor".

It was great in one way to see all the young people heading for university. Confident and civilised. But lonesome because this was the start of leaving Glenlatin for good.

I let the car take me where it wanted but the sign for The Reeds was like the pull of the moon on the tides. When God was making the world I'd say he dipped his finger in a desert and rubbed it along the ocean leaving a spit of sand between two seas.

The last day I was here it was a pet day in October and there was warmth in the Indian Summer sun. Dolphins swam in the bay and jumped up and down for sport. A gannet swooped for fish and surfers curled themselves round waves until they became part of the motion itself.

Today was wild and windy. Off the end of the pier little fishing boats were bobbing and weaving like a boxer on the ropes. The waves were full of themselves. No surfer would corral them ashore today.

I walked up and down through the sheltered sand dunes and I became very sad. I saw the remains of a white seabird torn to pieces by a hawk or a fox. The carcass was cleaned by the nocturnal dune vultures. All that remained was a headdress of feathers kept from being blown away by the rigid wisps of coarse marram grass.

I was sad for the cruelty of nature and sad for the little bird. I was sad after my Dad and sad after my Mam. Sad after The Hero and sad after the man I never really met because he never really existed except in my head. The man I once thought I could be.

I wondered when it is we start to slip inexorably from the goodness and simplicity of childhood. Bit by bit you compromise right and wrong until in many cases you don't really know right from wrong. It starts off in a small way. The odd lie, a small fiddle. As the years roll on, you compromise the idealism of youth more and more until your very survival depends on dishonesty to yourself and to others. It's the easy way out. The truth is hard to tell and can make you unpopular in the short term. But there's a difference between popularity and respect. I try to look back and feel what it was like to be young in an honest innocence. I try to feel for it and drink from my memory so that the drink from that cool, clear well will keep me right.

I will have to be honest and open with Paula. I'm trying to think of what I'll say to Mary O. I desperately want to see her, to apologise and explain.

The sea rolls in and curls up cosily on the beach after panting and thrashing further out. The tide is soon for turning and is gathering up its forces for a frontal charge on the shore. Out in the bay the waves gather in a frenzy of rage and surge until spent they cuddle up to the foreshore.

The rhythm of the waves and the certainty of their coming and going and their final soft falling shush on the beach calms me as does the notion that my salvation lies in rediscovering the voice I listened to when I was a boy.

Again I access my past to bring me from the depression the past itself induced.

I remember the women slipping into the snug next to the grocery in the Mayo Bar. The Hero would put me on biscuit watch. There were twelve enamel biscuit boxes in the snug with glass fronts. Inside were Marietta, Goldgrain, Mikado and the newly-invented chocolate biscuits.

"Watch 'em," The Hero would say, "they'll eat us out of house and home if we don't keep them under surveillance. Eternal vigilance is what's needed."

The Hero could buy a round of drinks for a football team when bills from our suppliers were sticking out of the top of a drawer he referred to as his office.

So I would sit there listening to the women talking about rearing turkeys and geese for Christmas and passing on bits of gossip or cures for their aches and pains from hard work and having too many children. And I would never steal a biscuit myself.

The snug women probably tried to overcompensate for my lack of a mammy by trying to mother me themselves. I made sure they didn't swipe any biscuits though. My father, ever alert for me, whipped me from biscuit security when he felt I was turning into a bit of a maneen. In other words, I was a bit too precocious for my own good.

The remark I passed to Mrs Murphy about a hot water bottle pressed against the belly in bed at night being the best cure for period pain swung it. And so the retention of my youth was put ahead of the loss of a biscuit or two.

My father was always anxious I remain a child until it was time to become a boy and a boy until it was time to become a man. And now maybe it's time to take on some of the boy again and at the same time be man enough to face up to what lies ahead of me.

My mood improved as the sea air infiltrated my head and the smell of the kelp and the salt air is a tonic in itself. Today the depression only lasted a few hours. Maybe I have found the cure. There's too much humour I can download for it to last more than that. If there were good times in the past, there will surely be good times ahead.

CHAPTER THIRTY

A BACKWARDS HAIL MARY AND A FORCEFUL SOLICITOR

I HADN'T BEEN IN the solicitor's office since The Hero died. Tommy Junior's practice was thriving. The names of five or six lawyers were engraved on the brass nameplate, the waiting room was full, the front-of-office space was the engine room with phones ringing and people running here and there with files. Clients were ushered into offices and hurried, confident, jacketless lawyers dropped messages and dictation tapes on the desks of their secretaries.

"Have you an appointment?" asked the make-up caked receptionist as she looked me up and down.

"I have an open appointment," I replied.

"I never heard of that before. An open appointment?"

And she raised her pencil-thin eyebrows to emphasise her incredulity.

"If you tell Tommy Junior that Sandy Sullivan is here, he'll see me for sure."

"I will see if Mr O'Reilly Junior is available. He may have left the office for a consultation."

Then she straightened herself up, pulled her shoulders back, wiped away an imaginary speck of dust from the reception desk and aligned herself into the challenge posture.

"Are you sure this can't wait, Mr Sullivan?"

"No, I need to see him right now."

"Well, it's customary to call for an appointment first. Mr O'Reilly Junior is a very busy man," she said, disappearing behind a door.

I could tell you all about her even though I didn't know her. The husband and herself would have bought a detached bungalow in the second most fashionable housing estate in Ballymore. They had one point zero children and a dog called Zack which was the name they picked for a kid if it was a boy. The house was huge for only three people, with two guest bedrooms no one ever stayed in because they didn't like visitors. A huge mortgage meant no social life. Wooden floors would have been put down in the last year and the three-year, deep-pile carpets which took so long to source and so long to pay for were thrown out. So passé and, anyway, wood was in.

The receptionist would be thinking of adding on a conservatory like the house two doors down. The problem was the husband and herself had amalgamated the car loan, the credit card debt and the overdraft into an even bigger and longer mortgage after they saw an ad on television promising cheap loans.

She would get extremely annoyed when she heard someone in the neighbourhood was changing her car or going off to Madagascar.

The husband, already neutered in the metaphorical sense, was sent in for the snip after the baby was born. The end result was that they could now just about afford to pay a babysitter and go out for a drink on a Saturday night. And I'd say she calls her mammy 'mummy'.

The receptionist came out again.

"Okey dokey then. Mr O'Reilly Junior will see you now."

By her insolent manner and the cocky way she waggled her arse into the office off the reception area, I'd she had something on Tommy Junior.

Tommy welcomed me. We shared a flat for a while in college. I knew he wouldn't let me down. Even if we weren't friends he had a reputation of being fiercely loyal to his clients. He had already "heard the whole shocking story".

"You really are a Hero now but a flawed one in the Shakespearean sense," he said. "Come on in. Sit down and unburden yourself."

Tommy was a handsome, big-boned man. He had the build and the presence to go with the status and the big office.

I apologised for the lateness of the visit and the lack of an appointment. Tommy said friends were welcome day or night and he called for the receptionist to bring a bottle of whiskey and two glasses.

She leaned over to place the drink on Tommy's desk, exposing a tanned bosom filigreed by a skimpy bra, which covered barely half her breasts.

"That's fine Dorsey, you can go now. Thanks."

With an "okey dokey, Tommy" she waggled off.

"Dorsey?"

"Short for Doreen."

"Okey dokey?"

"It means okay."

Tommy pretended he was looking for a pen as he scattered pages and rough notes. That was enough. Anyone calling his secretary Dorsey and breaking eye contact was definitely knocking her off. You'd think they would have taught him that one in law school.

Then it dawned on me that I actually knew Dorsey. I suppose I should've warned Tommy but I remember Dorsey's Nana being caught stealing from the shop. When my father accused her she started saying the Hail Mary backwards. It was an old piseog thing, a communion or an invocation to the devil and the lads. The Hero went into a blue funk and stared shovelling sweets and biscuits into her bag until they spilled out over the top on to the floor.

I told Tommy the whole story about the assault on Moran and the priest. He advised me the incident in the church would cost me a lot of money and there was every possibility of a jail sentence. After some time, Tommy suggested that here might well be a way out, but that some "very embarrassing questions" would have to be asked. I was not to take any notice because he had heard of every kind of sexual deviancy both "on and off the pitch" as he termed it.

"He buggered you didn't he, Sandy? The priest? You poor bastard. It must have been awful for you."

"No, he did not Tommy. I don't know where you got that one from. Moran used to beat us up but the priest never laid a finger on me."

The lawyer shook his head and looked me in the eye.

"Sandy, you are obviously in denial. I have a shrink who will give us a report to the effect that you are the victim here and that you were looking for closure. That should mean if you are convicted the worst that will happen is that you will be left off on Probation. You might even get off."

"He never laid a hand on me," I repeated.

Tommy started to doodle a sad face with an upturned downwards-facing mouth and eyes. Then he rat-tat-tatted the sterile end of the pen in a silent drum solo on the sketch pad.

"My heart goes out to you Sandy, but don't be embarrassed. I've done two murders and six rapes."

"You've murdered and raped eight altogether so is it? And you got yourself out of it. And they say a lawyer who represents himself has a fool for a client. Well done, Tommy," I said with as much sarcasm in my voice as I could muster.

But Tommy kept at it.

"Sandy, you haven't changed, still at the old jokes. Listen. Ballymore has a higher murder rate per capita than New York. Nothing surprises me. There isn't a Monday that goes by that someone doesn't come in with a divorce case based on some bizarre tale of sexual deviancy. Did he bugger you, he did, and say he did. Just say yes, you needn't say anymore than that for the moment. He did, didn't he?"

"Tommy, he never touched me."

He let out a few "tut tuts" and continued his inquisition.

"Sandy, there's nothing to be ashamed of. That lot shagged half the country. Just lighten up and tell it as it was. Look it's okay to just nod if you can't say the word yes." And he nodded his head by way of encouragement.

"Lighten up, Tommy," I shouted. "Lighten up. Jesus are you still on the wacky backy. Lighten up and you telling me a priest buggered me when he didn't. Jesus, I'll kill Liam."

"Liam is on your side. Would it be easier for you to outline the abuse to a shrink? He buggered you didn't he? The bastard."

"Tommy, for fuck sake. Are you listening? He never touched me. He never fucking touched me."

"Have it your own way . . . We'll just have to go on the violence against you at school so. I'm up against it when my own client won't give me the ammo. Did he put his hand on your privates maybe?"

"I'm getting out of here. Read my lips. He never touched me."

I pushed my chair back from his desk. I was half way out of it when Tommy relented.

"Alright, he never touched you but maybe he talked dirty to you or started playing with himself in front of you."

"That's it, I'm gone."

And I headed for the door. Tommy stopped me by grabbing hold of my arm.

"Jesus Sandy, keep the head I was only doing my job."

With the door half-open, Dorsey saw her chance and arsed in with some paperwork.

"Can I go now, Tommy?" she asked. "I have to bring Samantha to ballet."

"That's fine Dorsey. Thanks."

"Goodbye Sandy." And she threw me a ride-me-sometime look, if the time and place is right. And I thought of the backward Hail Mary's.

"We can stick to the violence so Sandy, if that's the way you want to play it."

He respectfully peeled the foil off the top of the whiskey bottle and poured one for each of us. He took a little sip and then a big one before he started off again.

"Look, have you any witnesses to the school stuff?"

"I can get witnesses."

Tommy started to scribble on a pad as he spoke.

"We must send a letter to the other side counter-claiming for mental and physical abuse over a sustained period. They know we know it's statute barred but I will tell them you were suffering from a mental disability and were therefore incapable of bringing a case within the statutory period."

"But I wasn't suffering from a mental disa-fucking-bility Tommy, you liardy bollix."

"Ah you were, Sandy. Oh, definitely you weren't right. Ah, there's no doubt whatsoever about that."

"How do you figure that one out Dr Tommy. I didn't know you were a psychiatrist as well."

"Trust me," Tommy answered.

"I trust you completely Tommy, you know that. But I was not ever, nor am I now off my frigging game."

"Anyone," continued the solicitor, "who did what you did has to be a bit unbalanced. They might get windy if there is a risk the evidence of the beatings gets out and maybe Moran will pull the case. Remember everything you say in a witness box is privileged and can be reported by the newspapers without any fear of defamation. My guess is that Moran is after cash. Knowing that smarmy git I'd say he's dreaming of a new fountain in that garden and a couple of new gnomes. It would probably help keep you out of the slammer if we paid him off in advance of the criminal case."

"How much is he looking for?"

"Who knows? It depends on his medical reports. Maybe he'll take three if we rev up the violence thing against you. Three would be fuck off money. I can't promise anything. It's early days."

"I can live with three . . . just . . . Tommy, there's something else."

"It's the adoption again Sandy, isn't it?"

"Yes Tommy I know I have you pestered. Can we force her to reveal where the child is? Surely dads have more rights now?"

"Men have shag all rights Sandy. I have a filing cabinet full of files where dads, as you call them, are grudgingly allowed an audience with their kids once a week if they're lucky. I'll check it out with a barrister who specialises in the area."

"What you do think?"

"It's a long shot."

"Tommy, I only want what's fair."

"I'm afraid Sandy, my old friend, you're in the wrong place for that."

CHAPTER THIRTY-ONE
MARY O'S REVISITED

IT WAS MY FIRST time back in Mary O's since that terrible Easter Sunday all those years ago. The latest in a long line of family collies was fat, his coat stringy and he looked bored from lack of work. He didn't even bother to bark or cartwheel or sniff around at my heels. There was no bellowing of cows or the hungry cries of weaned off calves. The milk quota was sold off a few years after Tom Tie passed away to a big farmer who was now a small farmer himself.

Most of the Tom Tie land was planted by the forestry. The little stream near the house was still singing but there was no life in the song. The water was a boggy dark brown from the run-off from the trees. Rushes and thorns had grown over the side of the banks and if you didn't know there was a glasha there you wouldn't give it a second look.

A satellite dish was grafted onto the side of the old cottage giving it the lopsided appearance of a man with only the one ear. Van Gogh Cottage. The half-door, which was capable of being opened in two to let fresh air in and keep hens out, was replaced by an ugly block porch with an aluminium door. The whitewash was sanded away. The walls were now painted magnolia. The Hero hated magnolia – and cream for that matter.

He always insisted on primary colours. Cream and Magnolia made him feel impotent, he said.

I pulled across the sliding door of the porch. While I waited for someone to come out, I could hear the whirr of a tumble dryer and the hysterical screeching of an American lady by the name of Fay who caught her boyfriend in bed with her brother and a woman called either Pearl or Petal.

Joey and Molly O arrived at the door at the same time. Molly O shook hands with me first and then kissed me.

"You are very, very welcome, Sandy."

I could smell the sizzling bacon. The ends curled into the shape of a jumping trout. Free-range eggs were bubbling and spitting in a huge pan on the gas cooker. We made small talk as Molly O sliced up a few home-made black puddings. They were so fresh and moist that they broke up a bit in the cutting and stuck to the carving knife.

The smell of the cinnamon in the black puddings brought back memories of the many great feasts I had in that house. Last in were the tomatoes and they sizzled and hissed and the red skin blackened a bit but not too much. The inside would be luscious and the skin tarty and barbequey.

Cakes of freshly baked brown soda bread and white pyramids of griddle bread lay cooling on a boxed blue cotton tablecloth on the sideboard. Molly O shuffled over to the kitchen table which was laid out with a white linen cover and dainty blue china with handles so small on the cups you would have to catch them by the waist to drink out of them. The electric kettle cut itself off when it boiled and she heaped in several spoons of loose tea into a porcelain, hair-cracked teapot with a design of man driving cows across a leafy stream. It was the sole survivor of the Easter Sunday breakage. The last member of my family to drink tea from it was The Hero.

"When will you be going in to get the hip done?" I asked.

"A few more months now Sandy, and I'll be on the pig's back." It was the way of the old people not to complain too much about anything.

She cut the ends of the stems from the bright red roses and arranged them carefully in The Hero's vase.

"There was no need of those. Roses in November."

I knew she loved roses. There was always a few growing in pots near the wall of the cottage. Bright yellow ones. The bushes were a going away present from her neighbour in England. She lingered for a minute to admire them again before taking up the breakfast.

When the fry was consumed, I praised it to the moon.

"You have The Hero's gift of the gab," Molly remarked, delighted I cleaned my plate.

Joey asked permission to light up a cigarette. It was a signal it was time to get down to business.

"I wanted to clear it with you about Mary O. I'd like to see her."

Molly was a hospitable woman and hated to disappoint a guest whatever the request.

"Sandy, I'm sorry," she said, "but she's gone very hard and bitter over what happened. Mary O, I'd say maybe, isn't the same girl you knew. Even her accent is gone back to English. I'm afraid she has no wish to see you."

"I won't force my company on her Molly, but I have a lot to explain and I want desperately to make contact with my child."

Joey supported me.

"Mam," he said, "I think Sandy should be given that chance. He was very young when all this happened and but for The Hero and Sandy I could be in some cell in England with innocent blood on my hands."

"I know all that Joey love, but it's Mary O's decision. I have to say she was bitter when you sent word you never wanted to see her again and that she should put the child up for adoption."

I stood up for a second but I sat down again immediately.

"I swear I never did such a thing. I swear on my child. On my mother and father's grave, on Paula. Oh Christ, but how could she ever have managed to think that?"

Poor Molly was incapable of telling a lie. I knew that for sure.

"Mary O," she said, "was told this by Fr Fitz and The Hero in this very house. She is telling the truth. I was present myself."

I sensed Molly wanted to believe me. I told her Dad and myself wanted to contact Mary O. I admitted I should have tried harder when Mary became pregnant but I would never send such a message.

"Never. Please believe me. It was a lie. A lie," I repeated.

Molly spoke in a low voice.

"I believe you but Mary O won't. The priest came to me at the time. I was going to keep the little baby at home with me. Rear her myself to give Mary O a chance to make a bit of a life for herself. We were going to pretend she was my baby and take it on from there."

Joey motioned at me to continue on.

"Molly," I asked, "do you think you could tell Mary O lies were told and that I'd like to meet her?"

"If she agrees I will but please don't force it or she might bolt again and that will be the last I'll ever see of her. And I'm dying to meet the grandchildren. I'm old, Sandy. This is my last chance to make it up to Mary O for not standing up to her father."

Then she started to cry.

"Mary O is afraid to come home," Molly said. "She has too many bad memories. It makes me so sad."

Joey had his mother's hands in his and was looking earnestly into her face. He spoke in a very gentle, loving voice.

"We know you did your best mammy. You were a wonderful mother. Tom Tie was impossible. And there were good times, thanks to you. You did everything for us."

It was lovely to see the two of them but it made me feel sad I never had such a moment with my own mother. Then I asked the question that brought me to the cottage.

"Molly, the reason I'm here is to ask you to get Mary O to meet with me. I can travel. That's no bother. All I want is to say I'm sorry and trace my kid."

"I will do my best, Sandy. I promise you that."

I knew she would. When women of that generation gave you their word you could be certain they would never go back on it.

Joey accompanied me to the car. He passed me a scrap of paper with

Mary O's address.

"Just in case she refuses to see you. You could write to her."

I couldn't believe The Hero would do such a thing to me. A savage resentment towards him was building up inside me. I began to wonder if anyone could be trusted. Then I thought of Dad, The Snipe and Paula and it kept me from my room.

THIRTY SIX HOLES OF INDOOR OUTDOOR GOLF

CHAPTER THIRTY-TWO
THIRTY SIX HOLES OF INDOOR OUTDOOR GOLF

AS EVER, THE BAR was waiting for me when I returned home. Seven days a week. Open every day of the year except Good Friday and Christmas Day. On with the shop face.

I stayed open a little bit later than usual tonight and had a few beers myself to help me get to sleep. There was no fear of the guards.

They were afraid if they raided me I'd re-bar The Bore Brogan and they'd be landed with him again.

He was back in tonight for the first time since the barring, sitting on his usual stool, back to the wall so he could see everyone and ensure no one would escape his stories. He was clicking his heels together with the delight of being allowed the opportunity to tell his classic tale of the retraining of a recidivist donkey.

I heard The Super had to hide in the cells for two hours last Tuesday rather than face another interview with The Bore.

Liam assured me the Sergeant would be on-side once The Bore was allowed back. He too was worn out from him. What's more, the file on my case hadn't been sent to the DPP. It was mislaid, he said. He knew where it was mislaid. In fact, it was mislaid under his mattress in the station on the other side of the Square.

Liam laid it on the line.

"The Super's gone against us now. Will you please let that boring oul' bollix back in before your life and mine becomes a misery? Do you want an end to Home Rule for the Glen? Well, do you? Is that what you want? And me maybe to get transferred and get killed by some drug head or a drunk outside a chipper in Ballyanywhere in Ireland on a Saturday night?"

That was that. I was beaten. I could hold out no longer. The best I could hope for was a pyrrhic victory.

I called to Chez Bore, grovelled, apologised and listened to home bacon, the Ballymore River walking with the white trout, cycling ten miles to dances and the girls chaste, and ludo.

By closing time, there was just the two of us in the bar. The Bore and myself. He had sent everyone else home with his stories. He went on again about the glory days of yore. I felt like dragging him out the door and kicking his backside up over Fat Arse Hill to the cemetery to show him the names of small babies on their parents' tombstones. Babies who died in the good old days from diseases that can be cured now by a couple of teaspoons of penicillin.

I played thirty six holes of golf in the Playstation in my head while he rambled on. The only problem with mental golf is that if you went for a real game the next morning you would be exhausted before you even started.

Then, in a rare lull in The Bore's litany of tales, the phone rang. Some respite at last. It was Joey. A message from Molly. Mary O had no wish to see me.

CHAPTER THIRTY-THREE

YAHOO AND YIPPEE

TOMMY JUNIOR INFORMED MORAN'S solicitor that he would put an advertisement in The Bugle looking for kids who were mistreated during the "reign of terror" in Glenlatin school.

"There was a strong possibility this would lead to numerous claims," Tommy stated. "A class action in more ways than one. The priest would be sued as well. He was manager of the school and as such was liable on the grounds he knew or ought to have known the extent of the physical and mental abuse."

The end result was that Tommy agreed I would pay costs without admission of liability which wouldn't amount to big money as the case hadn't progressed very far down the line. I would also have to sign a release to the effect I would never sue Moran.

The Sergeant was well disposed towards a civil resolution to a potentially messy case. The file was still missing and he knew he would be in trouble over losing it. He told Liam that "the priest and the teacher are squared away. The Bore is back in The Mayo Bar. Fuck it, but we'll leave this one as it is".

I immediately phoned Paula.

"Yippee," was her initial reaction. Then she cried.

"I was so scared, Uncle Sandy. You must never go crazy. Never. Do you hear?"

We chatted and I agreed I was off the hook thanks to my friends and that I owed it to them as well as Paula to keep the head. She signed off by wishing me the best of luck in the meeting in Ballymore and promised to come home very, very soon.

The Dosser dropped in this afternoon looking for a few Viagra. I suppose he wanted to take advantage of Moran's absence from the family home during the meeting.

"What about the blood pressure?" I teased.

"I'll take my chances with that. Wouldn't it be a great way to go?" replied the Glenlatino lover.

"It's probably the antidote you need to take your mind off the other thing. But maybe you have 'em for emergencies like orgies and things."

The Dosser seemed to have it in his head that I was a second Hero.

"No doubt when I am your age Arthur, I will need the solution to your little problem in high dosage. It's a wonder you didn't need them far before now. You put up a great battle."

"But Sandy, I'm younger than you?"

"I can get some alright, Arthur. Call back in a half an hour."

I phoned Liam and asked him for a few of our little blue friends. He told me under no circumstances to tell The Dosser. He was annoyed that I was using him as a pusher but when I told him the name of the other beneficiary in the pharmaceutical dispensing he was over to The Mayo Bar in seconds. I suppose it's fair to say we took a great deal of non-sexual vicarious pleasure from the affair.

* * * * * * *

Fr Fitzgerald and Moran arrived into the lobby of The Ballymore Park Hotel at ten past eight. The meeting was due to start at eight. They were early. Glen time and Greenwich Mean Time seldom coincide.

The Snipe and myself were waiting at the door to welcome our supporters. Moran marched up to us at speed and then suddenly slapped on the brakes.

"I hear you are contesting the chair Sullivan? A blackmailer in the chair, that's nice. Oh that's nice. Very nice." He used exactly the same language as he used to use in his classroom outbursts.

"Sandy is my name," I snapped back. "You are no longer my jailer and are therefore not entitled to call me by surname, especially as your friend here probably charged my poor father a small fortune to christen me."

Moran squared up to me. His face was only inches from mine. He moved ever closer, staring me down like a boxer who eyeballs his opponent before the bell when the referee is giving his instructions.

"You dared to accuse me of cruelty. You liar. You will rot from the inside out like your father."

I could smell the aftershave lotion, feel the tainted warmth of his breath. A tidemark of grey spittle like you'd see on the side of an old bath had formed on one side of his mouth.

"Control yourself, Master Moran. Please I want no more violence," pleaded Fr Fitzgerald.

Moran raised his voice to the pitch of a bellowing bull.

"Leave him to the forces of my wrath, Father. Do as I say, man? Do you hear me? Do as I say, I said. Do as I say, like a good man."

Fr Fitzgerald was shocked and silenced. Moran moved the priest back by pushing him on the shoulders. He turned on me again but I held my ground.

"You sent off your child and you give out about me. Shipped off your own little baby to God knows where," Moran whispered.

His spittle hit my face. He made as if he was going to hit me, raising his hand up and edging towards me until he pushed his chest into mine. I didn't budge, or speak.

Do you know the way cartoon characters see stars when they fall off a cliff into a chasm? Well, I saw stars floating around my head like translucent butterflies when he hit me in Senior Infants. Another trigger. I was afraid. Not of him but of myself.

Fr Fitz intervened again.

"Please, Mr Moran. Please."

People were gathering all around and looked on in amazement. The Snipe was moving ever closer to Moran.

"And you are the man who stole my childhood. Do you have any idea how much suffering you put the little ones through? Well, do you?" I asked.

"I never laid a hand on ye. I was too soft. Nice thanks. Nice . . ."

"Master Bater," I interrupted, "if you don't mind we must be off now."

Moran was dancing from foot to foot with temper. His fists were clenched tight and the blue bulging vein on the side of his neck was as fat as a slug.

I beckoned to The Snipe. We just walked away.

There was well over a hundred people in the hotel conference room. Moran and Fitz finally arrived in and sat up at the top table, drinking glasses of water and whispering. The teacher was pointing his finger at the priest who was talking face down towards the table. Moran lifted up the jug and waved at a hotel employee who was bringing in extra seating. When the man ignored him, he smashed the jug on the table breaking it into three big pieces.

Almost at that very moment Paula and about twenty of her friends trooped in – just off the bus from Dublin.

They shook hands with their neighbours and kissed their mothers and fathers. I never expected this and neither did the enemy. Moran looked as if he'd love to come down from the stage and wallop the lot of them into oblivion.

Paula finally got to me. She threw her arms around me. "Go for it and just say it as it is," she said. "Everyone here is on your side."

The crowd started to chant 'Sandy, Sandy'.

I stood up and proposed "a round of applause for our young people who travelled a long distance to be here to vote tonight".

There was a spontaneous standing ovation.

Moran then announced he was withdrawing from the meeting, saying that even though he was confident of victory he "did not want to split the village".

There was loud applause when he and Fr Fitzgerald left the top table and climbed down off the ballroom stage.

Paula proposed me for the chair. Maura seconded me. There was no other nomination.

I stood up to speak and thanked everyone.

"We mightn't have rolling acres and banks of money but we have mighty men and women with heart and fight and brains," I said.

As I spoke, I saw Fitz and Moran slip out the rear exit. The priest looked old and frail. He almost tripped up on the steps and was unable to push open the heavy fire doors. Moran bullocked his way through, barely waiting for the priest. The door closed and Fitz struggled to get out. He stood there confused and alone. Then the door opened again. Moran grabbed the priest by the arm and shunted him out the door in a rough fashion as if he was arresting him.

We formed a new committee. The meeting went on for nearly two hours. Finally, I proposed we adjourn to the hotel bar. There was another huge cheer. The young crowd couldn't stay. They had jobs in the morning and lectures. I walked out to the bus with Paula.

"Thank you, Uncle Sandy. It was a great night. A night to remember. I was very proud of you. Up The Glen. Yahoo."

"Yippee," I replied.

I promised the city Glen gang a good night out at Christmas. The

Snipe loaded a couple of crates of cider and a bale of sandwiches on to the bus. You could hear them sing the rousing 'Glenlatin for Battlin' verse of 'The Hero of The Glen' as the rickety old boneshaker left the hotel car park for the long haul back to the city.

I saw Maura to her car when the bus pulled off.

"You're in now, Sandy, and there's no getting out."

"Sorry Maura, I don't understand."

"Sandy, you're a politician now. You might even have to stand for election."

For a second I thought Maura said "stand for erection".

Then it dawned on me that Moran left the meeting early. Maura and The Dosser would be at his mercy. In the mood he was in tonight, anything was possible.

"Hello, this is the Moran residence," Sally answered in an out-of-breath, barely audible voice.

"Sally, this is Sandy. Your husband left the meeting early."

"Oh Jesus. Thanks. Thanks."

And then she hung up.

CHAPTER THIRTY-FOUR
A Parcel To England

MY FIRST CALL THE very next morning was to the computer shop on Ballymore's Main Street. They never had much imagination when it came to naming the streets in Ballymore. There was Main Street and River Street and Cork Street and Church Street. The colonial names such as Nelson Street and Waterloo Hill were done away with shortly after Independence and a couple of statues were pulled down, but Ballymore had several heroes and it couldn't be agreed between the different parties which street should be named after which hero.

I purchased two packets of print paper, a new printer, a compatible ink cartridge, a large bubble wrap envelope, a pen, a writing pad and a roll of cellotape.

Next stop was The Dosser's cottage – 'Old Trafford'. There was a dozen squawking, starving turkeys bought from the turkey factory only last week to be sold off the field as free-range birds by The Dosser for sale to the ever-increasing organic Christmas market.

I looked in the window but there was no sign of life.

His bed, with Manchester United duvet and matching pillowcase, looked as if it had not been slept in. Maybe The Dosser was gardening or maybe Moran beat him up and he was in hospital? The latter seemed the more likely explanation. I made arrangements for The Snipe to look after the birds. I phoned Sally from the pub ready to drop the phone if Moran answered.

"Hello, the Moran residence."

"Sally, is The Dosser there?"

"Sorry, you have the wrong number," she said out loud. And then in a whisper, "I'll see you in the pub in ten minutes."

Sally arrived an hour later. Her hair was tossed but she wore a nice blouse which was open near the top showing the foothills of her milky white, untanshopped bosom and it dawned on me Mrs Moran was now a woman.

Sally apologised for being late and asked to go into the kitchen where there would be more peace and quiet. Moran made her give him a haircut, she said. He had purchased a special hair-cutting device in the city "when the robber baron barbers in Ballymore put up their prices".

"Arthur is in hospital," she said.

Her voice was higher than usual and thin and shaky.

"I have a terrible headache. I'm afraid I had a little too much sherry last night. I don't know what to do. I am so sorry for bothering you but I didn't have anyone else to turn to."

I told her not to fret, that I would help her any way I could.

"When himself came home last night, Arthur was badly hurt. I don't know what to do. I just don't know what to do."

"Did Moran beat him up, Sally?"

THE LAST OF THE HEROES

"No, nothing like that," she said. "Arthur jumped out the bedroom window when my husband came in. His legs were caught in his pants and I'm afraid he broke his leg in the fall . . . Sandy, I know it's an awful thing to do and I'm ashamed of my life and I know this will come as a terrible shock to you but Arthur and myself are having an affair."

She finished the sentence on a high note, almost crying the last few words out as if she had admitted committing a terrible crime.

"An affair . . . Jesus, I'd never have guessed. My goodness. Ah sure, there's no harm in having an affair when you're married to a tyrant. It's par for the course."

"Is it?"

"Oh yes," I replied in the consoling voice of a doctor. "That's a well-known fact. Did your husband find out about the . . . tryst?"

"No. I thought Arthur got away until my husband found him this morning. Arthur was in a terrible state. He must have been there all night in all weathers."

"Was he suffering from exposure so?" I asked. I couldn't help it.

"I'm not sure," Sally answered, missing the joke. "Arthur told my husband he tripped over a garden gnome when he was coming in early to work. Arthur is in the hospital. I phoned and they said he was comfortable, whatever that means."

Sally went on to say her husband was in foul humour. He screamed at her and pushed her around the kitchen. He claimed it was her fault that Arthur was needed in the garden. She was, he roared, "an intellectual pygmy and a huge financial burden on him and was useless for everything and couldn't even cook a decent dinner or conduct an intelligent conversation".

By now, Sally was extremely distraught.

"Sally, you are a very nice woman. That's just the way he breaks people. Trust me."

"He phoned the insurance company to report the accident," Sally said.

"What will I do, Sandy? He'll kill me. You have no idea what he's like."

"Oh yes, I do know what he's like. Only too well. Your husband will take control of the whole situation and you Sally, if the evidence of the last fifteen years is to be relied upon, will be totally ignored."

When she managed to stop crying, she turned to me and asked in a very meek voice: "Is there anything else you think I should do?"

"Yes Sally. Leave the bollix."

"But what will I do? Where will I go?"

"Sr Maura will fix you up until you get the head together. Go back to your own people for a little while."

"What will I live on? I have no qualifications or money."

"Moran will eventually have to give you half his pension and half the house. I'd say he has a right bundle stashed away. Go through all his papers before you tell him what you're doing. Make copies of everything. Bank statements. Building society books. Everything."

"Okay Sandy. I know where he keeps his key to his filing cabinet."

"There will be no fear of you once you make the break. Sally, we weren't put on this world to be blackguarded."

I handed her Tommy Junior's card. Soon she would own half of Moran. I popped another one in my top pocket for her lover. He would need a good brief for the case of 'The Dosser v The Leery Leprechaun' and I headed off for Ballymore General.

* * * * * *

The hospital communiqué describing The Dosser as being comfortable was entirely accurate. He was reading a copy of the Racing Post. There was a pair of earplugs attached to a radio. The collar of his Manchester United pyjamas was pulled up, the starched corners pointing to the ceiling, a la Eric Cantona. He addressed the nurse who was checking his chart as "pet" and then "love".

"Dosser you're a genius," I said.

"I know."

"I have a bit of news for you. I think Mrs Moran, sorry Sally, is separating from the husband."

The Dosser pulled himself up in the bed on hearing my news of his lover's leaving.

"What? Is she gone gaga? Jesus, she can't do that."

The Dosser went very pale and for a moment looked as if he really belonged in hospital.

"What's going to keep her, Sandy? Where's she going to live?"

"Probably back to her own people for a while."

"Oh, that's great. Thank God. Well, I mean thank God for her. I mean she'll be well looked after by her own people. Ah yeah, there's no one like your own when you're in trouble."

He lay down again, greatly relieved.

"What's up with you anyway?" I enquired.

"My leg is broken or fractured or badly bruised."

"And you have headaches and a bad back as well, haven't you?"

"If you say so, Sandy."

"And the oul' neck isn't great?"

"Now that you come to mention it, there's a bit of a stiffness there alright."

And he grimaced as he moved his neck in a circular motion momentarily flattening one side of the collar.

I took Tommy's card from my top pocket and put it on the Dosser's locker.

"Sally is in a bad way and I'd say she's hoping you will comfort her. I know about the affair and I suggest you phone her on my mobile." I said this in a whisper.

"Sandy, just between the two of us," confided The Dosser in an even lower whisper, "I'm not saying I'm not knocking her but I'm not saying I am either. Sure she's being looked after by her own people. Didn't you say that?"

And I left him in the hospital, motionless for a change, but still drifting endlessly on the periphery of responsibility.

* * * * * *

I'm back home in The Glen now, here in The Mayo Bar.

A little earlier, I closed the door and put up a sign on the front window. 'Gone Fishing'. The fishing season is long over but it will give The Rumour Factory something to discuss. They're all a bit down in themselves now that the lesbian kiss saga on one of the soaps has been resolved.

It will take the soap a couple of months at least to build up to another gripping denouement. It's all the Factory has to live for now even though they still go to Mass – out of habit or as an insurance policy to ensure favourable treatment in the hereafter.

The printer is spitting out page after page of 'The Last of The Heroes'. The envelope is already addressed:

Mary Hargraves,
976 Milton Close,
Tunbridgeston,
Surrey GU28 8HK,
England.

CHAPTER THIRTY-FIVE

A HOLIDAY SNAP

MORAN HASN'T BEEN SEEN out since he received two solicitor's letters in the one week. The first from his wife and the other from her former lover, the gardener. It would make a catchy title for a film – 'The Teacher, His Wife, The Gnome and The Gardener'.

While he still attends to his parish duties, Fr Fitzgerald's heart isn't in it anymore. Almost overnight, he has become a disillusioned and bitter man. His golf game has developed a nasty hook and the poor man three-putted eleven times in the Christmas Hamper at Ballymore Golf Club.

He told Breda Biscuits she smelled of urine after The Legion of Mary meeting. "There was a hell," Fitzgerald said, "and it was called Glenlatin."

The Rumour Factory has reopened for business. Liam gave me the latest news hot off the assembly line. "You're having an affair with Sally, which is why she left Moran and that was the reason you were framed for Mary O's murder," he reported. "How do they manage to get their facts arseways all the time?"

Guess who had the answer? Yes, it was The Hero, our mutual ancestor.

"Sandy," he told me once, "your mother loved to knit and she was knitting a pair of socks for yours truly as the bad leg wouldn't fit so comfortably into shop socks. She was in trouble with the toe though. A school friend of hers was home for a month from Dublin to mind her aunt in Ballymore. The friend, I forget her name, she was a plain sort of a woman, used to call into the shop part of The Mayo Bar every day to see your mammy and the two of them would chat away. The friend was a tasty knitter even if she wasn't that tasty herself, the poor woman.

"Minnie May was always asking me who the stranger was. I wouldn't tell her or just fobbed her off by saying something like 'will the rain hold off?' or 'wisha, sure we won't find the time going now till the Pony Races are on top of us, so we won't'. It drove Minnie clean off the head. Then one day your mam's pal turned to your mam and said: 'Nora, I'll be back tomorrow to do the other toe for you.' Minnie May was sitting on a bag of sugar on point duty for The Rumour Factory. 'Ha ha, Hero, ha ha, Hero,' she said, 'you might have bate the Black and Tans but you won't bate Minnie Murphy. Faith then you won't. I know what your one is'. 'And what is she?' I asked her. 'She's a chiropodist,' replied Minnie triumphantly."

* * * * * *

Sally made an appointment to see me. I didn't tell her about the rumours. She has changed quite a bit, even in such a short space of time. Sally was dressed in jeans and a nice jacket. Her hair was Friends-straightened. She even wore a little line of undereye blue stuff. Looked very well, so she did.

Apparently, Maura had a friend give her a makeover.

"Sandy, now I know why he ah well . . . how . . . he . . . well . . . didn't like me . . . in that way."

"Ah sure, never mind The Dosser," I replied. "Ah, I'd say he liked you lots in that way. It's just that, well, he's not ready to commit." I couldn't believe it when I said that. Not ready to commit.

"No, The Dosser liked me very much in that way," Sally said. "I was talking about my husband, sorry ex-husband, well almost."

"Ah sure, don't mind him either. You've really come into your own now."

"Thanks to you."

She then handed me an envelope.

"My mobile number is on the back in case you're ever up my way. I have a job now. I'm helping out in an old folk's home looking after the patients. But I'm thinking of moving to the city to do a night course in college." And all sponsored by Moran, the great educator.

Inside the envelope was a six inch by four inch fading colour photograph of Moran and Fitzgerald. They were dressed in women's clothes. Moran wore a fur wrap around his shoulders with a fox's head at one end and his bushy tail at the other. The two ends were joined by a linked chain. A sky blue hat curled around his big head like a bandage. He wore sunglasses the size of saucers. Two smudges of some kind of rouge paste were daubed on his cheeks.

The priest chose an off-the-shoulder number nicely set off by mother of pearl earrings. A doughnut of lipstick circled his mouth. His balding head looked badly in the need of a wig or a hat.

"You can keep it," Sally said. "Tommy Junior has lots more. He thought you might like one for yourself. Because the photos and letters are part of the divorce proceedings we can never use them outside of the case but this one isn't in the court file so it's yours to do whatever you want with."

The words 'San Francisco, June 1976' were written in the teacher's perfect copperplate calligraphy on the back of the photo. He tried to beat the same style of handwriting into us – you'd swear we were being trained to carry out repairs on the Book of Kells. The names Moira and Angie were sloped and slanted in two-tone down near the bottom left-hand corner. Moira, I figured, might be a feminine abbreviation of Mortimer and could Angie be short for Aonghus? Who knows?

I turned the snap over to the front again and noticed Fr Fitz was wearing long white gloves up the elbow of his very hairy arms. He was an inch above Moran who was taller in real life. Fr Fitz must have been on high heels. I wondered did J Edgar Hoover, the FBI man, ever dance a tango with the Glenlatino cross-dressers.

It was a sad old sight in a way. Moran is a man I could not forgive but the priest never had a chance, did he?

Paula and The Snipe tell me I'm a very black and white man, like my Dad I suppose. I'm black and white with others but not when it comes to judging myself. I can shade myself with grey at will.

The priest was probably another victim of the system of vicarious vocation. He would have been chosen for the priesthood by his mammy while he was still in the womb maybe to atone in some way for the ride that led to his being put there in the first place. Mammy would have seen sex as her duty. Lie back and think of your rig-out for the ordination and tell your husband the ceiling needs painting just before he climaxes.

The boy of the cloth would have been treated differently to the rest of the family with his own room and if there was ever the slightest danger of him becoming friendly with a girl, he would have been packed off to an uncle far away. The girl's mother and father would have warned her that she was interfering with the career of an anointed one. He would have been sent off to a diocesan seminary school at puberty, cut adrift from family and friends, held incommunicado behind sweaty blue limestone or danger red sandstone walls, depending on the effect of the vagaries of the ice age in the locality of the seminary.

He would probably have been an easy victim for anyone who was in some way fucked up sexually. It was a self-perpetuating circle of lies and deceit and nearly everyone in the God game in those days knew or suspected it was going on.

In fairness to the man, he did look after the old folks and he was very nice to me when my Dad and The Hero died. The old priest did death well. He was probably bullied into becoming a priest by his mammy, and almost definitely bullied into a frock by Moran.

It was my guess that Fr Fitz didn't know what he was. It was most unlikely that he was a normal, honest-to-goodness transvestite. Most probably, he was wearing the secular frock because of a desperate need for intimacy of a sexual and non-sexual nature. Sr Maura understood it. "Pity the small boy whimpering for his mammy and daddy under the blankets in the cold dorm of a loveless seminary."

I know now why Moran had it in for me. He never stopped trying to best The Hero or anyone else who threatened his megalomaniac's quest for world domination and the infliction of misery. The Hero beat him and quietened him. Moran was going to get his own back on The Hero's grandson.

I also know now why the priest didn't help me out all those years ago. He was petrified of The Hero. The priest was trapped. He too was taken in by The Mayo Job myth. No doubt he felt that a man who was ruthless enough to shove Tans off a sheer cliff was well capable of pushing a priest over the edge.

Maybe I'm not just like my father but a bit like The Hero too. He would have kept the photograph and blackmailed both of them. Maybe I should send it to The Bugle or one of the tabloids. But the priest isn't inherently bad and evil like Moran. Fr Fitzgerald is like one of those emigré aristocrats waiting in vain for the restoration.

I put the photograph in a safe place for a rainy day. And there's a lot of rain in these parts.

CHAPTER THIRTY-SIX
LAST HURRAH

THE HAILSTONES WERE PLAYING a drum solo on the window and roof of the car. I drove up and around the rims of the hills that saucer the Glen. The sleet changed back to rain and back again into the slithery half rain, half sleet consistency of a melting ice pop.

Maura's car crawled slowly towards me on the narrow road. Molly sat in the front passenger seat. Maura thought it best to take Molly into town to give us our bit of privacy.

"Are you alright?" Maura asked through the turned-down window. The icy cold swept into the car.

"Fine Maura," I shouted back.

Molly said she was offering up a Novena and "asked me to be nice whatever happens". The Rosary beads were enchained in her thick, work-swollen fingers. There was a Holy Mary sky blue blanket wrapped around her shoulders and a tartan rug covered her legs.

The words "whatever happens" made me even more apprehensive. I drove on towards Mary O's.

The frost and sleet speckled the black slates on the cottage. It was as if a plasterer threw his mix at the roof and some stuck and some slipped off.

The dice-throw of white seemed to insulate the cottage from the real world outside. Like as if it was a house in an idealised winter landscape on the front of a Christmas card but it was never that. I walked up the sunken path directly into the worst of the rain and sleet.

Mary O came to meet me at the door.

"Mary O," I said as if I had seen a ghost emerge from the almost dark kitchen to the grey solstice light of the last of the afternoon. She looked thin and gaunt around the cheeks. Her hair was short now and well styled. The thinness of her face was emphasised by her high cheekbones. Her eyes were still the deep conker brown but they were sad. She wore jeans as she always used to and she looked very beautiful. Meeting her took my breath away. I couldn't speak.

"Sandy," she said.

"Sandy," she said again

Then in an English accent, "My gosh."

She regained her composure very quickly.

"Come in. It's awful weather, isn't it?"

I found it hard to look her in the eye. I suppose I felt ashamed.

"How good to see you," she said.

"Same here."

"How long? Twenty two tears less six months . . . I said tears didn't I?"

"Yeah," I replied, exhaling deeply to get the word out.

I offered my hand but she proffered her cheek and I kissed her. It was a strange feeling to be kissing Mary O again. Her cheek was warm and soft. Mary O looked at me for a second or two after the kiss. It seemed as if she was trying to connect with the times when we kissed for real. It was a long look. A figure-me-out look. For some reason I sucked in my belly and straightened myself. The fact she didn't go on the offensive calmed me and I was able to breathe normally again.

She laughed.

"My husband and I entertain a lot of French people. They do the second kiss thing as you know."

"Ah yeah, we get the odd mainly lost French tourist in The Glen."

"And The Hero is dead?"

"Yes. Over ten years now."

"I've read your story, Sandy. I must say I was moved, at times."

"Mary O, can I just say how sorry . . ."

I wasn't sure if she was rejecting the apology or trying to control the course of the reunion but whatever the reason she interrupted.

"He was one of those people you think will never die, just go on forever. Old man river, but he was a bubbly, fast-running river."

She stopped then and looked out the window towards the old shed where Tom Tie kept his three cows. I took my cue from her silence.

"Can I just say how really sorry I am?"

Mary O said "confession is good for the soul" in a casual, almost dismissive, manner.

Part of me wanted to break down and I think I would have had she maybe cried a bit but she didn't. She was very much in control at the beginning. As for me, I was back to taking big swallows and gulps to get the air into me.

She spoke again, slowly and in a fairly sophisticated English accent that had no hint of Glenlatin in it.

"The Hero was a real hero, you know. His version just rang so true. And he was so full of pity for the boys he killed. We had no secrets, he and I."

I was anxious to steer the conversation away from The Hero and on to the child which brought me there in the first place. I was bursting inside me. I was so close and yet I was desperately anxious not to hurt Mary O in any way. I owed her that at the very least.

I could see the faded poster of the can of tomato soup through the open door on the far wall of her old bedroom. Molly hadn't touched the room since Mary O left. That hit me as much as anything else. Molly kept the shrine and now all she had to show for the lost years was a faded poster of a can of tomato soup. It was so awfully, heart-wrenchingly sad. No apology would ever be enough.

"Mary O, can I just say . . ."

Again she interrupted me in mid-flow. It seemed as if she just didn't want me to express how I felt.

"You were amusing at times but I think you always held back something, but The Hero was such a passionate man. And so erudite and so very handsome for his age. In fact, he transcended age, don't you think?"

"Mary O, can we talk about our child?"

"That's what brought you here, I suppose?"

"Yes Mary O, it is."

"And you are not in the slightest bit interested in how I coped with a teenage pregnancy back in the dark ages and how I have managed since."

I knew I should have taken my time. I presumed that she would have known of my guilt and sorrow from reading these pages.

"I know you've been to hell and back but please can you just tell me if Paula is my daughter, our daughter. Please, I beg of you. I cannot really express how sorry I am. But can you please tell me? Please."

The net curtains covering the small cottage windows filtered and greyed the diluted low watt winter daylight. The kitchen was dark now. Mary O was almost a silhouette.

"That's the only reason you are here. You never loved me. It was sex, a scarce commodity back then except for little old me that is. I put out quite a bit. The village bicycle I wasn't though. It was more the village tandem. There was just the two of you."

"Two of us. What do you mean?" I asked in a total puzzle.

"Paula. It's all about Paula, isn't it? Not me. Paula. You wouldn't have bothered to come to see me today if I had a miscarriage or an abortion back then, would you?"

I felt Mary O was unravelling me, stringing me on, like a cat pulling at a ball of wool. What was she up to? What game was she playing?

"Mary O, I know you must be bitter. But can you cut out the riddles and the English accent and the posturing. Just tell me about my child," I said, my temper rising.

"Your child? How do you know it's your child?"

"Mary O, it had to be my child. Had to be."

Mary O looked at me for a second and then she said: "Paula is a Hero. That much we can be sure of. Definitely."

She had lapsed back into her Glenlatin accent. The affected Englishness was gone. She was smiling.

I hugged and squeezed Mary O as tightly as I ever did in the old days. There was hardly a pick on her and I had to stop myself from hugging her too hard. She kept her hands down by her sides as if she was an inanimate object.

"It's fantastic news," I almost shouted. "You have no idea, no idea how much this means too me. No idea."

"Well, isn't that all nice and pat? I leave, give away my baby and you and yours who caused me to leave get the baby. Like as if I was a surrogate mum."

"It wasn't like that, Mary O. I never suspected it was Paula until very recently, very, very recently."

"Your daughter. Well, not quite Sandy, but yes she is a Hero mind you. I'm not sure if you are getting the drift." She was English again. It was the "not quite" and "the tandem" comment that triggered me off as well as the posturing and the torturing.

"Not quite? What do you mean not quite? Is she or isn't she, you affected fucking bitch?"

"The Hero, your Grandad that is. It's funny I don't even know his bloody name . . . The Hero might be the father of Paula. Or it might be you."

I stood up, sat down and stood up again. For once, there was nothing I could say. I felt the rough timber edges of the kitchen table; my fingernails dug in to the soft white pine plane of the splintered surface. I crossed my toes inside my shoes to stop myself from kicking out. Mary O looked on at me in a detached manner like someone observing a lunatic from behind a one-way mirror.

"Sandy, listen to me. You were going out with that Cork girl and I heard all about it. I had my suspicions for months. I was heartbroken. I felt betrayed and disillusioned with everything and everyone. I used to meet you at weekends and I knew you were lying, but I couldn't let go. I loved you, Sandy . . ."

"But you and The Hero? I just can't . . ."

"The Hero was just nice to me. It started from that. It just sort of happened and I suppose I wanted to get even."

I had it in my head for a few moments to run to the graveyard, dig The Hero up and kick his bones around the cemetery. Then I lashed out, sending an enamel bucket clattering violently across the room.

Mary O moved behind the table. She took out her mobile and held it towards me.

"Stop Sandy, or I will call the cops. We can't have this. You're as bad as my father. Please Sandy."

I stopped. That stung me, being compared to Tom Tie. He was the last man who wrecked that kitchen.

I walked over to the dresser and back to where Mary O was still sitting. I was in a spin. I walked towards the windows and the door and back to the windows and back to the door, a bluebottle looking for a way out.

Mary O stood up. "Sandy, sit down. Please."

"It was a wonder you didn't bed my father as you were at it," I snapped. "Wouldn't that be some achievement? An Irish menage-a-trois.

The father, the son and the holy ghost himself, The Hero."

It was all too much to take in. My stomach seemed to be dropping out of me like a lift in freefall.

"I was told by my counsellor that I may have been looking for a father figure. My husband is twenty years older than me. Same age as The Hero was . . . back then."

I butted in sharply. "What age is your husband?"

"He was sixty three in August."

It was my intention now to wound.

"The Hero was seventeen in 1921. He would have been in his seventies when you and . . . Jesus, what were you thinking?"

"Stop Sandy. Please. I was damaged goods. He was kind. I hated myself. You were all I ever wanted. I was seventeen. Seventeen."

She was crying now. The control, the poise had vanished. Tears flowed and she was unable to speak.

"But he was my Grandad. You should have stayed put. Ah Mary O. I would have helped out."

"I know that now but I was just a girl. What was I to do? Who was I? A navvy's up-the-stick slut."

"We were both fooled, Mary O."

"The book you sent me, Sandy. It was only when I read it I understood. You did make an effort even though you didn't love me. I just wanted to hurt you at the start. I was jealous of Rachel and how you felt about her. I'm sorry."

"I should have left that bit out," I said. "Oh Mary O, I could have done so much more. I cared for you very much. Maybe we could have made a go of it."

"Maybe," she replied. She stopped to think for a moment of what might have been. Then she continued. "We were too young. The adults, except for your Dad, were conditioned to covering up. It was just the way it was back then."

"Can you forgive me, Mary O?"

"Yes, I can. I do. You suffered so much Sandy. But there's Paula and at least some good has come out of the whole thing. What will we do about her? I can disappear again. I'm so ashamed, not so much about giving her up but of not seeking her out and rejecting her offers to see me."

"No, you must stay in her life. Once is enough to be sent away. Paula will grow to love you. I am sure of that."

"What will we tell her? I've worried about the telling of how . . ."

She paused. "I couldn't tell her I slept with an old man if The Hero doesn't turn out to be . . . and how do we find out for sure?"

"Mary O, I always saw Paula as my daughter irrespective of who the natural father happened to be. Okay?"

"Okay."

"So Paula is my daughter, our daughter."

"Now you know why I couldn't come back."

"Now I know."

I put my arms around her. She placed her head on my shoulders and we just sat there without a word as the rain and hail splattered against the windows. I knew then what had to be done.

"Mary O, why don't we just tell Paula we're her parents. Tell her everything, except The Hero bit."

"You would do that even though you know the baby might not be yours?"

"I would do that. We can't have you going away again."

And so it was decided.

* * * * * *

It was dark by the time I reached The Glen. Houdini was standing outside the front door, dying to get in, like a drunk on Good Friday. He followed me through the dark bar to the kitchen, his bandy legs walking in four different directions but miraculously managing to take the shortest route between two points, a straight line. I threw the rest of Sunday's dinner on a plate for him.

There was a commotion at the door. I had almost forgotten. The Snipe had his own key and was calling in to open the pub for the evening. For some reason I thought I would be in the Mary O's all night. There was a few with him.

He stuck his head round the door.

"I'll serve these lads," he said. "Come out in your own time if you feel like it."

I took the print of Moran and Fitzgerald from the safe and levered the top of the range with the poker. I dropped the photo on the burning turf sods. I was no Hero, no more than I was a Tom Tie. The photograph burned slowly at first, curling at one corner and going up in a short, soft orange blaze. Moran's head was the last to vanish in the flames. An audition for the afterlife.

I walked along the causeway in the lino worn from thousands of journeys from the range to the bar. The path was as wide as the bottle trolley that choo-chooed in and out twice a day at opening and closing time with the regularity of a commuter train.

I then put on the shop face and strode into The Mayo Bar.

The Dosser hobbled up to the counter.

"How did you get on, Sand?" asked The Snipe.

"All right," I said. "I'll tell you some other time. It was some day but everything will be okay eventually. Snipe, go on away out you and have a pint. I'll take over."

"I won't be able to do no more work till after I get the compo," The Dosser interrupted. "But is it alright still if I come over for the dinner Christmas Day?"

"Of course you can, Dosser. No man is more welcome."

"Ah thanks Sandy, and I'll make my famous chestnut and sausage stuffing that I learned off the telly."

"Well Dosser," I replied, "it won't be the first bird you stuffed this year."

In no time at all I was caught up in the jousting and camaraderie of The Mayo Bar.

* * * * * *

Now I'm here all alone again, tip-tapping the tale of today. I have a lot before me and it will not be easy. But I am a lucky man. I had my daughter near me all along and I have a chance now to make it up to Mary O.

In front of me, over by the Sacred Heart, there's a print of my mother on the wall by the door leading to the bar. She's leaning against a full mid-summer hedge in a light, flowery dress. My mother seems to be squinting into the sunlight but laughing at the same time. Her pals are with her, and Auntie Annie. I'd say they had a lovely day.

Beside her on the wall is a framed photo of my Dad and myself at my First Communion. Me with the gap in my front teeth, my Holy Communion badge and my short pants and bony knees. Dad was in his good suit with his hand on my shoulder. His fingers are spread out over me, as if he's trying to mind me.

That hand was always there for me. Even now. That was it. The hand would always be there.

I have much to do and I will need to draw strength to do it. Tomorrow is a day I can always face until it becomes today. But I will do as I said I would. My mother and father gave their very lives for me. I will not let them down.

When Dad was dying he would roll with great effort to one side to get himself out of bed and struggle for ages to get his too-big-for-him clothes on to what was left of his once-strong frame. His face was thin and his legs and arms were sticks but his heart never wasted.

Then when he was already exhausted and not even out the door of his bedroom, he'd say, "Hold onto me, Sandy. Let's go now boy. I'm ready now."

I took him by the hand to make sure he'd stay up. His grip was strong even though he had no strength.

He was almost a ghost. He was a ghost. He was yellow and wasted but he had heart. Heart.

"Every day is a little new life, Sand," he said as he took on the stairs.

Dad summed it all up, didn't he? He chose his words for me with care in those dying days.

Every day is a little new life.